The Never Ones

ARRON AGNOLI

First published by Busybird Publishing 2018

ISBN
Print: 978-1-925830-09-5
Ebook: 978-1-925830-11-8

Cover image: Kev Howlett, Busybird Publishing
Cover design: Busybird Publishing
Layout and typesetting: Busybird Publishing

Busybird Publishing
2/118 Para Road
Montmorency, Victoria
Australia 3094
www.busybird.com.au

We are never bound to the path beneath our feet.
Every step forward is a chance to change direction.

FOREWORD

Arron Agnoli wrote many stories and two novels, 'Dark Blessings: Ascension of Shadows', and *The Never Ones* before he passed in 2015. While I never met Arron, I'm lucky to have read his words, and met his family, while launching *[untitled]* issue seven, in which his story, 'The Water Fox', was a standout.

I can't tell you what type of a man Arron was in a personal sense. I believe he was passionate, for one never puts pen to paper without a necessary modicum of passion. I know he was dedicated, for the writer's road is paved with many who sought to engage through the written word but never published work. And, though it pains me to say it, I can see that he lived a meaningful life. For writing is in itself an act of faith; an inextricable, inimitable way of saying that the people one loves, the places one lives, and the thoughts one has are worthy of sharing, and of deep contemplation.

I miss Arron as a peer, so I can only imagine how hard it is for his friends and loved ones, who grew up with and loved him. I take solace in his words, as I do with the words of many authors who left prematurely: deep thinkers such as B.S. Johnston, John O'Brien, and David Foster Wallace. Those willing to write of loss, of grief and sadness, in the hope that we might learn from their journeys.

What does it mean to write? It means to dream, to hope, and to be honest on the page, whether or not life is being fair, or honest with you. It means to take solace in the idea of sharing one's world, to leave thoughts, fears, and feelings behind, whether or not you will be there to talk of their greater meaning.

It means to live, love, and be brave, his words forever a gift for those who knew him, and those who would like to have known him.

Arron was the best kind of writer. He wrote not for himself but for the world.

We now have his words. Indeed, we always will, as a tribute to the way he lived, and the ones he loved, and who loved him, along the way.

Laurie Steed
2 August 2018

The Never Ones

1.

DEATH TO THE KING!

Pan stumbled to a stop and listened. His ragged breathing sawed through the surrounding calm. No cries could be heard here, no roaring of weapons. Nothing moved. The thin palm trees were asleep, their reaching leaves painted upon the black canvas of the night sky with a glossy green paint.

The darkness was a weight on his aching body, sending him to his knees like a defeated holy-man. Sand and grit explored his open wounds with tiny points and sharpened edges.

Only one other had made it out.

'Long day, Vin,' he said, brightening his voice as much as the dark would allow.

Little Vinny did not reply. He lay as the statement of their defeat, his glazed eyes staring up to the stars above.

With a hand gloved in blood and grime Pan covered Vinny's eyes. 'The others await you, friend,' he murmured, closing off Vinny's view of the world of the living.

The gash in Vinny's chest gaped like a mouth preparing to draw breath. Pan shifted the tattered shirt and hid the dark, bloody hollow.

He sat back and sniffed the stale air. His muscles were stiff. His clothes were shredded. Dried blood flaked and cracked across his skin as though he had been dipped in crimson plaster.

How long had they been fighting? How long was left?

He yawned, tilted his head back and prodded the wound on his scalp.

The stars of strong life blinked as though aghast. The dying ones were easy to locate. He imagined a teeny cry tearing from their light as they sputtered and coughed before going dark, lost forever to those below.

Perching himself in the trees, in the days before the fall of the endless night, cradled by warm winds and the therapeutic scents of the ageless jungle, he would count those ever watching sparks. He smiled. The bruised bulge on his cheek throbbed. They went on forever. Morning would always come, shrouding the glistening spread before he had managed to travel an inch across the sky.

He could count them all now … the ones that clung to life.

A rustling drew his eye. The sounds were clumsy and small.

Puffing, the child tromped into the clearing. His bright green eyes were wide, framed in brown paint and a sprinkle of dried blood.

'You survived,' Pan breathed.

The young child nodded. 'Vinny boy made it back?'

'He is gone, Sticks,' Pan returned.

'Gone?' Sticks paused, looked at Vinny and indicated the body with a finger. 'There.'

'Trust me. He is gone.'

'Oh. Coming back?'

'Probably not this time.'

Peering through the dim surrounding, Sticks's mouth formed a small O.

'The rest of the boys, Sticks?'

'All down. Won't get up.'

Pan searched the air above. 'What about Touch? They get it back?' he asked, looking to another star as it faded from the sky, screaming without a sound.

Sticks reached behind and retrieved the slender splinter of wood. He tossed it over. It landed in the sand with a dull thud as though impotent. Pan winced at the sound.

Touch was blackened by char. The small carved images on the hilt were hidden beneath a smeared coating of black and red.

With a tired hum Sticks fell onto his back, spreading his arms and legs in imitation of a mangled starfish. 'Stars going, too.'

'They are.'

'I'm not having fun anymore,' Sticks breathed, towards the sky. 'No?'

'Let's go play with the others. Let's, Pan.'

Pan moved to a nearby tree and rested his head against the craggy bark. He breathed the tree into his lungs, smelling the infection in the thing.

Sticks sat up with a start. Finding Vinny, he collected the cold hand in his. 'C'mon, Vinny boy,' he laughed, tugging at the arm, 'let's do something else. Let's go find the pirates.'

Vinny's body jerked at each pull, his shirt falling open to reveal the gaping wound.

Sticks huffed annoyance and tossed Vinny's hand to the sand. 'He's same as others. No fun.'

'I already said he is gone, Sticks,' Pan said. 'He is dead … Dead,' he repeated, with a hand on his jaw, feeling how the word worked his mouth.

'Gone dead?' Sticks leaned forward and inspected Vinny's face before turning to the remaining stars. 'Is it all … dead?'

'Soon.'

'Don't think I like that.'

'Same here.'

'Where'll we play when we go dead, too?'

'I will not allow that to happen.'

'You won't?'

'I will get it back.'

'We can get it back? Can we?'

'I can try.'

'Yes, yes, yes. Try, Pan.'

Pan pushed himself off the tree. 'I will get everything back. Everyone too.'

Sticks pounced to his feet and shot both fists into the air. With head raised to the heavens, scrawny arms waving wildly as he spun, he crowed into the night. Calming from his dance, he looked over and asked, 'How?'

'Well, they want the king to die, Sticks. They want him to go dead. When they kill the king they will disappear and our home will be freed from their grip.'

Sticks pulled on his bottom lip, thinking. 'Let the king go dead and we get home back?'

'Right.'

'But you're the king, Pan.'

Collecting Touch from the sand, Pan felt the added weight of the thing, now soaked with countless more lives, countless more stories.

'Pan. But, Pan, you're the king.'

The wooden splinter hummed as it arced around his position in swift curves. Despite the new heaviness it still moved like silk on a breeze.

'Pan! Pan! You're the king, Pan. You are!'

'Not for long,' he said, sliding Touch through his belt.

*

The window was a thin partition, a transparent barrier between the night beyond and the light within. Windows were the eyes of the house. Through them, past the reflective glaze, were truths, rarely expressed beyond the walls that held them. He had stood before many, silently witnessing, reminding himself of the necessity of his kingdom.

Through these windows words were thrust like sharpened things; fists and screams and tears, and ornaments turned projectiles. He had seen all these emotions as they swelled and gushed forth in all their hideous frenzy. He watched as this hurt and jealousy and fear was left behind, safely stored, when they entered the world of surfaces; the hollows filled with smiles and accommodation and courteous gestures.

He ran a finger along the cool glass, leaving a clean strip of greater detail. Inside this small home were two unlike many others. They too, contained seething things within. But their furies went unexpressed. They were muted little creatures, tight containers supporting fiery materials that were never released.

The breeze bound him up and drew him into the depths of this foreign night. This will be no easy task, he thought.

2.

MEASURED STEPS

The storm clouds contained hidden boulders which collided and shattered with resonating detonations. Unconcerned for the danger above, cars rushed along the street beneath. Their tyres hissed on the slick asphalt and spat at Alley as they passed.

Hugging her middle, she steeled herself against the grey sheets of drizzle layering upon the town. The chill was a toxin, seeping through her clothes and skin to infect her bones. The shabby windbreaker she wore was poor armour against winter's raid.

Her steps dragged, scraping the sidewalk and dissecting the puddles. Water had been quick to find the failings in her shoes and penetrate all the way to the spaces between her toes.

Alley scrutinised the distance of her stride. One, two, three … she would count. After the eighteenth step she could raise her head and view the surrounds for the next set of eighteen.

The tacky shop fronts passed beside her. It was still early. None were open. Their security shutters were down, displaying the crude artworks of local delinquents.

… *Eighteen*. Alley dropped her head and counted the steps; *one, two, three* … ensuring they were consistent and evenly spaced.

Deep puddles could not be avoided as her foot came down at the right distance.

… *Eighteen.* She looked up and to the window at her side. Her shambling reflection stared back as though embarrassed someone had caught sight of it. The light rain had worsened the mess of long hair into a frayed mass of black.

'What are you staring at?' a little voice said.

Alley turned to Cale. 'Nothing,' she said, dropping her head. *One, two, three,* 'I'm freezing. We need some warmer clothes,' she said, *ten, eleven, twelve,* and watched her left shoe dive into the depths of a murky puddle, causing wild seas for the unsuspecting cigarette butt boats.

Cale reset the bag on his back and peered through the falling mist.

Alley raised her head and looked to her little brother. He walked with a slump, his shoulders, neck and chest leaning towards the ground as though he was about to topple.

'You should walk straighter,' she murmured.

'What?'

'Bad posture.'

'What?'

'Nothing.'

… *Eighteen.* Alley lowered her sight to her feet. An unexpected flicker of light punctured the surrounding grey. A gleaming speck darted behind her back. She halted her steps, paused her count, and spun to catch the source.

'What are you doing now?' Cale sighed to the dreary sky.

Another flicker danced in that unseeable space over her shoulder. It was like a shard of mirror, held in a trembling hand, deflecting bullets of sunlight into the corner of her eye.

The glimmer shot along the brickwork of a shop front, rounded the side of the building, dropped and scooted under a dumpster parked askew in the laneway. Gloom resecured its hold.

'Did you see that?' Alley said, eyes on the dense shadow beneath the dumpster.

'Beanie Lady,' Cale announced quietly, 'coming in at nine o'clock.'

Alley peered into the depths of the lane. Shuffling towards the main street, hunched upon herself, was a large woman. Four stained beanies stretched over the top of her head were all the local kids needed to brand her as the legendary Beanie Lady.

'Whoa, she's coming right at us,' Cale whispered.

Like the instincts of a hunted thing, Beanie Lady only made use of the laneways and backstreets. She was skilled in merging her sizeable form into the small shadows of thin avenues. She rarely travelled close to the main roads, capable of traversing the entire town unseen by the local residents.

As Alley watched the lumbering approach of a mountain of grubby material, her thoughts stumbled. *What was the number?* The glimmering trail of the speck lingered in her vision, striking through her mind and across her thoughts as though the whole lot was incorrect.

'Alley,' Cale grated, through his teeth. 'C'mon.'

Beanie Lady's right foot dragged as she moved closer. The flaking old boot was paired with a collection of holey socks on the other.

'Alley!'

It was rumoured that Beanie Lady had killed a man in every state. They said that she lived on stray pets, carrying them up into the surrounding hills where she roasted them on an open fire. Toby Polster swore on his mother's grave that she ate his Doberman pinscher last May and returned the collar with a thankyou note.

It was all ridiculous, but Alley could not dismiss the eerie feeling trampolining on her stomach whenever she saw her.

On the odd occasion Beanie Lady drew too near another being, she would shy away as though magnetically repelled. Alley did not have a clue what to do when the woman redirected her shuffle towards her. A hint of panic pinched her insides. Her feet refused to rise and fall without the numbered sequence.

She glanced to each foot, to the path, to a wide-eyed Cale, then up to Beanie Lady as she swayed to a stop before her. The thick aroma of tree bark and damp earth drifted out from the large woman in waves.

'Morning,' Alley said, in a small voice.

Beanie Lady stared down with black eyes. The darkness of her skin hid the level of soot that was caked upon her face.

'Anything I can help with?' Alley asked, cringing as the question was released.

After a long moment of consideration Beanie Lady bent forward. Opening her mouth beside Alley's head, Beanie Lady said, 'Beware, poor sufferer. He will tear this all apart just to hold a dying thing.'

With her words said, Beanie Lady twisted her body and tilted into her lurching gait.

'What the hell was that?' Cale said.

Alley watched the woman fold in upon herself as she moved down the street, her arms squeezed close to her sides, her head retracted into the mounds of her shoulders.

'I've never seen her do that. She actually spoke … to you. I've never seen that. What she say?'

Turning to the path, Alley focused on the feet beneath her … *seventeen*. She concentrated on the last step in the count and raised her head for the following eighteen.

'Well,' Cale said, falling in beside her, 'what did Beanie Lady say? This is like first contact or something. This'll go down in the history books.'

'I don't know. Something about dying.'

'Dying? I don't get it. What does it mean? It's weird. Sounds like crazy talk.'

'Maybe. But it sure meant something to her. You should've seen her eyes. She looked …'

'Like a lunatic?'

'Strong.'

After a moment of thought, Cale said, 'She doesn't have a home, you know? People say she's all messed up in the head. Did you hear what happened to Toby Polster's dog?'

'I heard.'

'They make fun of her. Don't let her get that close again. You can't let anyone see you near her. Not you, okay?'

'And why's that?' she asked, wearing one half of a cynical smirk.

Dropping his shoulders and leaning into his trudge, Cale kicked at the loose chunks of pavement before him.

Alley poured her concentration upon her measured steps.

'Heads up and face masks on, everyone,' gravelly words rolled their way through the grey cold.

Finishing the count, Alley looked to see the bus stop before them. Bryce sneered in their direction. Cale remained intent on the ground beneath him.

The two boys beside Bryce were slouched against the bus stop signpost, attached to the object in an inanimate way.

Bryce eyed Alley and Cale, chewing the inside of his mouth. 'Wrong bus stop, you two.'

The two boys looked at him with inattentive eyes. One cracked a smile. The other, Trent, the school's vice-captain, remained straight faced, scrubbing the rain from his hair with his fingertips.

'The bus leaving town is over there,' Bryce nodded down the street.

Alley and Cale stopped a short distance away. She glanced to two girls entwined on the knee-high brick fence behind. They sheltered beneath a red and white umbrella, giggling like a pair of demented parakeets.

'Or, the bus for Deep Moss is over that way.'

'Bryce,' Trent huffed, massaging his forehead. 'It's a Monday morning. My head is pounding. And you're talking that shit right into my ear.'

'Hey, I'm just performing a community service, helping a couple of our native nutters get the help they require.'

'*Native nutters* …' the sheltered parakeets mimicked, twittering and laughing between themselves.

Trent turned his eyes on Alley. His brow was dark and levelled like a ruler. It added squareness to an already square jaw and structured his cheeks. He was as tall as Bryce, but not nearly as well-stocked around the middle. Trent was fit, moulded muscles visible beneath his white button-up school shirt.

Alley used to imagine Trent modelling for some Italian renaissance sculptor; shadow and the copper gleams of ancient candles battling upon his chest and stomach, the smell of granite and aged timber condensing into droplets on his skin.

She was much more mature than that now … usually.

Breaking away from Trent's eyes, she studied her unpolished fingernails.

Bryce shrugged and considered the sky with a frown. 'But I doubt Deep Moss could handle their level of freak. It may be an international concern. It's gonna take the world's stocks of mental pills to shut off their crazy.' His humourless chuckle was ceased with a wince. Tenderly touching his fingers to the split on his lower lip, he saw the fresh blood and hid it within a fist. 'Or, we could just put them down. That's more humane for hopeless cases. And much safer for the rest of us.'

'Get-lost, Bryce,' Alley said, towards the ground.

'Excuse me, freak? Your mentally insane gibberish is difficult to understand.'

'Want to walk?' Alley murmured to Cale.

'We'll be late,' Cale returned, kicking at the cracks in the pavement.

Alley bowed her head, studying the dark fissures made amongst her folded arms.

'Let's go,' Cale said, leaning into a trudge, upper body in a constant fall towards the ground.

Alley followed at his side, arms wrapped around her middle, head down, counting, *one, two, three, four …*

3.

DRAWING BREATH
IN THE MUDDY DEPTHS

Three, four, five … Alley's sodden shoes squeaked as they padded across the linoleum, a pair of gossiping mice betraying her movements in these deserted halls.

Neither the principal nor the teachers were concerned for these instances of tardiness. Alley knew it to be an unspoken expression of condolence, which she accepted with a grimace.

'Hey, Alley,' a voice chirped.

Alley stopped and raised her head. She gingerly removed a pen from her pocket. Keeping a steady eye on Carla, Alley wrote the number five on the palm of her hand with a discreet movement. She was not going to have a repeat of what happened with Beanie Lady. 'Hi.'

Carla's mouth was stretched wide, beaming, exposing her orthodontic braces back to her molars. It was the happiest chain of metal Alley had ever seen.

'We got our photography assignments back the other day,' Carla said.

Alley raised her hand and placed her thumb nail between her front teeth. 'Oh. I haven't checked,' she mumbled. Watching her work develop caused a full ten minute cringe. The image always looked clichéd and contrived when it was preserved everlastingly on photographic paper.

'You did really well. I love how yours came out. How you made marigolds look so menacing, I do not know.' She released two sharp notes of laughter that rocketed through the halls.

Alley looked behind to her awaiting classroom.

'Hey, you should come with us after school sometime. Give Micko a few pointers. It'll be fun.'

'What?' Alley's teeth came down hard, removing a decent chunk of nail from her thumb. It was tossed around the inside of her mouth before she swallowed the little blade and said, 'I mean, I don't know. I don't have any equipment of my own.'

'You should buy some. A good investment for someone like you.'

Alley scrunched her nose, attempting a modest smile.

'Mrs Cleary will let you borrow the school's equipment. I'm getting the whole class involved. I know it's the end of the year, but it's something we can keep going after school. Keep analogue photography alive, baby.' She pumped a fist into the air. 'Digital's killing the art, you know? Too much technology is dehumanising. That's what Mrs Cleary says. We'll start a club if we get enough people. Right now there's just me, Micko and Maria.'

Alley shifted her weight. 'Maybe,' she shrugged. 'I should go. I'm running late.' She remained where she stood, watching the headlight brightness of Carla's radiator grill smile.

'Think about it, Alley. It'll be heaps of fun.'

They stood facing each other until Carla spun and strolled away.

Alley read the number on her hand and continued walking, *six, seven, eight* …

No one noticed her late entry into class. The electric scent of hysteria was in air. The gradual approach of a prophesised tsunami was on the horizon; The End of School. Listening to the chatter, it was clear everyone was far more interested in Romina's end of school celebrations than the actual end of school.

The classroom's seating was set out in neat columns and rows, a grid of compartments into which the students were deposited.

With the room buzzing like an agitated beehive with an AWOL queen, Alley struggled to navigate her way while maintaining intent on her steps – fifteen from the door to her desk at the back.

Reaching a set of legs stretched across the aisle, Alley stopped and committed the number to memory. She looked down at Sarah who angled a soft smile upwards.

'Alley, sweetie,' Sarah said in her saccharine tones, 'you look like a homeless person in that jacket.'

Alley stared at big, blue, shining eyes below her for a beat then shrugged.

Sarah held her smile steady. Her thin eyebrows arched high, first the one of pity, then the one of expectation. Alley wriggled out of the windbreaker. The eyebrows lowered and the gate of legs withdrew.

Avoiding the remaining obstacles, Alley threw her jacket on the ground and slotted herself into her little compartment, the far corner where the arms of sunlight never ventured. A shiver shook her limbs. Retrieving her notebook, she returned to the spiralling pattern she had been designing since second term.

With her head close to the page, Alley listened to the whispering scratch of her ballpoint as it glided in its swirl around the paper, a little ice-skater with a thin, blue wake. It did little to drown the manic yelping of the others.

'Yeah, she's supplying all the booze.'

'Rich wogs rock.'

'Free beer is the only thing I care about anymore.'

Hard words shouldered through the conversation. 'Get back. You're too close.'

'Chill, Bryce. I'm just sitting here.'

'Get away from me.'

'Aww, what's the matter, Brycey boy?'

'Don't touch me!'

The clatter of toppling desks quietened the remaining voices. Bryce had thrown one of the boys across the room. Laughter bounced between the walls as Bryce's opponent, Sam D, scrambled out of the jumble of classroom furniture. He cradled his arm with the other, his expression taut with restraint. Bryce glared, daring Sam to speak any objection. The injured student skulked in retreat. The chatter reignited.

Alley watched Sam as he lowered himself into a seat, collected a pen and chipped away at the corner of the desk. A glimmering speck dropped from his pocket, hit the floor and sped across the carpet, swerving around feet and bags. It moved at a pace where Alley could not latch onto it with her eyes. She was always a microsecond behind.

The speck darted around a foot, performed a sharp U-turn and disappeared within the shadows of an open bag.

From beneath her brow, Alley examined the others. None appeared to have seen anything. She blinked slowly, staring down at the intricate pattern beneath her nose. Had she even seen anything? Were the fractures in her mind opening up even further?

The door swung inwards. None paid it any notice.

'Alright, you miscreants,' Mr Henderson's husky voice barrelled through the room. 'Take your seats. Now! Come on. Come on … And what are those desks doing like that. Joseph, pick them up.'

'It wasn't even me, sir. It was bloody Bryce and Sam.'

'I don't want to hear about it.'

As everyone found their seats, Alley glanced up. Henderson had not entered alone. A new student was standing beside him. He was an explosion of wild hair, bright eyes and exposed teeth.

'Got another one,' Henderson said.

'Ha!' a student cried. 'It's only like a month till the end of school.'

'Not even,' laughed another. 'Why'd ya bother?'

'Quiet,' Henderson barked. 'I'm sure …' his eyes fell to the paper in his hands, 'Pan has his reasons.' He looked to the one beside him. 'Pan?'

'Yes?' Pan returned.

'Pan what?'

Pan turned his open eyes on the teacher.

'Pan what?' Henderson repeated.

'Pan.'

'Pan Pan … that's your name?'

A few laughs trickled through the room.

'No. Just Pan,' Pan said, turning to the room, and mirroring the humour before him.

'Yes,' Henderson said, his irritation compressing each word into separate statements, 'Pan is your first name. What is your last name?'

'Last name?' Pan questioned him. 'Pan was my last name. It is my name now. And it will be my name after.'

A few more laughs broke across the room.

'What the hell's with this guy?' Bryce said. 'We don't need any more lunatics in here.' He sniggered in the direction of Alley's corner.

'Bryce,' Henderson admonished.

'Least he's cute,' Sarah said, glancing to Cynthia at her side. They both went through practised motions of preening their blonde-streaked waves of hair.

'Alright, Pan, take one of the spare seats,' Henderson said, turning to the whiteboard at the front of the class.

'Over here, Pan,' Sarah and Cynthia sang together, patting the chair in front of them.

'Here, here,' another of the girls said, withdrawing a seat from the neighbouring desk.

Pan wandered through the room. Bryce followed his movements with a snarl. 'I smell freak on you,' he breathed.

As always, the seats surrounding Alley were empty. Pan moved to the one beside her and sat down.

Alley watched him from the corner of her vision. He stared towards the front of the room, viewing something much further away. The girls were not deterred, casting their flirtatious glances in his direction.

'Pens and books out,' Henderson said, scribbling an equation on the board. 'This will be in the exam. You should all know how to do this by now. If you don't, then my pities go to your parents. So, write it down. Figure it out. You talk, you're out.'

Pan looked down at his desk. He had not entered with a bag and besides the belt around his waist, he held no other items.

Alley lent towards him, arm extended, offering a piece of paper and pen. Pan stared at the objects for a long while before collecting them. Without acknowledging her, he turned and placed them on his desk.

A large ball of paper zipped through the air and collected Pan in the forehead with a dull slap. Laughter broke through the room, mainly from the boys.

'Bryce!' Henderson grunted.

Bryce was turned in his seat, watching Pan as though awaiting the results of a scientific experiment.

Calmly, Pan bent down and retrieved the tight ball of paper. He pushed himself from his desk, held it forward and asked Bryce, 'What for?'

A glare was Bryce's first reply, 'A game,' was his second. 'I throw the object, the object bounces off your face, and it amuses me. Those are the rules.'

'Return to your seat, Pan,' Henderson called out.

'I like games,' Pan returned.

'I'm glad. There'll be plenty more coming.'

Pan strolled across the room and stopped over Bryce. 'Let me see if I understand.'

'Pan! Seat!' Henderson bellowed.

Pan's knuckles were white as he gripped the ball of paper. 'Is this it?'

With his smile unfaltering, Pan swung his arm, driving the ball of paper and his fist into the scowling face below him. The strike was solid enough to throw the large boy from his seat. Bryce collided with the neighbouring two desks, sending two more students into a tumble. They were quick to climb from under the furniture and get to their feet. Bryce was not moving. He was out cold, blood bright as it dribbled from his nose and mouth.

With Henderson, the class was silent and still, eyes switching between Pan and a crumpled Bryce.

Breaking from his stupor, Henderson hollered, 'Christ, Pan! Wait for me outside!' He rushed towards Bryce, pulling a chair off him and rolling him onto his side.

Pan walked from the room, smiling as he went.

Alley found herself smiling also.

*

The scene simmered with roughhousing, brazen posing, surreptitious glances, exaggerated laughter and death stares. Lunchtime was a cauldron of hormones and restlessness, volatile and ready to explode at the slightest bump.

Alley moved through the common grounds. Huddling upon her folded arms, she dodged wayward balls, sidestepped preoccupied clusters of wanderers and amended her trajectory away from tight social circles.

The navigation of the grounds was made more difficult when measuring the distance of her steps. She could only examine the area and choose a path on every second set of eighteen.

Alley had perfected the skill. On every second set of steps Alley scanned the area, examined the flow of students and chose a clear path that would not send her head-butting an obstruction when her sight was down and measuring. Using this method she was able to walk with an unbroken stride the entire length of the common area, imitating the walking manner of a normal person.

On the far corner of the grounds, beneath the spindly canopy of a paperbark, a mildewy wooden bench sat. Two girls were seated on one side.

'Hey, Alley-cat,' Megan said, dragging the words along with melody.

Taz was sucking on the end of a liquorice stick, viewing the jittery mass of students from behind dark sunglasses.

'Hey,' Alley greeted the two, finishing on eleven on an unmeasured set. She dropped her bag and climbed onto the table to sit crossed-legged on the edge.

'Did you see it, Alley? It was your class, wasn't it?' Megan said, picking through her chicken wrap, discarding the lettuce, tomato and cucumber. '*Are they bloody serious!? Carrot, too.*'

'Wish I was there.' Taz chuckled. 'K.O-ing the big boy... brilliant.'

'Great way to make a first impression,' Megan said, sucking the mayonnaise off a chicken chunk and tossing it over her shoulder.

'Establishing dominance,' Taz explained. 'It's what you gotta do when entering a hostile environment. Pick the biggest, meanest mutha in the room and knock the living shit out of him. It's actually a big part of the social contract in the southern states, Megs.'

'Really?' Megan mused.

'Yep. Schools, workplaces, department stores, book clubs … You gotta go in swinging, babe. That's the kind of world we live in.'

'Sounds scary. I'm never leaving this side of the country.'

Stifling a smile, Alley collected a notebook and absently scrawled random shapes in the back. 'I don't think it had anything to do with that. It was like Pan already knew enough about Bryce to cut to the inevitable.'

'Pan?' Taz huffed. 'Is that his name? Such inspired parents …'

Megan laughed her agreement. 'Yeah. Is his brother named Pot?'

Taz's long stare was enough to ensure Megan's terrible lapse in judgment would not occur again. 'You're lucky you're hot.'

'Damn straight, ho.'

Alley had never been overly close with Megan and Taz. She had been attached to their tight duo thanks to their mutual friend, Milly. When Milly left school a year and a bit ago, like the formation of a new molecule, Alley remained bonded to Megan and Taz.

Despite knowing she was, and always would be, the backup singer to their duet, it was a tight lunchtime alliance. Megan and Taz, like Alley, were situated on the peripheries of student life. It was not that the other students disliked them; the majority saw the three as curious spectacles, or unsolvable maths problems not worth devoting too much attention to.

One thing Alley did appreciate about these two was their penchant for privacy and an unconscious reflex for disregarding odd behaviour. They never asked about Alley's personal life, knowing that Alley was not prepared to share.

'Check it out,' Alley huffed, slamming her book closed, 'the jerk's at it again.'

Deep into the common grounds Bryce had a hold of one of the juniors.

Alley shook her head. 'What's wrong with him? I would've thought that getting flattened would knock some sense into him.'

'He obviously can't find Pan and now this kid's gonna be the consolation prize,' Taz said, through teeth clamping on another liquorice stick.

Like an unruly pet, the junior hung from Bryce's hand by the scruff of his neck. It appeared Bryce was attempting to coerce his victim into some deviant behaviour. Another student was quick to step in and swat at Bryce until he released the kid with disdain and swaggered back to his friends.

'Gimme some of that,' Megan grinned, leaning towards Taz. She parted her lips and aimed them for the liquorice dangling from Taz's mouth. With the liquorice joining them, Megan and Taz massaged their lips together for a few beats before retreating.

A collection of juniors became noticeable as they angled their way through the grounds. Their destination was clear. Alley eyed them from beneath her brow. As though handcuffed, the leader of the four held his arms behind his back stiffly. Alley tensed.

'Looks like we've got some spectators,' Megan said, pointing to the four kids, halting Taz as she lent in for another kiss.

Taz turned and found the four. She pulled down her sunnies to lance the group with a harsh glare. 'Piss-off, shit-bags.'

One of the boys, a brown haired, brown eyed, ball of a kid, collided with Taz's words and came to a halt. The other three continued forward with caution.

'You that kid's sister?' a boy asked, hands behind his back.

Alley stared at the boy, body lost amongst a swell of nameless panic.

'Did ya hear what I said, Freckles?' Taz growled, rising from her seat, planting her fists on the table. 'I've squashed bigger bugs than you four.'

The round kid at the rear spun and bolted in the other direction. Freckles remained strong, eyes on Alley as though seeing a dead body for the first time, frightened and fascinated. He stepped forward.

'Go on,' Freckles's friend whispered. 'I wanna see it.'

Even if Alley knew where her arms were, she would not have been able to raise them in defence. Frozen by a familiar terror, she could only watch as the kid stepped forward. He swung his arm from behind his back and presented his hand to Alley. A large serving of mud sat on his palm.

Freckles reached forward and wiped it, almost kindly, on Alley's arm.

As the filth spread across her skin, Alley felt it seep into her pores, infecting her bloodstream. The mud raced through her system, befouling every capillary. It found her heart and smothered it, before crawling into her lungs. It poured in, filling them, suffocating her, drowning her in muddy water.

Her body trembled. The world faded.

'Get it off, get it off, get it off,' came the frantic chant.

A hand reached towards her. Her body jerked away. 'Don't touch me!' she screamed, falling from the table top.

For a moment the blow of the fall knocked the panic from her. She felt the chill of the grass, saw three sets of white-fuzzed legs before her face. It was a momentary sensation. The terror engulfed her once again, sucked light from the world, leaving only a blank void, her trapped screams, and the sight of the mud on her arm.

'Alley-cat …' the echoes of a voice slapped upon the surface of the panic. 'Lemme help.'

'No,' Alley pushed the word past the mud filling her throat.

Gagging and coughing, she tore through the common grounds, aiming for the toilet block on the far side, unable to see, all movement executed on memory.

'Freak out, freak out,' the voice of Bryce followed Alley's flight like a national broadcast.

The step count was lost amongst her wild run. Her mind shattered like a fragile piece of glass, a light globe under the repetitive stomps of a heavy boot.

Restraining her whimpers, Alley barrelled into the girl's toilet. She fell across the sinks, shoving her arm beneath the tap. The water was unleashed to its maximum. She collected soap from the wall dispenser and scrubbed.

As the storm of panic subsided a drone was left in its wake. Alley's body numbed as she repeated the motions of soap, scrub, rinse, soap, scrub, rinse, soap, scrub, rinse.

When a physical pain punctured the numbness her vision un-blurred. She had scrubbed through the skin. Diluted blood was swirling a pink path across the white porcelain of the basin.

She closed the tap and checked her nails. She had not chewed her middle and ring fingers low enough. There was just enough edge on them to grate the skin.

Raising her sight to the mirror, she peered into the dirty muck of her eyes and reprimanded herself with a vicious stare. Her reflection looked back as though it was not herself; a relative, maybe, someone who knew her messed up mind and was preparing to cast their judgement.

Tears filled her eyes, smearing the vision in the mirror. Alley dropped her head into her hands and let her tears run, soundlessly, as she knew to do.

When chirping chatter signalled the approach of two girls, Alley wiped her face, lowered her head and shuffled out of the toilet block, not meeting the eyes of the two girls that passed beside her.

Measuring the distance of her steps, Alley did not notice the figure standing in her path. Her head bounced off a solid chest.

Stumbling back, Alley looked up to see Pan.

His face fell into a sombre examination of the one before him. 'Why are you crying, girl?'

'I …' Alley said, catching the words that tumbled towards her lips. 'I'm not.' She placed a hand on the oozing wound on her arm and secured it.

'What's your name?' he questioned.

'My name? You want to know my name?'

He nodded.

'Hey, you. Pan,' the boisterous holler of Romina collided with them.

Alley turned to see the dark haired, dark eyed girl marching towards them with an embellished sway and a curve on her glossy lips. Sarah and Cynthia were at her flanks, their fair-skinned blondeness highlighting the Mediterranean shade of Romina.

'You were right,' Romina said, loudly, half turning to Sarah, 'he is cute.'

Alley's instincts compelled her to walk away. Romina had an invisible barrier around her, a repelling force that drove people like Alley into the background. It was Pan's eyes that held her in place. He only glanced to the three girls as they stopped close to his side.

'I'm Romina,' she bubbled.

'Hi,' Pan returned.

'I've been told that I just have to meet you.'

'Is that so?'

Romina tossed her hair over one shoulder and turned slightly to display her best side. Pan did not notice. Her lips skewed, she shifted her stance, restructuring her hips, and then settled a steady glare on Alley.

Alley engaged Romina in the silent exchange as long as her courage would allow. She dropped her eyes to her hand clasping her forearm.

'Some verbal charity, Alley,' Romina sighed, her razor thin eyebrows arched high like little *n*'s. 'You should take better care of your hair. Your head looks like the shaggy ass of a wet dog.'

'Yeah, no offence,' Sarah added.

Watching Alley, Pan chuckled at the comment. Romina's head tilted to the side as she looked to Pan, content with the world and where all its objects and items were placed.

Alley sought out her feet, turned and walked into the background, counting her steps.

4

THE UNTOUCHABLE
WATER CREATURE

The ocean endlessly crumpled and creased with its white edges, never content with the appearance of its jagged mess. The storm clouds above darkened the water, blending menace into the view. Hidden dangers awaited swimmers within that liquid world.

Cale sat on the edge of the pool, legs dangling in the brine, staring at the angry ocean beyond the composure of the pool's surface.

The outdoor pool was originally a natural cavity in the rock platforms that bordered the ocean. With a little shaping, an inner coating of concrete and a sky blue sealer, a fifty meter saltwater pool had been formed.

'A much more effective design than Mother Nature's half-assed attempt,' the Member of Parliament was rumoured to have said when he cut the ribbon with a gleaming smile. 'Women, eh? Stick to the kitchens and bedrooms,' he apparently laughed, and found a job at the timber yard the following term.

Cale looked to the other kids finishing their laps. On occasion, when the ocean was calm and absent of rips, the swim team would venture into the unbound waters. Cale preferred the pool, with its limits and inability to surprise.

A rogue wave had enough strength to climb the break-wall and spew white froth into the pool. The push of effervescence jostled the swimmers in the first three lanes. The minor interruption gave them excuse to plant their feet, pop their heads up with exaggerated expressions of confusion, and suck at the air. Mr Lowen, or Coach, frowned at the three, with all the unimpressed frustration of a seasoned high-school teacher. His slow, extravagant arm flap, as fists were set on hips, was enough to send the kids skimming along the surface once again.

The stragglers, arms out stretched, slapped the wall on their final lap. They snatched the concrete lip and hung their heads, recuperating from the endurance swim.

'Nice work, everyone,' Mr Lowen bellowed. 'Cale, much better than last week.' He flipped through the pages on his clipboard. 'Cale came first, everyone.'

Mr Lowen's commending hand came down on Cale's shoulder. The touch of unfamiliar skin, those alien fingers upon him, delivered a surge of septic electricity. It seized his muscles, halted his lungs and threatened to halt his heart. He was stopped, all the cogs that made him move fused to immobility. Terror was the only thing left to slither around the stilled factory of his organs.

It was only a light touch, but potent enough to hold him down. He awaited the invasion, the plundering, the savage thievery.

But the hand withdrew and Cale was allowed to breathe again. He shimmied away from the figure beside him … and those hands that were not his own.

'Mitchel,' Mr Lowen said, turning away, 'looks like you've got some competition.'

Mitchel targeted his eyes on Cale like they were loaded and ready to fire. 'Whatever you think, Coach.'

Cale peered down into the water, his recovering trembles hidden amongst his cold shivers. He wondered how long he could hold his breath in that liquid world.

'Alright, we'll call it quits for today,' Mr Lowen said, tossing the clipboard amongst his gear. He turned to the gaggle of middle-aged women decorating the park benches of the grass slopes above. 'Your lovely mothers look like they could use a hot cuppa tea.' He stretched his arms, sending his sleeves sliding to his shoulders. His biceps bulged as he rested his hands on his head.

Cale withdrew his legs from the chill and pushed himself to his feet. He collected his towel. It was a tattered scrap of faded brown material. The other boys called it a dog blanket. He did not have another. After a moment of hesitation, Cale closed his eyes and wiped the water from his hair and body.

Throwing on his clothes and runners, he watched the last few mothers muster their sons and, side by side, amble over the grassed rise to the car park beyond. He stared at the backs of the last pair, side by side, his upper lip pulling back and his chest tight.

As Mr Lowen broke into a run to follow on the tail of the mothers, Cale became aware of the four boys assembling themselves and their bikes on the concrete boat ramp. They were mounted and glaring at him like a savage dog wanting to taste blood.

Cale dropped his head and made a beeline away from the pack of four. His stride was swift, but, as though a wild dog was truly at his back, he knew not to run. Running was an invitation for the animal to chase and maul.

Pedals clicked and wheels hummed as the bikes were kicked into motion. With his head down, Cale watched the four bikes swerve around him and slide to a stop. His grip on his towel tightened.

No words were said as Gavin threw down his bike, strode forward, drew back a fist and drove it into Cale's face. Sight, sound and smell exploded in a flash of light and a lingering cloud of pain drifted about his head.

On his back, Cale peered up at chunks of storm clouds melding into one another. His whole face ached. He rolled to his side. The sole of a shoe shoved him flat again.

'You only get up when we tell you to get up,' Gavin instructed.

The clouds grumbled in an exhausted way. Cale wondered if he would make it home before those surging monsters unleashed their remaining stocks.

'C'mon, man. What are you still doing here?' Mitchel asked. 'How much longer are you going to make us do this to you? You're only hurting yourself.'

Cale waited, feeling the weight of the stormy sky upon his body.

'Pick him up,' Gavin said. 'Let's throw him off the rocks. We haven't done that one in a while.'

'No,' Mitchel said. Lowering his voice, he said, 'Don't touch him, Gav. I've told you before, you idiot. You can't put your hands on him.'

Gavin squinted at the order, before asking, 'Anyone need-a piss?'

At the suggestion Cale's eyes shifted, checking their response.

Grinning, the two other boys untied their boardies.

Mitchel glanced to his two friends digging inside their shorts. He looked to Cale. 'Stop. Wait.'

The two boys hesitated.

'Just go for his towel,' Mitchel said, redirecting their aim for the tattered thing.

'Yeah,' Gavin laughed. 'It's no better than a piss rag anyway.'

The two boys cackled, shooting a warm jet on the brown towel with good aim. Gavin stood back, arms folded, watching with a satisfied sneer.

Cale studied the sky, his surface numb, his inside swirling and twisting itself into strangle-knots. He listened to the liquid whizz, felt it splatter on his grip on his towel and halfway up his arm.

'Take the hint, dickhead,' Gavin said.

'At least get yourself a new towel,' Mitchel said, as the two boys put themselves away and retied their shorts.

'Yeah, you're a bloody embarrassment, Cale,' Gavin added.

A light scattering of laughter fell over the scene. Everyone turned to see a figure standing on one of the benches, hands on hips and head angled back.

'Who the hell are you, asshole?' Gavin called upward, surprise providing a megaphone for his voice.

'Pan,' the young man called down upon them.

Gavin watched Pan from beneath his brow, weighing his next move. 'C'mon. Let's get outta here. It smells like piss around here, anyway.'

'Enjoy your piss rag, Cale,' one of the boys hollered. They all erupted into forced laughter and sped over the grassed hill and out of sight.

Cale pushed himself to his feet. The towel dangled from his hand with an added weight. He felt his towel would no longer be known as the dog blanket.

Feeling an uncomfortable pressure on his back, Cale turned to see the guy watching him, unmoving. Cale shot his harshest glare up at the grinning figure, spun and headed for the ocean. He would wash out his towel the best he could, knowing that he would be unable to clean it completely.

5

HOVEL, SWEET HOVEL

The lawnmower repair shop was a dilapidated, weatherboard, one bedroom house. The pastel yellow paint of the walls was flaking, revealing the greying rot beneath its skin. One side wall, including the bathroom window, had been decorated in a rainbow spray of graffiti, exclaiming the various artists' discontent in glaring expletives. There was little point in Mr and Mrs Duhent cleaning the wall. The graffiti was repainted as soon as the canvas was renewed.

Mr Duhent's workshop was his garage. It was a cube construction of foraged materials, connected to the sallow house like a brick and corrugated iron tumour.

The conjoined buildings sat on a large plot of land, one of the borderline properties that separated the town from the steep, forested cliffs surrounding.

Their mailbox was a large cookie tin, balancing precariously on the end of the shaft of a rusted golf club. Mr Duhent was creative when it came to fashioning new mailboxes whenever the previous ones were destroyed by the local kids.

Alley checked it as she walked past. No mail. She headed around the side of the house, aiming herself for the back of the property. Alley and her brother's shelter rested at the back of the Duhent's land. It was a shack, originally built by Mr Duhent as the workshop. He gave it to Alley and Cale three years ago, rent free. He had known their father many years past; was even at the hospital when Alley was born.

She stopped, noticing the roller-door of the garage was up. Hearing the sounds of clinking tools, straining metal and the incomprehensible grumbles of an old man, she changed her direction.

Mr Duhent was squatting above an over turned lawnmower, stabbing at its underside with a screwdriver. His face was a scrunched, brown paper bag with ears attached.

'Hello, little one,' he said, in his jagged Russian accent.

Alley offered him a brusque smile. To Mr Duhent all people under the age of thirty-five were known as *little one*.

'How school go?'

Alley shrugged, eyes wandering the ancient tools and apparatuses of the garage. It looked like an archive of torture devices from the dark ages.

'School no good?' Mr Duhent grunted, prying at something stubborn and uncooperative.

'No. Not really. Same as usual,' Alley replied. She moved to the side and collected a short handled gardening scythe, the blade rusted to the point of fossilisation. She wondered how he used this tool to improve the motor of a lawnmower. 'School's not really good for me, Mr Duhent.'

'No, no, no,' he stuttered. 'School important. Very important. Education important.'

Alley lent against the side bench. It whined and flexed under her weight.

'Learning …' he grunted. 'World eat people who not learn. World eat idiot people.'

According to Mr Duhent the world was waiting to eat a lot of people; the kids who spray painted his house and wrecked his mailboxes, the people who sent him bills and asked for his money, and a high majority of his customers. All were just waiting to be eaten.

'Learn now. Soon, it all over, yes?'

'Yeah.'

'Then, then, work, work, work.' He waved a knobbly finger in her direction. 'But you finish the learning, yes?'

Alley wondered what she was going to do when her exams were over. The first thing would be to compile a résumé, list all her skills and talents … *can count to eighteen with the proficiency of a mathematical genius; well versed in methods of freaking out; can imitate the shaggy ass of a wet dog with great precision …*

She blocked the flow of her thoughts. Thinking about next year made her physically ill.

'How's Mrs Duhent today?' she breathed, pushing away from the bench.

'Miss Mumbo Jumbo mad. She no talk to me.' He sat back with a wheezing groan and stared ahead with his drooping eyes. 'Good thing, good thing,' he nodded. 'Quiet good.' With a similar groan, he lent back into the lawnmower.

Mrs Duhent was a psychic. She followed the movements of the stars and celebrated the first full moon of every month, when she remembered it. She called it Esbat. The living room of their small house had been draped in tasselled blankets of dark purple and deep blue. Incense always burned in that room. Walking into it was like burying your head in a basket of Indian spices. Troubled, misty eyed people would arrive at the door to have their palms read, or for Mrs Duhent to flip through the tarot cards and peak under the veil of the shrouded future.

The medicines and scientific treatments for her rare form of leukaemia were only silly annoyances of lesser beings without her spiritual acuity. The medical nonsense was tolerated solely to silence the whinging of her husband. She claimed it would be her innate understanding of the mystical world and her truckloads of positive karma that would banish the illness within her.

Her accent was not as thick as her husband's … except when she was with a customer. She also had a greater grasp of the language.

Mr Duhent said that eloquence was a waste … not that he used the word *eloquence.* Anything that can be conveyed in five words can usually be expressed in two, sometimes one.

'Hammer,' Mr Duhent called to Alley as she stood daydreaming. He indicated the side bench with a crooked finger.

She retrieved the tool and presented the handle. Mr Duhent's hand shook as his fingers closed around it. His second and fourth fingers were too crippled to secure the grip.

'Um, Mr Duhent,' Alley murmured, sweeping forsaken screws into a small pile with a foot, 'if there's anything to be picked up from the post office or deliveries to be dropped off, I'm happy to do them.'

His dark orbs swivelled to the corner of his eyes. He watched her without turning from his work. 'Sorry, little one. Business quiet. No deliveries.'

'That's fine,' Alley said, forcing brightness into her voice. 'You know where to find me if you do need any work done.' She released a short laugh and she did not know why.

'Okay, okay,' Mr Duhent said in a low voice.

Alley left the garage, feeling the eyes of Mr Duhent follow her. She pictured his face drooping much more than usual, a brown paper bag beneath running water.

As she headed around the house the rain fell. She sensed her hair snarling at the water's touch, imitating *the shaggy ass of a wet dog* with great precision.

Their home was small; sixteen Alley-steps long ways, eight the other. The front door opened into the middle of the living room. A three seater couch sat against the rear wall. Its grey material was torn, blowing bubbles with the off-yellow foam inside it. A bathroom was left of the lounge room. There was a functioning toilet and even a shower. A kitchenette sat on the opposite side. It had a sink and a stove top and a bar fridge that housed their milk and the few vegetables that were offered when the neighbouring ethnics harvested their sprawling vegie gardens.

The only bedroom was behind the kitchen. It was large enough to fit her mattress and a rack for her few pieces of clothing.

Cale lived in the lounge room. His wardrobe was a duffle bag sitting in the corner. His bed was the couch. He said he did not mind the arrangement. He said he liked falling asleep to the fuzzy black and white images of the small TV that Mr Duhent had salvaged from the Stenosen's rubbish collection pile. It sat on an overturned milk crate in the corner opposite his wardrobe.

Alley smiled and nodded at him whenever the subject was raised. But she always felt his pleasure was exaggerated. The alternative would be to live within foster care or in a home with others in a similar situation to themselves. That was not an option for Cale. He was no longer able to share walls with anyone other than his sister. He even seized up and shut down when Mr or Mrs Duhent drew too near.

Alley dropped her bag and fell onto the couch. She retrieved her windbreaker and held it before herself.

Sarah was right. It did look hideous.

The windbreaker was thrown into the wall opposite and a book was collected from beneath the lounge. Alley wriggled herself down into the mess of foam and material until she was almost buried up to her neck. She pulled the book close enough to her nose so the pages wrapped around her head, preparing to draw her in, and send her tumbling onto the moors of Wuthering Heights.

Sometimes she would construct her own endings to such stories; ones where Catherine and Heathcliff run off into the sunset together, escaping their lives, and themselves, and finding their happiness at last.

'*Wow. What a bastard I've been to everyone!*' Heathcliff would say, in all his untamed gypsy-ness.

'*Yeah. I've been a bit of a nutter myself, darling. And I can't believe I married that little twerp,*' Cathy would reply, delicate and fierce together.

'*Yeah, well, what about me? What the hell was I thinking!? Let's just run away together … me and you, babe. And then we'll finally be happy. Wadda ya reckon, eh?*'

'*Oh, my love. That was all I wanted to hear …*'

It was only a child's game. Deep down she knew their sufferings were necessary. There was no Catherine without her mad, self-destructive passion. And there was no Heathcliff without his agony and brutish wrath. They needed to suffer in order to exist.

Sometimes there are no happy endings. And that is the way it has to be.

Three words into her first sentence and the door swung inward. Cale entered.

Alley lowered her book into her lap and said, 'Hi.'

Cale raised his head in response. His eyes landed on the glaring wound on Alley's arm and turned his attention to the couch beside her.

'How was swim practice?'

He walked into the kitchen. Organising a drink of water, he drank it slowly as though savouring the blandness. Placing down his empty cup, he braced himself against the stove top. His swim-shower towel remained in his hand the entire time.

From her position, Alley could see the swollen lump of his left cheek. His eye was bruising. It would be a dark shade by tomorrow morning.

He looked to her with a blank expression. 'I need something.'

Alley watched him.

'I need to buy something.'

'Yeah?' she said, hesitantly.

'A new towel.'

'A new towel?'

He clenched his teeth. The muscles of his jaw bulged.

Alley glanced to the one in his hand. 'You want a new one?'

'This one's shit,' he burst, holding it forward in a white knuckled grip. 'It's embarrassing. It's no more than a bloody rag. I want a new one for swimming.'

Alley looked down at her jeans. The skin of her knees was visible through the tears. She looked up. 'I'll swap you. Mine's a bit better than yours. You have my towel and I'll have that one.'

Cale bared his teeth as he looked around the floor for something lost. He threw his head from side to side as though shaking off wasps and walked to the front door. Flinging it open, he tossed the towel out into the rain. 'Don't touch it,' he mumbled, beneath his breath. 'It's mine,' he said, closing the door and heading into the bathroom.

Alley pulled her book up to her nose and stared through the pages to the wall behind.

6.

THE SEEPING DARKNESS

Was he getting worse? Alley could not tell. Was she like that when she was his age? She could not remember.

Her strides were a mess. Failing to land her step at the right distance, Alley squirmed in her skin. She felt her mind constricting and choking on its own thoughts with each mislaid step.

She had seen him once at school that day. He sat on the perimeter of the grounds, hunching over his sandwich. His head was lowered and his eyes darted to and fro at those whizzing around him. He looked like a caged rodent in a laboratory; one wise to the power and cruelty of his captors, anticipating the moment when that cage door would open and those gloved hands would reach in.

The Duhent's property drew up alongside her and disappeared behind. It was an arduous uphill trudge to the headlands. No longer did it shorten her breath.

As the road steepened, Alley fell into her rhythm. The camera, snug in its padded pouch, swung out on every even numbered step and then collided with her hip on the odd ones. Carla had taken it upon herself to ask Mrs Cleary if Alley could borrow some of the photography equipment for some personal projects. Because it was Alley, no return date was attached.

Carla had handed over the camera with a smile filled with expectation. Alley accepted the camera amiably and evaded a commitment to Carla's photography club.

The camera slapped her hip again. She dug her windbreaker out from within the depths of her bag. Unsure why she searched the weed-thick properties beside her and the road behind, she pulled it on. The camera was pressed against her body now, unable to swing. It somehow felt safe beneath her jacket; her hidden eye ready to emerge and capture the state of the world.

Reaching towards the cliffs, the road then curved back inland, prowling the rolls of the climbing hills in its escape from the town below. The forest track was cloaked by encroaching shrubs and low hanging branches. Without raising her head, Alley left the road, ducked the tree limb stretching out like a boom-gate and was enveloped by shadow and thin shards of sunlight.

Massive pines dominated the area. Like gigantic moulting beasts they shed their needles, creating a thick carpet over the ground, a protective layer against the mud and Alley's shoes.

The smooth roar of charging waves beyond and below filtered through the forest. Attached to the call was the smell of salted seaweed.

The pines thinned and were replaced by a sculpted promontory that looked out across the expanse of the oceans.

Heading north along the rocky cliff, she came to a stubby rise of stone, the lofty throne of forgotten people. She scrambled up its side and took her seat in the centre. Raising the camera, Alley adjusted the focus, transforming the smear of colours into the world she existed within.

She traced the run of mighty cliffs travelling the coast. The town rested within a gouge in this wall of rock that stood against the ocean. It was as though a giant ice-cream scoop reached in and took a dollop of land, leaving a half-bowl cavity in the ample mass of highlands. The two miles or so of yellow sands was the line separating town from sea.

Nestled deep within the cliff's protective huddle, the town had housed the majority of miners that burrowed into the surrounding cliffs like coal-hungry termites.

Alley scanned the distant slopes, hunting for the step in the forest that indicated the railway track. Once the mining company shut down operations the track became a thin memory slowly fading beneath the creeping tide of vegetation. She focused and pressed the button, storing the view away.

She recalled a quite poetic letter-to-the-editor in the local paper by a grizzly old man by the name of Mr McCoy. Underlying his plethora of complaints was the mine's closure two decades earlier. He claimed sealing the mine entrances did not stop dark things seeping from those subterranean voids they drilled into the world. As though they had hit a spring of darkness, a terrible blight continued to pour upon the poor town of Coalcliff.

Anger and resentment engulfed the once quiet and peaceful streets. Neighbour turned against neighbour, children against their parents, husband and wives against each other. Alcohol and drug abuse rose rapidly. The din of domestic violence replaced the nightly song of creaking crickets, whispering trees and the soft cheer and sigh of waves as they spread themselves on the sand after their lengthy travels.

After a few years of the flow of darkness from above, crime, like the abusive graffiti staining the streets, became an accepted annoyance that needed to be endured. Hate-filled youth prowled the darkened hours. They were infected, oblivious minions of the blight, according to Mr McCoy.

Alley lowered the camera. Even her father had succumbed to Mr McCoy's seeping darkness.

From what little she learnt of her father, the ex-miner spent the majority of his new found free time at the local bar. When the sun set and the whistle blew after a hard day's drinking session, he was travelling along Cliffside Drive when he left the road at Hopes Lookout. The speed with which he found the tree caused his ute to meet the trunk as tinfoil. Even if he managed to avoid that solid growth, the cliffs, a short distance beyond, were ready and waiting to seal his fate.

No one ever did explain to her why her father was at Hopes Lookout that night. Cliffside Drive was fifteen minutes past their home. And Hopes Lookout was a further twenty up a road of hairpin turns most people did not have the stomach for when they were sober.

Mr McCoy was sure the mines had awoken something malevolent. When people responded with facts and statistics on the abysmal unemployment rate, the collapse of small businesses and the epic amounts of foreclosures, Mr McCoy agreed with a short hum. 'It was all a big, tangled ball of string,' he replied.

One thing they all agreed upon was that the town was in a state of decay.

Alley was able to see small truths in Mr McCoy's disgruntled ramblings. She looked upon the town and saw the drabness that coated it. As though the rains washed the ashy residue of coal from the heights onto the town, a thin film of grey coated every surface. Everywhere she looked, to the sky, to the sea, to the leaves of the trees, was a dullness. Life within and around this town was awash with gloom.

But, as though the town was a crippled plough horse, too stupid to stop, too stubborn to die, it clung to life.

The one source of nourishment offered to the expiring beast sat in the distance.

Peering through the camera, looking over the town to the northern cliff, Alley brought Deep Moss Heights into focus. Framed by the viewing window, the simple, deep grey blocks of buildings looked like the ruins of an ancient city, built by the hands of an unimaginative, austere culture. Her finger hovered over the button.

Deep Moss was originally the headquarters of the mining company's national operations. After the closure of the mines, the state brought up the land and buildings for a penny. Deep Moss was transformed into a high profile hospital for the mentally ill and rehabilitation centre, in order to ease the pressure of the city hospital three and a half hours north. The hospital accepted patients from the entire state.

Before her finger fell to the button, Alley dropped the camera and hid it within her windbreaker.

It was fortunate for her mother that when the woman was committed she was only forced to travel twenty minutes up the road.

The new hospital needed managers, book keepers, nurses, groundsmen, maintenance crews, and security and transportation officers. As a government initiative, those willing unemployed of Coalcliff were offered training and a position at Deep Moss.

And just like that, the town was hooked up to a massive, concrete life-support machine.

As though the hollow veins of the cliffs bled its dismal grey upon the town, Alley imagined the hospital spilling the insanity it housed into the streets, contaminating the unsuspecting townspeople. She felt as though everyone was soaking in madness, stewing in it, slowly losing their minds … or maybe that was just her.

She shook herself, stood and turned her back on the town and Deep Moss in the distance. She headed south along the precipice.

Stopping at the edge of a drop, Alley looked down to Mystics Bay. It would have been a tranquil little hideaway if not for the massive reef break just beyond the bay's mouth. With five to six foot waves breaking upon a reef cushioned by only two inches of water, only a couple of local surfers dared the break.

'Told you it's here.'

'Yeah. I could smell it. It stinks of home.'

Alley froze.

'Shit, you're right. That's one of 'em. A damn Water-home … Makes me wanna vomit, it does.'

She peered into the forest, searching for the three owners of the three voices.

'Let's burn the thing.'

Only trees and broken shadows could be seen.

'What? We gonna burn a beach? How the hell can you burn a beach?'

'You can burn anythin' with enough fire, you can.'

'Well, we gotta trash it somehow. C'mon, let's find a way down … Over here.'

There was a shuffling of feet and the breaking of branches. They were heading towards the precipice. Alley's thoughts stumbled. She lost the number … no, it was seven. It was too late. Three young men swaggered to a stop as they found Alley standing on the rocks.

All three were darkly dressed. As though on proud display, they ensured their right arms were visible and the mark on the back of their hands. The thick black tattoo was of a jagged anchor, starting above the wrist travelling down, and finishing with the hooks on the back of the hand. The marking at the end of the appendages appeared to hold a strange weight. They stood at an uncomfortable angle, bracing themselves against the uneven load.

Alley, along with the rest of the townsfolk, was familiar with the logo. It indicated the three were of a delinquent gang that had invaded the town recently, the Anchors. Their numbers had swollen over the past month, aided by recruiting local youths.

'Who the hell are you?' one of the young men hacked.

Alley shook her head. 'No one.'

'Is that so, is it? Does that mean no one's gonna miss you after we toss you over the edge?'

Alley heard the waves colliding with the rocks far below. She took a step back. 'Eight,' she breathed.

'Eight what?' one asked, his expression contorting from some new taste in his mouth. 'Eight seconds to reach the bottom? I reckon it's more like three, girly.'

'There's only one way to find out, there is,' said another.

The sound of movement amongst the trees halted them all. Alley only knew of two people who surfed this break, and here was one of them.

Eran, in only a pair of shorts, board tucked under one arm, moved through the scattering of trees with his head bowed. There was no hesitation in his step as his bare feet came down on sharp stones and the prickly pine needles.

'Hi, Eran!' Alley called out loud enough to shake the birds from the trees.

Lifting his head, he found her and the three Anchors. His face, as always, supported an unchanging solemn gaze. He was in Alley's grade, but was rarely seen at school. The days he did attend, he usually spent out on the lawns, lying on his back, sleeping.

Eran stopped. His board maintained its position under his arm. 'Hello, Alley.' He turned to the Anchors. 'What are you all doing here?'

'Whatever the hell we feel like,' one scoffed.

'Wait,' another said, to his colleagues. 'You know who this is, don't yas?'

The other two scrutinized Eran.

'Can't yas smell him? That putrid blood in his veins. It's one of *them*. A dirty little tribesman,' he sneered.

All three looked to the bay, then back to Eran, their expressions opening.

'What are you doing here?' Eran repeated.

'A few things, dirt-eater. First, we gonna kick the shit outta ya. Then we headin' down there,' he pointed to the bay, smirking.

Eran reached out and planted the tail of his board at his side.

Alley wanted to stop them. She knew if she opened her mouth nothing more than a whimper would escape.

More sound, a heavy thump, flowed from the guts of the forest. A large shape shifted amongst the trees. Emerging into the light was the massive form of Croco.

Like Eran, he only wore a pair of shorts. His board was tucked under an arm that looked like some kind of hydraulic pistons covered in skin.

'Croco,' Eran greeted his friend.

Croco glanced to Alley then eyed the three Anchors. 'What's going on here?' He planted his board in a similar fashion to Eran and rolled his shoulders. A tattoo of a crocodile curled around half his neck. It wriggled as Croco's muscles rippled under his skin.

It was said that Croco spent a few years on the pro circuit. He denied it. True or not, he surfed like a pro. He handled the break of Mystics as though he controlled the waves himself.

Alley could only guess that the waves, like everyone else in town, were intimidated by the bulk of the man and the restrained anger simmering behind his tiny eyes.

The three Anchors shifted their attention to various objects, their gazes only capable of sweeping over Croco, never wanting to linger too long on the man.

'Looking for trouble, boys?' Croco said. His lips stretched wide. The two runs of small teeth managed to dominate half his face. 'Why don't you all run along before I decide to tear your arms and legs off?'

'Your time's coming, old man,' one of the Anchors said, finding his courage. He tilted his head back and a rattling issued from his throat. He then hacked up a large blob of phlegm to land square on Croco's chest.

Croco's hand was around the Anchor's throat in the next beat, squeezing a blue tinge into his face. His bared teeth were enough to halt the advance of the other two.

Alley watched Croco's fingers enclose the cylinder of skin and muscle that connected head to torso. His thumb and finger tips were meeting at the undulating ridge of the Anchor's spine. She was sure Croco was going to crush the young man's neck. When she expected to hear the gooey snap, Croco released him and the Anchor dropped to the ground like a body taken of all its bones.

Collecting their gasping colleague, the three Anchors cautiously edged their way around him.

'Your pal's forgetting something?' Croco grumbled, lowering his chin to his chest.

One of the Anchors moved forward with a glower. Reaching towards Croco, the young man scooped the slippery gunk out of the mat of hair.

'Be sure he gets that back,' Croco said, and watched as the young man wiped the phlegm on the recovering man's arm. 'Bye,' he added, directing his teeth at the three as though they were enough to repel them to distant places.

When the shadows of the forest had swallowed them, Croco turned to Eran and said, 'Little pests.'

Eran grimaced. 'More than that, Croco.'

Croco laughed through his nose. 'Nah. They're just little pests. Flies that need swatting every now and then.'

'And when they start swarming?'

Croco retrieved his board.

'Do you all know each other?' Alley asked.

Throwing his board under his arm, Croco turned his small eyes on her as though he misunderstood the question.

'I mean, it just seemed like they knew you two.'

Croco glanced to Eran. 'How's the break?' He moved to the edge and nodded his approval at the ocean's savage pummelling of the cove.

Alley threw her ring-finger nail between her teeth. That should keep her mouth busy. A small burst of light exploded before her. Flinching from the unexpected attack of bright, she scrubbed her eyes of the visual shock.

Clearing the momentary blindness, Alley saw a speck of light race towards the precipice and drop over the edge. Blinking away the luminescent streaks scorched on her retinas, she moved towards the cliff. Amongst the scrub bordering the bay below, a glimmering dot rushed. It zipped towards the ocean, turned, and began a stuttering race around the rocky shore.

Her hands found the camera at her side. Aiming the camera in the direction of the cove, she zoomed and fired off a few shots.

'Oi!' Croco's small eyes had thinned, two hyphens typed beneath his brow, as he looked to Alley's hands. 'Not a good idea to be taking pictures of the cove.'

Alley tucked the camera back within her windbreaker, trying not to make the move look like that of a guilty five year old.

'Just wanna keep this place a nice little hidey-hole for us lot.'

Alley nodded.

'There's some out there that shouldn't know 'bout this place. Won't appreciate it like us. We don't want any more of those,' he nodded on the trail of the three Anchors, 'sniffing around here. It'd be bad news, get it?'

'Okay.'

'This is a special place, girl.' Croco turned. 'It might be best you don't come here again.' He leaned into his lumbering stride towards the cliff side path that led down to the bay.

Hung up by strings to keep her from crumpling into a pile, Alley stood in the aftershock of Croco's disapproval. Was she so dim-witted that she could not see Mystics Bay the way Croco knew it to be? Or was she just so un-special that she had zero affinity with special places?

Eran did not move to follow after Croco. He turned to Alley. They looked to each other like a national and a foreigner, both aware of the density of the language barrier. This was just another feature of Eran, these long periods of absent words. Starting conversation with him was like trying to kick over a fifty year old tractor; difficult, but not impossible.

He was well known at school, praised for his talent on a board. His friendship with the revered recluse, Croco, also elevated his social standing amongst the others. Yet his ears seemed un-attuned to their small talk. And his careful, abstract comments brought awkwardness to conversations like a battering-ram.

When talking to him one on one, Alley received a sense of what it might be like to be the socially adept one in conversations.

'I didn't expect to see any of those Anchors up here,' she said. 'They usually just hang around town.'

'Expectation opens you to unwanted surprises,' Eran nodded, eyes on the ocean visible over her shoulder. 'You go to school today?'

'Yeah. I didn't see you there.'

'I felt tremors of bad tidings in the ground.'

'Tremors?'

'In the ground. Up into my feet. Bad tidings.'

'Oh.'

'Hmmm,' Eran agreed. 'I know it has something to do with him,' he said, to the sea.

'Him?'

'The new arrival.'

'Pan?' Alley questioned. The interest in that new student was inescapable. Every classroom she walked into, every hall she moved through, were the whispers of Pan's name.

'A darkness follows him, yes?'

'Um …'

'A dark trouble,' he clarified.

'Well, not really. He's usually, kind of … bright, I guess.'

There was a twitch to the corner of his eye. 'There's darkness,' he corrected. 'I've been running into Anchors all day.'

'I don't even know why they're up here.' She felt a rumble through the ground as a giant set of waves threw themselves upon Mystics' reef.

'They're rallying. Spreading.' He lowered himself, crouching over a large caterpillar inching its way towards the vegetation. He allowed the creature to crawl onto his finger and lifted it to Alley.

'Um, cute.'

Eran stepped to a nearby tree and released the caterpillar to the trunk. 'This town is dying, Alley. The Anchors are its disease.'

'Sounds like them.'

Eran twisted his lips as he returned to her. 'I fear the authorities here don't have the strength to fight them.'

Alley placed the nail of her middle finger between her teeth. 'I don't think it's that bad, Eran.'

'Something's stirring. I can feel it. And it won't be good.'

The wind blew hard against them, moaned as it blundered its

way across the cliff face below. Alley watched Eran's eyes focus on something distant. She had never really noticed the darkness of his eyes before. Tilting her head to the side, she recalled her encounter with Beanie Lady the other morning.

Eran turned abruptly, depleted of all his conversation. 'I'm gonna catch some waves.' He paused, turned his head, and said, 'Croco's right. This place is too special to be risked.'

'I don't understand.'

'You never will.'

Alley, held up like a string-puppet, watched him head towards Mystics Bay, with the nail of her middle finger between her teeth.

7.

A LONELY HOWL

How far could he swim? Push himself through the breakers to the dark expanse beyond? Crawl across the endless heave to the thin line separating ocean from sky? Further, perhaps?

Cale huddled upon the damp shelf, looking out to sea. Further down, the waves collided with the solid foundations of the earth, scrubbing them with white suds as though the ocean knew this place beneath their feet was filthy down to its core.

What would he look like to someone on the surrounding cliffs? Hugging his legs into his chest, bowed forward, chin resting on his knees, he must have looked tiny, a dust mote settled upon the jagged edge of this craggy spread.

An uncomfortable thing surged inside him, seeming far larger than the body that contained it. If it broke through his chest and escaped into the world, it would be giant, hollow and dark. Its head would be lost in the mist of the clouds, sending a great shadow over Coalcliff. Everyone would arch their heads back, almost falling backwards, and gush, 'Wow. I've never seen something so big,' and it would lumber its way out into the ocean, the water never reaching higher than its belly.

The long yellow stretch of sand to his side was empty. The ocean was absent of its riders. Cale imagined the town had been taken of its people. He was the last person in Coalcliff, the last person in the whole world.

He was now a wild child, with only the untamed ocean as a companion. He would not bother to live in a house, or even bother heading into the town at all. Here, on the beach, he would be. He would catch fish and crabs, and cook them on fires he would make on the beach at night. All he would need was a sharp stick to spear them out of the water. A bit of driftwood would do, sharpened with a rock, or an oyster shell. Those things were damn sharp. After a huge meal he would relax beneath the stars until his dinner settled. Then, he would dance around the naked flames of his bonfire, howling to the full moon, howling and howling, ensuring the world understood that this was his place, his kingdom.

He raised his head and spotted the bent crowbar of the moon, prying its way between the clouds. 'Howooo,' he sang, quietly, and listened to the waves wash his call from the night's surface.

He threw his head back, closed his eyes, drew a massive breath until his lungs were ready to explode and released, 'HOWOOOOOOO!' to the moon above.

His cry peeled out across the rocks, rolled across the tops of the waves and spread across the ocean. The hollow giant in his chest shrunk back from the mighty call.

Cale glanced to the side. His brown, tattered towel was half sunk in a rock pool. It drifted back and forth, swaying between baubled necklaces of seaweed as it soaked.

Steps were heard behind. Someone was coming. The giant expanded its arms, pushed against the inside of his chest.

Did they hear him howling? Did they think he was crazy like the rest of his family?

The sound of steps drew nearer. Cale froze. The steps reached his back, moved to the side, walked around him and displayed the body that made them. It was the young man from yesterday, the one with that wild hair who did not help him against Mitchel … not that he wanted help.

Cale watched him as he continued along the shelf, picking his way across the jags and around the large rock pools. He reached the edge and looked down into the waves as they playfully barged the short wall he stood upon.

For a long while the young man stared into the dark and white churn below.

Cale spent most of his time on the edge of the ocean. What was so interesting down there that he had never noticed?

He straightened his back and stretched his neck, but he was sitting too low. Cale climbed to his feet. Standing, he was still unable to see down into the water. He stepped closer. Nothing curious could be seen. He took another step and another. Soon he was close enough to be heard. The young man turned with a heavy look. Seeing it was Cale, he returned to his inspection.

Cale walked closer, watching for any hostile reaction, ready to flee. Reaching his side, nothing was said, so Cale looked down into the briny stew, searching for the object of interest.

'I don't see anything,' Cale whispered, squinting in the dark water as it surged and fell, surged and fell, exposing nothing but itself.

The young man only looked down, concentrating.

'This is stupid,' Cale said, after another long, unimpressive moment. He stood back and looked at the guy. 'What are you doing?'

'Listening,' he whispered, not taking his eyes from the water.

'Listening? To the ocean?'

'Yes … You can almost understand the words if you listen hard enough.'

Cale looked from the absorption in this guy's expression, to the water, and back again. 'Are you crazy?' he asked. 'I have a sister who's crazy.'

'Shoosh,' he said. Without looking up, he grabbed Cale's shirt and brought him closer to the edge. 'Listen …'

Cale obeyed. All he heard was the slushing and sucking of water as it hit rocks and drew back. 'I don't know who you are, but …'

'Pan.'

'Okay. But the ocean doesn't talk. It has no mouth.'

Pan looked up, his eyes gleaming in the dull light of afternoon. He stared at Cale for a long time before throwing his head back and laughing to the sky. His humour roared upwards as it rolled like foothills from his mouth.

Cale stepped back, amazed, but not afraid. He was almost laughing himself. 'It wasn't that funny,' he said.

Pan calmed himself and wiped the tears from his eyes. '*It has no mouth* ... That was a good one.'

'No, it wasn't,' he said, reflecting the smile beaming at him.

'Of course I am not listening to the ocean talk. I am listening to those within it.'

'The people in it?'

'Yes. Sound travels faster in water. It is clearer. I read that in a science book, kid.'

'I know that,' Cale said. 'I do science.' He paused. 'So, you think the ocean grabs sounds out of the air and carries them around?' he asked, wondering how far his howl had travelled.

'It is mainly from those within the water. And you have to listen hard enough, and know what to listen for.'

'You sure it works like that?'

'I think it works like that,' Pan said, scratching the top of his head and reading something in the storm clouds. 'I can hear them sometimes.' He shrugged.

'But I don't hear anything.'

'Most don't. But some do. And it is easier if you are in the water, too. Or at least a part of you is.'

Pan reached forward and took hold of Cale.

Cale seized at the touch.

'Come over here,' Pan said, tugging at his arm.

Cale found his legs moving. The constriction was not really there.

Both lowering to their knees, Pan directed Cale's hand down into the water.

He felt the chill of the ocean cold rise and fall over his fingers and palm. Water shouldered the rocks, breathing dense mist into the side of Cale's head. His mouth and eyes fell open. Like a coherent seashell held up to his ear, he heard the talk of the ocean.

'I hear it,' Cale said. 'I do.'

It was difficult to interpret, as though each word was joined and soaked by gurgling water. He was certain that those who were speaking were enjoying themselves immensely. There were bright squeals, and warbling laughter like the bursting of many bubbles.

'What do you hear?'

'Something … like laughing and messing around.'

Pan rolled his eyes. 'They are always messing around and causing mischief.'

'Sounds like they're having a great time. Wait … They've gone quiet.' Cale looked to Pan. 'Hold on. They're humming. Can you hear it?'

'I can.'

'No, they're singing. It's a song.'

'You hear their song?'

Cale remained motionless as the bubbly words rippled up his arm to find his head. '*Scarred and beaten, born and broken, child of water, fear your fate …*'

'You can hear it.'

'*… Your life shall be laid upon a crumbling throne—*'

Pan yanked Cale's arm clean out of the water.

'Hey,' Cale said, stabilising himself on the rocks. 'I almost fell.'

Pan stared into the water, chuckling. 'Trouble makers.'

'Who are?'

Pan climbed to his feet. 'No one.'

'Are they your friends? Do you have friends?'

'I know them. They are not really my friends.'

Cale's eyes fell onto the ocean, and continued falling until he was staring at his bare feet. 'There's nothing wrong with me.' He felt Pan look to him. 'I'm not crazy. And there's nothing wrong with me.'

'As you say.'

'I'm just messing around when I howl. Did you hear me? I'm just playing.'

'It is a good thing that you howl. You should do it all the time. Sticks crows,' Pan said.

'Who's Sticks?'

'You will meet him sometime. He crows like a rooster announcing the start of a day.'

'Really? A rooster? That's a bit stupid, isn't it?'

'Roosters are strong and proud. And what is more important than stopping the night and starting the day?'

'I guess.'

'And he got that from me. But he can have it, because it is good to call out to the world. All the best warriors I know do it.'

'Yeah?'

'They do. They howl like you. The water-wolves. They do it to remind the world that they exist, that they are here and they should not be forgotten.'

'Water-wolves … I've never heard of them.'

'They started out as boys like you and me. They liked playing at the beaches and swimming in the rivers and lagoons all day. That is where they met the Great Wolves.'

'Great Wolves?'

'The Great Wolves were the wisest and strongest things in the land. But there were these people. They sailed in from a dark horizon. They landed their ships and found a way to kill them.'

'Why would they do that?'

'It is hard to say. These people like to take things. All they do is take.'

'Did the Wolves fight back?'

'They did. But these people cannot be stopped. It is like trying to plug a spring. You might stop it for a while, but the water is always there and will just find another place to pop up. So the boys who played at the beach decided to help the Great Wolves. But the Great Wolves were proud and did not like the boys even though they were nothing like the ones who take. Their leader told the boys to stay away. The boys were not deterred. Not in the slightest. No way. They had the spirits of warriors, of kings. They trained themselves to fight like the wolves. And one night, when a great amount of ships sailed in on the darkness, the boys swam out to them. Using their teeth and nails, they chewed and scratched their way through the hulls and sunk them. The boys were the best swimmers. They fought in the water and killed every last one of those who take. The Wolves saw the battle and accepted the boys into their pack, calling them the water-wolves. And whenever one of the Elder Wolves passed into the next life, they shed their fur and gave it to the water-wolves. Soon all the water-wolves had their own Great Wolf skin and were recognised by everyone in the land as great warriors. They feared no one and no thing. And they protected the boundaries of the land for a very long time, standing against the ocean, howling to the horizon to remind those who take that they were there and they were not afraid.'

'Good story.'

'It is.'

'I'm a swimmer. I reckon I'd make a great water-wolf, if they were real, I mean.'

'They are real … Well, not anymore. They are all dead.'

'Dead?'

'Yes. A new danger made itself known,' Pan said, studying the horizon. 'It caused an endless night to fall. And when the water-wolves fell in the following battles, they could not be awoken. They were dead, for good. Ended. The Great Wolves, too. All of them.'

'That's terrible.' He watched Pan watching the water. 'It's not true, but. It's just a story, isn't it?'

'It is true.'

'No, it's not. I know it's just a story. Wolves can't talk to people.'

'They can where I come from.'

'Oh, really? And where's that?'

A smile was Pan's reply.

Cale returned the look. Pan was clearly crazy. But a good kind of crazy, not at all like his sister or mother. He was definitely not a freak.

'Anyway, I have to be getting back,' Cale said.

'I will walk with you. I think you live near my place.'

'Where's your place?' Cale questioned, walking back over the rocks.

'You know the long fence that traps the horses?'

'You mean; Reed's horse farm? That's behind my house.'

'I live in the forest behind that.'

'I didn't know there were any houses over that way.'

'Not yet. A few more days and there will be the best one in the world.'

Nearing one of the rock pools, Cale collected his towel from within the water. He looked to Pan. Pan looked back.

No words were said and they headed home, Cale dragging his towel behind like a broken tail.

8

THE CALL TO WAR

There was something disappointing with the way the boy had gripped his towel. It was too tight.

Pan turned his back on the small home, leaving the boy to his dreams and drifted away with the night breeze. He moved through the streets, between the resting houses and into the bulk of the town.

Creeping amongst the solid structures, held by steep banks of cracked cement, was an ashen-coloured stream bearing a feathery coat of fog on its back. In a lethargic squirm, it made its way amongst buildings and beneath bridges, drains feeding it a steady diet of dribbling sludge as it slipped beneath them. It carried the scent of ancient creatures.

As the thing sought out its oceanic freedom, Pan retraced its journey. The concrete solidness of the town subsided and gave way to natural rock and large trees reaching out to one another with balding limbs.

Further on, deeper into the darkened forest, the stream fractured and dispersed and disappeared in a swampy territory of reedy ponds and thin ridges of muddy earth, all frosted with a soupy mist. Here, the trees were malformed and tubby. Their trunks twisted violently as they reached up and out, forming a thick canopy to shield the heavens from sight.

Pan lightened his steps. He avoided slapping at the squadron of mosquitos that hovered like a cloud about his body. The grating chorus of bullfrogs intensified the deeper he lurked, concealing the squelching of his steps.

'*You hunt as well as a drunken ox.*'

Pan froze. He searched the flooded surrounds. Through the bullfrogs' rusted mantra shot a clean musical note. Like a metronome maintaining the existence of time in this marshy realm, the steady twang repeated again and again, each tone chasing the flight of the one fired before it.

Straightening from his prowl, Pan sloshed through a stretch of water, navigated a thicket of contorted trees, and came to a clearing. Sitting as an island in a large pond was a mound of damp earth. Upon it was a ramshackle little dwelling, constructed from warped plywood boarding and sheets of corrugated iron. Against one side was propped a surfboard, speckled with grimy wax. From the slanted roof of the shack, hanging from a bent nail on the corner, was a lantern. The wobbling flame released a dull orange light that only held enough strength to reach down and paint a creature reclining beneath.

Slumping in an aged deckchair, blackened feet outstretched to perch upon a block of wood, was a mass of muscle dressed only in a pair of tattered shorts. In his lap was an acoustic guitar missing all but three strings. With eyes closed, he bobbed his head along with the beat he plucked from the thickest string. The crocodile tattoo around his neck seemed to tap its stubby legs and swing its tail along with the rhythm.

Pan waded through the water and ascended the bank to stand before the minimalist musician. 'Just like home,' he grinned, setting his fists on his hips.

His beady eyes opened slowly and viewed the one before him. The vibrating string was silenced with a flat palm. As the bullfrogs amplified their croaking to compensate, he raised a finger to his lips and released a gentle, 'Shhh.' The surrounding bullfrogs obeyed, leaving their cousins in the far reaches to carry on their song. 'I wasn't expecting to see the likes of you in these parts,' he grumbled, placing the guitar behind his seat.

'How did you get here, Croc?'

'Ha,' Croco returned, without humour. He reached to a cooler at his side, removed the lid and retrieved two bottles of chilled beer.

'There is war,' Pan said.

Croco paused, stretched his jaw and then leaned to the side to return one of the bottles to the ice. He replaced the cooler's lid and sat back, cracking the top of his bottle and guzzling.

Large flying insects charged the glass of the lantern, attempting to shatter the barrier and attack the flame. Pan followed their charge, curious to see if they would succeed. 'I sense the Tiger in these streets.'

'She's a broken woman.'

'Impossible. Not her. Not the Tiger.'

'She's broken.'

'How?'

'She faced your darkness.'

'She found it?'

'She is the child of the Panther, ya monkey,' Croco derided. 'A blood-born hunter.'

'What happened?'

'All I know is that she fled here in defeat. And now, this place,' he sniffed at some foul odour, 'ain't doing her any favours.'

'What of her people?'

'Scattered. Here, back home, and everywhere in between.'

'I need them to stay together. Our land is weaker without them.'

Croco flicked his brow, dismissing Pan's concerns. Resting his bottle on his stomach, he spent some time scratching at the hair on his cheeks and the thick carpet on his chest. Satisfied, he took another long drink before asking, 'I heard you and your boys made a stand?'

'We did.'

'And?'

'Only one other survived.'

Croco halted his inspection of the swamp and turned his small eyes on Pan. 'You lost.'

'I am still here.'

'Shameful.'

'The boys … they do not return when they fall.'

'Dead,' Croco said.

Pan nodded. 'Dead.'

They both turned to the mist rotating on the water's surface.

'And the old enemy is not as we once knew them to be,' Pan added. 'Never have we lost a battle. That thing …' Pan shook his head. 'It has changed them. It is leading them.'

'Wrong,' Croco grunted.

'Is that so, old croc?'

'It doesn't lead 'em. It doesn't conspire or devise plans. It just is.'

'But they follow It.'

Croco shrugged his large shoulders. His painted crocodile seemed to shrug also. 'They worship the damn thing, I expect.'

'How do you know all this?'

After a swig, Croco mumbled, 'The maidens.'

'You are friends with them now? Is that how you came to be here? Fleeing to a little Water-home like a frightened guppy?'

With a swift movement Croco was on his feet, standing over Pan, his small, sharp teeth glinting within the lantern's flame. 'I do not flee. And I am no one's friend.'

'We have fought together. We have won together,' Pan said, matching the stare weighing upon him.

'I fight for my own reasons. I fight for myself. I'm on no one's side. Now, get lost. The smell of death is thick about you.'

'Help me fight It. I have a plan to victory. There is a child …'

'You can't fight It, ya fool. Only an enemy can be fought. And this thing ain't your enemy. It is death. Your death. It can't be avoided. No one can. It ain't an enemy.'

'I will make It my enemy. I will fight It and I will win.'

Croco sneered, chuckling as he lowered himself to his seat. 'The desperate words of the dying king.'

'You will see, crocodile. And when I reclaim what is mine, it will be I who decides what manner of wild creature may return to my home. So maybe you should start looking for a more comfortable chair to sit on, old croc. You may be here for a long, long time.'

With Croco's bared teeth targeting the meat on his limbs, Pan turned, laughing as he wandered away.

9

RIBBONS OF NIGHT

'Alley? Darling?' a voice sung through the window.
Swinging open the door revealed Mrs Duhent.

Her cheeks were withdrawn. She was dusted by an ashen hue. But Mrs Duhent would not halt this bi-annual tradition for any illness. 'Are you ready, my child?' the elderly woman asked.

Alley nodded.

In silence they left the property and walked a distance down the road. They waited for the bus, entered it when it arrived, and exited on the far side of town all without a word between them.

Beneath a heatless sun, they travelled up the steep road, Mrs Duhent having to stop and rest at regular intervals. By the time they reached the cemetery gates, Alley had a hold of the woman's arm, bearing the weight Mrs Duhent was no longer able to bear.

The tombstones seemed to glower in their greyness at the two animate beings shuffling between them. Alley and Mrs Duhent came to a stop before a small slab of stone entitled Nadia Duhent. On their first visit, years earlier, Mrs Duhent, with a shake to her head, explained that the meaning of Nadia was *hope*.

The elderly woman retrieved two envelopes from within her shawl, stepped towards the gravestone and tenderly balanced them on its top. She stepped back and, with Alley, watched the wind toy with the letters.

Mrs Duhent always wrote two. The second was for Grigory Duhent, back in Russia. He was fourteen years old when he was killed on his homeward bound journey from school. Like the focused attack of a lightning bolt, the motorcycle had struck the side of the bus and extinguished only one life. The motorcyclist survived with a concussion and a broken clavicle. Mr and Mrs Duhent left Russia the following year, never to return.

Two years into their new life, the Duhents prepared for the coming of their second child. And, as though in homage to her Russian blood, Nadia arrived six weeks premature in the depths of winter. Her four months of life were spent in a transparent box, tethered to a variety of scientific contraptions that Mrs Duhent prayed to devotedly until Nadia's last breath.

In the telling of this story, Mr Duhent said he was fearful of the rage he expected his wife to fly into. He found her silence was far more terrifying as she stood from her child's side, pushed past the doctors as though they were fictional creations and left the hospital building without a glance behind.

Alley's eyes stumbled over the epitaph, inscribed in the blocky Russian letters. Researching the words on the school computers revealed it to be a quote from an accomplished poet by the name of Vasko Popa. It read:

> *"… From every hope*
> *We Cherish*
> *Sprouts a star*
> *That moves unreachable before us …"*

'My child,' Mrs Duhent said, turning to Alley, 'is there anyone you wish to visit today?'

The question was routine and delivered with hopeful expectation. Alley returned her regular response, 'Not today, Mrs Duhent.'

As they returned through the cemetery, Alley's eyes were drawn to the far run of graves she usually refused to acknowledge.

Attached to, and spread about, a specific headstone, as though targeting Alley with insult, were dozens of black ribbons fluttering in the wind. An unseen thing swooped in, silent and dark, and sucked all warmth from her body. 'Why would someone do such a thing?'

'Do what, my darling?'

Alley indicated the distant headstone and surrounding plants.

Mrs Duhent shook her head.

Dropping her arm, Alley looked between the dark streamers and Mrs Duhent. The woman was not seeing them.

'Alley, darling, whatever is the matter?'

'Nothing,' Alley replied, twisting her lips into the shape of a smile. 'It's nothing, Mrs Duhent. Let's go.'

Seeing Mrs Duhent safely onto the bus, Alley explained she wished to walk the return journey, needing to clear her head. Mrs Duhent nodded and said she would be waiting with some tea when she arrived home.

Alley's numbered steps came down hard as she descended the steep road. It was one of those days when the town seemed lifeless and hollow. She imagined she had entered, and now explored, the two-dimensional world of an oil-painting. The scene seemed to congeal in its pigments, locking everything in place. A haunting quiet hung in the air. The sunlight was an inferior imitation and the painter's brush made the distant forms of people seem unnatural on the landscape.

She tucked her hands into her pockets, afraid of smearing the dull colours about her, and measured her steps as they brought her to the town's park, Kensington Gardens. It sat as the centre of Coalcliff and was a shrivelled, parched plot of land. The town was opposed to verdancy and dashes of painted bright. It preferred the cratered stretches of asphalt, bordered by drab strips of concrete sidewalks. The park, knowing it was unwelcome, had laid down and given up.

Alley walked the perimeter, watching a mangy dog race about the innards without any apparent objective.

'What are you counting?'

With a start, she turned to find Pan. All understanding of speech disappeared from her mind.

'What are you counting?' he asked again.

Alley peered at him, attempting to decipher his motivations by the arrangement of his facial features. 'How do you know I was counting?'

'I saw your mouth. You were counting numbers without speaking them.'

Alley placed the nail of her ring-finger between her teeth.

'She can't stop it ...'

'She's not right in the head ...'

'She's going the way of her mother ...'

The concerns of the adults had grown grimmer the older Alley grew.

'A child's games can progress into a teenager's quirks, and then into a young adult's mental disorder ...' the counsellor had explained.

She trained herself to be mute when counting her steps. It was now an inbuilt mechanism, her soundless counting, like the tic of her heart or the inflation of her lungs.

On occasion, when she was deep in the canyons and valleys of her mind, her lips would work involuntarily, mouthing the numbers that continued incessantly in her head.

'What are you counting?' he asked a third time, as though the question would repeat forevermore.

Alley stared at him. Not once had his eyes dropped from hers. 'My steps,' she heard her voice say and a black hole opened up in her chest, sucking everything in and leaving only negative space.

She realised her hand had fallen from her face. It raced back and covered her mouth, sealing her lips.

What on earth had made her say it?

Alley turned, almost falling as she spun. Preparing to rush away, she stopped and watched thin streams of darkness emerge from the shadows of the park and slither across the ground.

The misty tendrils gathered speed, gliding without sound across the pale earth. A dog barked as though it was warning of a collapsing sky. Alley watched the mangy mutt dart around, lost in madness, dodging the dark ribbons clawing for it. A ribbon reared back like a cobra, struck and latched onto the dog's hind leg. The dog yelped and tore towards the bordering streets, trailing the black behind.

Alley, dazed, glimpsed the approaching car. Dark streamers slithered across the bonnet and wove themselves in and out of the front grill. The dog raced, blind with terror, mouth foaming and its body wrapped in vaporous night.

The streamers binding the dog and the streamers clinging to the car reached out like stretching gum. They connected and contracted, bringing the two hurtling masses together.

A solid THUNK reverberated through the streets, followed by the screech of tyres skidding to a halt.

The dog rolled to a stop and lay still in a twisted mess. Its head was angled back to the ridge of hair on its back. Its tongue lay like a piece of raw steak on the road, in a spreading pool of dark red.

Alley's hands trembled in time with the flutter of her heart.

'It is coming.'

Alley turned her bewilderment on Pan. 'What?' She felt sick.

'It is coming,' he repeated.

'What is?'

'The end.'

Were those things real? Was this what had been in her mother's head? *Oh, god!*

She turned and fell into her stride; *one, two, three* …

'The stars,' Pan called out after her.

Alley stopped. Half turning, she said, 'What?'

'The stars. That is what I count … What I used to count.'

Alley gaped at him before returning to her feet; *four, five, six* …

10

A HOME AND ALL ITS TRIMMINGS

Alley's head swarmed with images and memories and voices, all shaped oddly and attempting to assemble. She did not want to go home. She needed a friend, a partner with which to engage in mindless chatter.

After measuring the distance of eighteen steps, she raised her head and changed direction.

Milly had been her closest companion in school. She had dropped out to pursue a career in fashion design and modelling.

Since a young age, everyone had pegged Milly as a model; hair like a sun-backed waterfall, eyes like the azure sky contained by lashes as thick as painted fingers.

Everyone said she was gorgeous. Her mum, Mrs Greene, – when she was conscious and coherent – always pointed out the fact when Alley was over, running an unsteady hand along the cheek of her daughter.

The boys could not get enough of her either. They always hassled her for dates. She conceded most of the time, heading out with them on late night excursions that started and ended in a beaten up car in some parking lot somewhere. The boys did love her … even if it was only for short stints.

Their house was easy to spot. The front yard was a wilderness. The grass was waist high, concealing the white pebbled path leading to their front door. Trees with broken branches lent over the house like the skeletons of crippled giants. Damaged furniture had migrated into the yard and settled down for a long stay as rot and rust atomised their existence.

The father left four years ago when the second child was born. No one else in the house was concerned with the state of the front yard. There were heavier matters weighing upon the lives of the remaining few.

Alley picked her way around the discarded items – it was eleven steps from the mailbox to the porch. Reaching the door, Alley hesitated. She stared at the peeling white paint, feeling her heart racing itself to somewhere deep. As her legs turned her away, her arm shot upwards. Her knuckles rapped on the door like a conscientious woodpecker.

Her hands held each other as she chewed her bottom lip and waited.

Sounds were heard within. Someone struggled with the door knob. After a few attempts, the door swung inwards. A little boy was standing on a chair that had been propped up against the wall alongside the door. He stared up at Alley with big eyes.

'Hi, Lukey. How have you been?' Alley said brightly, bending forward to reach his level.

He stared back as though she was speaking a different language.

Luke was four years old. He did not speak much, but he had become proficient in some tasks four year olds were not expected to perform, like opening the door to potential strangers.

His head was topped by a greasy splatter of light brown hair. He was already in his dark green pyjamas, or perhaps he had not left them.

'Remember me, Lukey? I'm Alley.'

'Could I have water?' Luke asked, as though singing a tuneless song.

'You want water?'

Luke threw his head up and down with an exaggerated nod.

'Okay, let's get you a drink,' Alley said, moving into the house and closing the door behind.

She was doused in a heavy gloom and a pungent odour. The lounge room was in disarray. Shelves and side tables had been emptied and cleared, their objects organised into small piles on the floor that Alley's adult mind was unable to interpret. The large LCD screen of the TV was muted, the faces of afternoon newsreaders calmly expressing devastating events in silence.

The kitchen was clean. Besides a few glasses, no plates and dishes had built up to be washed. To the side was a round, wooden table. On its surface were balls of tinfoil, little squares of empty satchels and gas lighters. The glass pipe, charred at the bulb on the end, sat like an exclamation mark in the centre.

Alley remembered the embarrassment of Milly's mum whenever she accidentally left it out and exposed like a verbal announcement when any of them were moving through the house. She stumbled through excuses about degenerate friends leaving their shit in her house. Over the last year she had become comfortable with the thing lying about when guests were over. She overlooked it, as though it was too common in her life to be considered an object of interest. It now sat on permanent display.

Glancing to the quiet little body at her side, Alley noticed Luke eyeing the item along with her.

It was such a simple instrument, that little glass tube. To his innocent eyes, Luke would have no idea of the drama such an innocuous looking thing could cause … or maybe he did.

Running a tap, collecting the water in a glass, Alley handed it to Luke and watched him pour it into his mouth and over his face. He gave her a satisfied grin and extended his arm upwards, presenting the empty glass.

Alley set the glass down, grabbed a tea towel and dried the boy, finding that he was coated in a thin layer of grime.

'Where's mum, Lukey?' she asked, wiping down all of his exposed skin, careful not to get any of the muck on her hands. She did not want to traumatise the boy by having a freak out in front of him.

'Ahhhmmm,' he hummed, eyes to the side.

Alley waited for any conclusion. None came. 'What about sis? Is Milly here?'

He nodded, vaguely pointing in the direction of her room. Alley turned and a tiny hand latched onto the tatters of her jeans.

'I'm hungry,' Luke stated, head bowed as though confessing to some wrong doing.

She opened the fridge. The milk was off. The juice was empty. The eggs looked wrong. And the beer was not a good choice for a four-year-old. Alley went through the cupboards and found many bare shelves. She located some baking soda, half a kilo of rice and a few old cans of corn.

Pulling a can down, she showed it to him. 'Do you like corn?'

He nodded vigorously.

'Want me to cook it first?'

He shook his head with just as much enthusiasm, accompanied by his outstretched hands clasping at the air in its direction.

Peeling back the can's top, Alley placed the yellow bits in a bowl and presented it to Luke with a spoon. He sat himself down on the kitchen floor and began gobbling as though it had the potential to evaporate away.

Alley turned and headed through the hall to Milly's room at the end. The door was closed. She stared at tiny images of supermodels on catwalks, pinned to the door at eyelevel. She knocked softly. No response. She knocked harder. Again, nothing. She slammed her knuckles upon the smiling face of a brunette in white lingerie and white angel's wings spreading from her back.

'What?'

'Milly, it's me, Alley.'

'Oh, my god. Alley. How are you, girl? I was just catching up on a bit of sleep. Come in.'

Alley turned the handle and pushed it inward. Her eyes landed on Milly, nestled beneath a puffy white doona. Her face, eyes darkly rimmed, was the only body part exposed.

'Haven't seen you in a while,' Milly said.

'Yeah. Just came to see how everything's going.'

Alley looked around the room. Nothing had changed. Pictures and posters of supermodels papered the walls as though it had been decorated by an adolescent boy. The carpet and furniture were white. Besides the posters, no objects tainted any surface. It was pristine, sterile. A large, built-in wardrobe sat at the far end of the room. Mirrors coated the surface of the sliding doors, reflecting the room, doubling its space.

'What time is it?' Milly yawned.

'Almost six.'

'In the arvo? Wow, I thought it was still morning.'

Alley looked to her with a raised brow. 'You've been sleeping all day?'

'I've just been so tired lately. Plus I was out at Glaze last night …' her head fell to the side, 'or was it the night before. Anyway I was with these guys who are doing an intern at Macabella's magazine. Sleazy bastards, but they said they'd try and hook me up with a fashion spread.'

'Sounds fun.'

'What I remember of it.'

'Hey, your mum's not home.'

Milly pulled the doona up over head. 'Sooo tired,' she yawned, again.

'Where is she, Milly?'

Milly threw back the doona. She pushed her body up and onto her feet. She wobbled as she found her balance.

'Milly …' Alley breathed. 'You've gotten so skinny.'

'No,' Milly refuted. 'There's still some work to be done.' She shuffled across the carpet, heading to the mirrors of her wardrobe. Her tight tank top hung as an oversized shirt. Her pyjama bottoms were tied around her waist, the ends of the draw string almost reaching her knees.

Alley watched her, not knowing what to say. Milly had always been skinny, but now she was a skeleton with a thin, fleshy covering.

Milly stared at herself in the mirror, plucking at the flesh sitting on the sharp bones of her hips. 'Still a bit of work to be done,' she whispered.

'You look like you're starving to death.'

Milly released a weak chuckle. 'I wish. I just can't get rid of the chunk around my middle.'

'Seriously, Milly, I can't see any chunk. I think you're just picking at skin there.'

'Nah. It's there. It's ugly … u-g-ly.'

Alley shifted her stance. She caught her own reflection. She looked away and noticed the blackness under the bed. It quivered and bristled as though displaying barbed quills. Stepping back, *twelve, thirteen*, Alley watched the dense shadow retreat a few inches and settle down. It appeared to be sleeping, or waiting.

'Alley, hon, what's the matter? You okay? You look spaced,' Milly said, looking to her through the mirror.

Alley rubbed her eyes. 'Just tired. Need sleep, I think. And I saw this dog get hit by a car today. It was … strange.'

'Ew, gross. Don't tell me about stuff like that.'

'What about you? You doing okay? Eating enough?'

'Food's the enemy, girl,' Milly smiled into the mirror.

Alley watched Milly's expression, the human skull that held it up. 'I think your brother's hungry.'

'I was planning to do a grocery run. I just needed a nap. The day got away on me.'

'Will your mum be home soon? Do you think she'll bring some food?'

Milly drew in a long breath. It was an exhausting move. She looked through the glass to Alley. 'I wish I had your cheek bones.'

'My cheek bones?' Alley's hands rose to touch her face. 'Why?'

'They're spectacular.' Milly held out her hand, drawing Alley alongside her to look in the mirror.

Alley peered at herself. Her hands tried to smooth her long dark hair. 'Do you think my hair looks like a wet dog?'

'What? Don't be silly,' she replied, considering the dark waves as though it was artwork in need of analysis. 'It could use a bit of improvement though. Here, take the jacket off.'

Alley positioned her arms so Milly could remove her windbreaker.

'Nice camera,' Milly said.

'Oh, yeah, it's the school's. I forget it's there sometimes.'

'Blah. No school talk. I couldn't stand that place then, can't stand it now.'

The camera was slid over her shoulder and tossed onto the bed. Alley held her eyes on the thing. The film was still undeveloped.

Milly drew Alley from the camera to the mirror. Her hands collected Alley's hair and draped it over a shoulder. 'See, it's beautiful. You're beautiful.'

Alley shook her head, laughing, wiping unseen things from her arms. 'Stop playing.'

'I'm not.' Milly collected the full length of Alley's hair into her hands. She twisted it and pulled the length upwards into a tight coil above her head. 'See. Beautiful.'

Alley refused to look.

'Remember those stupid makeover nights we had when we were little?'

'Yeah, they were fun.'

'Yeah. We should do it again sometime… I could use a night in.'

'What about after my exams?' Alley said in a voice she had not heard herself use in a long time.

'Yeah, let's do it. We'll get you looking stunning. You'll get any boy you want. Remember when Trent had that crush on you?'

'That was a lifetime ago,' Alley said, holding the healing wound on her forearm.

'It was more like an obsession,' Milly said, pulling at a few strands of Alley's fringe so they fell alongside her face. 'You should go for it.'

'Okay. I'll get right on that. I'll let Trent know that I'm good to go.'

'Ease up. I'm serious. Feelings like that just don't disappear. If all that shit about your mum and uncle hadn't gotten out …'

'He wasn't my uncle,' Alley whispered, pulling away. Milly let the dark hair slide through her fingers.

'I better be getting home,' Alley said, collecting the camera and her windbreaker from the bed. Milly was staring at herself in the mirror again, plucking at the skin on her hips, engrossed. 'Cale might be wondering where I am.'

'Huh? Oh, yeah. Cale. Say hi to him, for me.'

'I will.'

'Girls night in,' Milly added, half turning to examine the profile of her thighs and rear, 'don't forget.'

'You or your mum should probably go get those groceries soon. Lukey's going to get hungry again.'

'Yeah, yep. Definitely.' Milly spun, checking her other side.

Alley closed the door as she left and wandered into the kitchen. Luke was curled up in a ball beneath the chair of the kitchen table.

She picked him up, managing not to wake him, and carried him to an armchair. She found a blanket in the corner of the room and wrapped his little body in it.

'Good luck, Lukey,' she whispered in his ear and headed out into the darkening street, trying not to think of mothers, or the lack of them.

11

BEYOND THE NEVER

The clearing in the forest consisted of a gentle slope of dried leaves, travelling down to a slow moving stream. A massive fig tree hunkered in the middle, billowing up and out like an explosion. Its roots had burst up through the loamy earth as though there was not enough world beneath to contain its feet.

Where the limbs reached outward from the trunk, boards had been laid, forming sections of flooring. The platforms were connected by suspension bridges, roped and secured with entwined vines.

The solid tock-tock-tock of wood upon wood drew Pan around the tree. On the other side, amongst the tall roots, a small figure sat. In his hands was the sharp-edged Touch. It was being used as an axe to split a long, thick branch into planks.

'Sticks,' Pan greeted the child.

Sticks looked up from his work and compelled a smile to his face. It did not last long.

'This will be one of the best Tree-homes you have ever built.'

'I'm tired,' Sticks said, throwing down the wooden blade. He looked to the side. 'And I remember things.'

Pan turned his back on the fig. 'What do you remember?'

Sticks's eyes grew large. 'A man and lady,' he whispered. 'The roaring and roaring and roaring. And no water. It won't turn and no water comes out.' He moaned. 'It's in my head again.' He placed his hands on his top as though it was a fragile artefact needing to be steadied on its pedestal.

Pan nodded. 'This place will do that to you, Sticks.'

'I don't want to remember.' He squeezed his eyes shut, tilted his head to the side and tapped, attempting to dislodge the memories from within. 'I wanna go back, Pan. I wanna. I don't like this anymore.'

'I need more time.'

Sticks stood and stretched his little arms. 'Can I see the new boy yet? I wanna show him Tree-home.'

'Soon. And remember, he will be crowned king.'

'His brothers?'

'He only has a sister.'

Sticks dropped his arms. 'Is she gone mad yet?'

'Well …' Pan walked over and collected Touch from amongst the leaves. 'She is already a little crazy, I think.'

'But is she gone dead mad? Like the other ones?'

'No. I will not let it happen this time.'

Sticks angled his lips, peering at Pan from the corner of his eye, his green orbs glowing. 'It will.' He giggled. 'They always do.' He laughed, a sound that morphed into a piercing rooster crow that ripped the stillness of the surrounding forest.

With a straight face, Pan waited for the boy to settle himself.

Cackling, Sticks said, 'You can't stop them dying mad.'

Pan looked down at Touch in his hand. He could smell the gallons of blood leached into the wood, coalescing with the life of the weapon.

'It's funny. They're so silly, going dead mad because of you.'

'Shoosh, Sticks. Do not forget who I am'

'I know.' Sticks wiped the smile from his face, leaving a dirty smear across his mouth. 'I know. You're the king, Pan.' He scanned the surrounds with a frown. 'I feel bad.'

'Have you been drinking water? I told you to drink water.'

'Yeeesss,' Sticks sighed, pointing at the stream down the slope.

'I will go and collect some food tonight. And be sure not to leave the clearing. It will hurt if you do. Here, take the sword,' Pan said, handing him Touch. 'Keep it close. It will help.'

Sticks walked over with slow steps. Pan could see the restraint on his face, the attempt to hide a devious grin.

As Touch's hilt reached his little hand, Sticks spun, swinging it towards Pan's stomach.

'Too slow,' Pan mocked, jumping back. 'You cannot take down a king like that.'

'Ha ha,' Sticks hollered, swinging the wood above his head. 'No, no, no. You're the pirate. I'm the king! King Sticks!'

'I am always the pirate.' Pan rolled through the leaf litter in search of a sturdy branch to defend against Touch's razored edge. A misstep could see him with one less limb, or his entrails staining the golden and brown carpet at their feet.

'Die, dirty pirate!' Sticks charged, his face twisted in maniacal delight, swinging the wood as though swatting flies.

With their laughter zipping amongst the surrounding trees, Pan wondered how in the world this kid managed to survive beyond all the others, and why.

12

SEARCHING FOR THE BRIGHT SPECK OF SANITY

The darkness was a dense cube of ink. She was suspended in its centre, the nothingness compressing upon her position. It layered itself upon her skin, ran through the soft fuzz on her arms.

If her hand was rising, she could not tell, only imagine as her fingers sifted through the viscous black. Her touch pushed into the ink and collided with the switch. The safety light of the dark room exploded, driving itself down through the black, splitting and separating it, pushing it against the walls.

Alley emerged from the nothingness into a dull red gleam.

The roll of film hung before her, shedding drops of fixer solution as it dried. She listened for sounds beyond the dark room. It was early. No one should be outside the door, ear to the timber, listening to the rapid thump of her heart, or her subdued breaths.

There was something creepy about these school buildings when they were absent of students and teachers. She felt like an intruder in some secret government institution, a rogue operator with a sinister agenda.

Collecting the film, she placed the right negative in the enlarger. The faded projection on the easel was of Mystics Bay in spectral form. Alley lowered herself until she could smell the chemical scented timber of the stand. Her eyes travelled the ghostly shore, but located nothing resembling a fallen star upon the rocks.

She needed a sharper image.

A piece of photographic paper was situated on the easel. She waited. Retrieving the paper, Alley methodically washed it in each of the three solutions, before hanging it on the line of string above.

A small earthquake rumbled through the walls. Art class had begun. Alley stepped from one foot to the other and back again.

Indifferent to her lack of time, the image dawdled in its materialisation. Igniting the fluorescents above, Alley unpegged the photograph and scoured each particle of the paper for an extraordinary bright dab.

Her eyes reached the bottom right-hand corner of the image and toppled from the paper to the floor. There was no hint of a bright abnormality.

She stared at the abyss beneath the counter. What did it mean? The blackness churned. Was she getting worse? The black reached outwards and laid itself at her feet. Were her mental quirks marching her along the plunging path her mother had trodden?

Knock, knock, knock.

Alley jumped.

'Hellooo? Anybody in there?' Mrs Cleary sang.

'Ah, hello,' Alley replied, with a cringe. 'It's just me, Alley.'

'Oh … Alley …'

She switched off the lights and exited the dark room, *eight, nine, ten, eleven*, to be confronted by the open gaze of Mrs Cleary and the restless mess of students behind.

Mrs Cleary was young, but held a distinctive aged aroma of mothballs and stale peppermint. 'Some personal projects?' she asked, looking to the photograph in her hand.

'Um, yeah, kind of.'

'Oh, wonderful. Anything good?'

Alley shook her head. 'Not really. Just a landscape.'

'At-mos-pheric,' Micko complimented with a rhythmic drawl, as he transported some equipment nearby.

Alley lowered the photo.

The teacher craned her long neck to the side. Alley tilted the photo so Mrs Cleary would not sprain her muscles.

'Oh, that's wonderful. May I?' she asked, reaching for it.

Alley held it tight. Would it be weird to fold it up and gobble it down like a sandwich?

Mrs Cleary collected the photo in her long fingers, her massive bejewelled rings framing the photographic paper like a royal portrait.

'It's so mysterious. Like a different world.'

'Nice work, Alley. Spooky,' Maria said over Mrs Cleary's shoulder as she passed behind.

'It's just Mystics Bay,' Alley said along the nail of her index finger.

'But the way you captured it. Look, Alley, look at the deepening tones as your eyes are drawn to the edges of the bay; the hint of mystery captured in the surrounding forests. This deserves a place on the Wall.'

'No, no,' Alley said, reaching for it back. 'It's not an art photo. I wasn't really supposed to be taking pictures there.'

'You weren't? Why not?'

'Actually, I don't know … You know what? Put it up. Let everyone see it …' *even the un-special ones.*

'Here,' the teacher said, 'I'll write your name on it.'

'Wait, no … I don't …'

It was too late. Her name had been branded upon the image of Mystics Bay and attached to the wall, displayed to the populace in open defiance of Croco's specific instructions.

Croco would never see it, but Eran … She was sure she could retrieve the photo before his next day at school.

With Mrs Cleary still lost in Mystics Bay, Alley exited the classroom. She straightened as she noticed Pan across the hall. He smiled, lounging upright against a doorframe, with arms tied across his chest and one foot folded over the other. Alley moved on, watching him; the boy who counts stars, or used to.

When she was forced to swivel her head back to the front, she stopped. A cold breeze flowed through her as she realised she had left her step count at the classroom door, several feet behind.

Her mind was not in a hysterical breakdown. She felt calm and normal, and Pan's eyes upon her back.

13

IN THE LIGHT OF TREE-HOME

The afternoon was icy. The sky was clear, but held a deep grey pall as though the freezing winds had slain it and placed a death shroud across its face.

Alley waited out the final, gloomy hours of the day in the park, taking photographs of the dead flora decorating the estate. She spent seven whole shots on the last seven leaves on the skeletal tower of a liquidambar. She then waited and watched four of the seven detach and dance in their descent, all the way down to lay in the graveyard with their fallen brethren.

Every whispering rush of a car beyond, or distant echo of a barking dog, drew her attention. Her camera was poised, ready and waiting, to capture anything unusual.

When night dominated, Alley sighed and headed home.

De-shrouded windows of passing houses cast gleaming, orange shapes upon the night's floor. As though they were sticky, Alley's stride was slowed before them. Between measuring the distance of her steps, she would study the warm innards of these alternate worlds.

For the space of fifteen or so slow steps, Alley saw the mundane activities of families as they settled themselves down for the night. There were conversations around dinner tables; games being played and kids spread upon the floor with books and papers before them. There were stilled families, packed together on lounges, dozing within pale blue plasma glows. Sometimes there were smiles and laughter and exaggerated movements. Some houses bubbled and fizzed on the inside. Others were a soothing flow of gentle movements.

Sometimes she imagined herself within them. She imagined setting the tables amongst the smells of rosemary and simmering meat and steaming gravy. They all had their assigned seats. She would ensure her cutlery was positioned straight when not in use, while the man nods with loving attentiveness as the little boy and little girl regale the table on all their discoveries and accomplishments of the day. She would enter the kitchens, her fingers running along the ornate objects on her way, and readjust the tea towel on the oven's door to be that little bit neater.

It was all ordinary and unexciting. And sometimes Alley found tears on her cheeks as though the building pressure in her chest could only find release through her eyes.

She knew it was weird, and probably a borderline criminal offence, but she saw it all as a child's storybook. When each house was passed, the page was turned, and when she arrived home, the book was closed and returned to the shelf.

In a passing thought, she considered taking a photograph, taking the story back to her dark, cold, compact home. Besides the weirdness and illegality of the act, she knew that these quiet imaginings were only for brief entertainment and never to be considered too deeply.

Alley stepped onto the Duhent's property. Averting her eyes from the windows of the Duhent's house, she climbed the few steps to her door, entered and froze.

Cale sat upon the couch. The shoebox of a TV crackled drowsily in the corner. In the centre of the room, bright and colourful against the drabness, was Pan.

With fists poised on his hips, Pan watched Alley with a cocky grin.

'What are you doing here?'

Pan looked to her, pink lips moving as though he was holding back a laugh.

'He needs some food for his friend,' Cale answered.

'What?'

'I do not have any,' Pan said.

'What makes you think we do?' Alley returned.

'Your house is the closest to mine.'

Alley shook her head, not fully grasping the situation.

Cale leapt to his feet to stand at Pan's side. 'He lives in the forest behind the horse farm.'

Again, Alley shook her head. 'There are no houses over that way.'

'Not yet,' Cale said, glancing to Pan with a half smile.

'Well, we don't have any food, either,' Alley said, walking into the kitchenette – seven steps from the front door – needing to evade Pan's eyes.

'That is fine,' Pan shrugged, sweeping his sight around the room, 'I will tell him to drink more water until I have found some food.'

Alley peered into the sink, focusing on the clean patina of the stainless steel. 'Who are you talking about?'

'A little boy.'

'Your brother?'

Pan's smile twisted for a beat. 'I guess you could say that.'

'How old is he?'

'About this.'

Alley looked over to see Pan with his arm out from his side, palm horizontal against the floor, just above hip height. 'How old is that?' she asked.

Pan looked from Alley to his hand. 'About this,' he repeated.

'He's young?'

Pan replaced his hand on his hip.

Alley bent to the bar fridge and looked inside. 'We've got a heap of green beans we can share with you.'

'We get them from old man Tom Macaulay who lives up the road,' Cale explained, staring up at Pan. 'Half his garden's filled with beans.'

Pan's face wrinkled. 'He does not like eating green things. He would think I was trying to kill him.'

'Well, he should face those fearful odds.' Alley stopped herself and looked at Pan from under her brow. 'The rest is for our lunches and dinners tomorrow.'

'Let him have my sandwich,' Cale said. 'I don't mind.'

'What are you going to eat?' Alley said. 'There's only four slices left.'

'I don't mind,' he said again, with a tiny shrug.

'You'll starve.'

'I'll live.'

Pan looked down at Cale and then across to Alley, the curve to his lips levelling.

With a quiet, grating breath, Alley said to Pan, 'Do you want Cale's sandwich?'

Pan nodded.

'He won't have anything else to eat tomorrow. He'll starve to death.'

'Alley,' Cale said.

She waited for Pan's response.

After a pause, Pan said, 'Give me his sandwich.'

Alley collected two of the last four slices of the loaf and smeared the sandwich spread on one slice. Throwing the two pieces together, she slammed the sandwich down on the side of the sink, leaving the impressions of four fingers in the top of the bread.

Pan walked over, grabbed the sandwich, sniffed it, and shoved it into his pants' pocket. He did not thank her or Cale as he made his way to the front door.

Stepping halfway out into the night, Pan stopped and turned. 'You should come and see my house tomorrow after school,' he said to Cale. 'It is brilliant.'

Cale's face lifted. 'Yeah. That'd be … well, actually, I've got swim training tomorrow.'

'Do not go.'

'I have to. I can't miss it.' Raising his head, he asked, 'How about now?'

'Sure.'

'Cale …' Alley began.

A look of annoyance was directed at her. 'I'll only be a few minutes. It's not that far away.' He turned to Pan. 'It's not far, is it?'

'Just over that little rise.'

'See,' Cale said, returning to his sister.

'Am I going to be able to stop you?'

Pan glanced to Alley before leaping outside and running into the dark, laughing as he went. Cale was close behind.

Reaching the rear fence, Pan did not slow. He thrust his hands before himself, clutched the top rail and used his momentum to flip himself over. Cale gushed behind. He knew he was unable to match Pan's acrobatics and was forced to clamber through the middle.

'This way,' Pan called out. His shadowed form collided with a staggered wall of shrubs and disappeared.

Cale followed without hesitation. He charged the plants, stumbling as they stood their ground and resisted him with prickly stems and needle-like leaves.

Battling through, Cale stopped. The forest was a mess of shadows and diagonal blades of misty moonlight. Quiet thickened the darkness, made the forest seem impenetrable.

A short roll of laughter bounced between the trees.

'Slow up,' Cale called out, and launched into a run.

To his right was a blur of colour. 'I'm gonna lose you, Pan.' A branch flexed and whipped back into place to his other side. He changed direction. The ground slipped from beneath him. He tumbled down a slope, rolling over and over, the world flipping around him. He gained his feet, his head spinning. 'Pan!' The trees pushed upon him from all directions, their branches reaching out with crooked fingers. Shards of laughter fell from above. 'Pan!' Cale stepped one way and was blocked. He stepped another way only to be halted by a slender hand that stretched around his body. Panic struggled through a sudden exhaustion sweeping upon him. He staggered, tipped and was steadied by a solid breeze. It nudged him, propelling him towards a sliver of copper bright. The glow widened into a thin triangle, opening further, enfolding him in a warm cocoon of light.

Like being awoken from the depths of a life-long sleepwalk, Cale found himself standing in a gentle wash of polished bronze. A hand was on his shoulder, keeping him from collapsing. He barely felt it. He barely felt his own skin. The air was warmed to a temperature that made it difficult to determine where he stopped and the light began.

'I feel …' His voice was muffled, as though the amber light was a syrup he was submerged in. 'I feel weird.'

'It will pass,' Pan replied. 'This taste of home is a potent spice.'

'Home?'

'The Never.'

Cale raised his arm. It lifted from his side, feeling like a limb not his own. Lowering this alien appendage, Cale felt the world accelerate to its normal pace. The haze in his head lifted.

'Wow,' he breathed.

Before him, majestic and large, a fig tree grew, its billowing crown expanding into the night sky. As though the fig was sprouting a home, a tree-house was being incorporated into its natural growth. Balconies and alcoves curved around the trunk. Tiered decks sat on extended limbs. Open rooms were skewered with branches to form benches and tables. Roped suspension bridges were hung like decorations, linking each feature. Wooden planks travelled in a gradual spiral down the trunk, becoming the central staircase, connecting the multiple levels.

It was luminous in a golden light, emanating from small points of bright, randomly spread around the tree and clearing.

The light stained all surfaces, made the carpet of leaves gleam in their golds, oranges and browns. It pushed at the surrounding night, halting the dark against its impermeable barrier.

Cale drifted through the autumn glow, the leaves cushioning his steps. He came to the tree and a large rectangle that had been carved into the trunk. Etched within its deeply chiselled border were the words, *Haven Hold My Cherished Whole*, in sharp, hard to read letters.

'This's amazing.'

'It will be great once it is finished … An outpost for the eternal lives of Never things.' Pan's voice had become soft. 'Our Tree-home.'

'It's not finished?'

'Not yet.'

'I reckon it's great already. I never built any tree-houses.'

'I know.'

'Did anyone help you? This would've taken ages.'

'Sticks,' Pan called out, swinging the name around him with a twist of his body.

A small figure lurched in and fell against the tree. The boy's drooping eyes hung on Cale.

'Wake up, kid. We have a guest.'

Sticks drew a long breath, turned to Pan, and then back to Cale. His brow crumpled as he straightened. A rosy shade emerged on his pale cheeks. His haggard expression tightened.

''Ello,' Sticks bubbled, pushing himself from the trunk. 'Who're you?'

'I'm Cale.'

Sticks walked closer, eyes open and running all over the body before him. When Sticks's small hand reached for the buttons on his shirt, Cale stepped back towards the tree. 'Did you really help build this?'

'Me,' Sticks replied, casting the syllable at the sky with a yelp. 'All me. Pan doesn't help. I'm the best at building.'

'Really? All by yourself?' Cale walked closer to the construction. 'But you're so little.' He noticed that all the slats and boards of timber had been grooved and slotted into the neighbouring pieces. No nails or screws or any other foreign matter had been used in its construction. 'Did your dad teach you to build like this?'

'No. Just me.'

'Really? You're not lying?' Cale ran his hands along the smooth joints of a projection above his head. 'How long did it take you to get so good?'

Sticks hoisted himself onto a low platform. Sitting on the edge, he dangled his legs in the air. 'How long? Um …' He looked to Pan. 'I don't know how long. Forever, maybe. I've been building like this forever.'

'But you're so little. How old are you?'

'How old?' Again, Sticks looked to Pan. 'That's like how long,' he mumbled to himself. 'I'm … um, forever.'

Cale turned a bemused smirk on the child.

'I'm forever,' Sticks said, nodding to himself as though cementing the fact in his own mind. 'Well,' he said, with a childish sneer, 'not here. I'm not forever here. Back home I'm forever.'

'I don't get it,' Cale said.

Pan leaped into the tree-house to stand alongside Sticks. 'We do not come from here, Cale. We come from a place far away.'

'The furthest I've been from Coalcliff is Ashfall Tops. That's the town inland a bit. I don't think about that place anymore.' Cale watched the dancing of a small flame sitting on the window sill of a half-finished wall. He could not see what it burned. When he stepped nearer it dropped from the sill to the ground. When he looked for it, it was gone. He returned to the two above. Both watched him without movement. 'So, where's the Never?'

Sticks turned to Pan.

'Our home,' Pan said, 'is hard to find for some. It exists out there,' he said, lifting his brow to the skies. 'It is here,' he said, stomping on the timber flooring at his feet. 'But that is only a bit of it. Where we come from, where our home is,' he said, jumping from the tree to land before Cale, 'is here,' he said, tapping the side of Cale's head.

Cale looked up to him. 'Inside my head?'

'That place that is yours and yours alone. The place without limits or walls, where things that can never be become more honest and dependable than the fragile truths of the world you walk through.'

'I don't get it.'

'Perhaps one day you will.'

Pan swept his foot through the golden and brown leaf litter. The dry leaves swirled in a tight eddy, climbing higher, drawing other leaves into the current. Reaching the weight of night above, they hesitated and wandered their way back to the earth, turning the clearing into an autumn snow-dome.

Cale raised his arms and held his hands up to the raining shapes.

'Our home is great,' Sticks said, beaming at the falling leaves. 'It's fun and we go on adventures and we build Tree-homes bigger and bigger, up into the clouds. And at home I don't get tired. Not ever. And I don't need to drink water and eat, if I don't want. Not one bit.'

Cale laughed at the silliness of it all.

'Ha ha ha!' Sticks joined in. 'And we have all our friends. And it's just us and no one else. Except for the pirates and Indians. But they're not with us. We kill the pirates. 'Cause they're the bad ones. And we never lose.'

Sticks leaned back as though his rambling thoughts had collided with a brick wall. He turned to Pan. 'Do we ever lose, Pan?'

'No. We never lose.'

'What,' Cale chimed in, 'against pirates? Like pirates with ships? With swords and cannons and stuff?'

Pan shrugged. 'Our home is filled with all sorts of things. The ones you must watch out for are those who just want to take everything for themselves.'

'Yeah?'

'They do. They take everything from you. They will even take your skin and what you are. You know people like that?'

Cale shifted the leaves at his feet. They were immovable objects to his touch.

'The ones who just want to take everything need to be stopped.'

'We kill pirates,' Sticks said. He held a splinter of timber in his hand. It was raised above his head.

'You really kill them?' Cale said, turning to Pan to see the young man's heavy glare upon him.

'We fight them back,' Pan said. 'We fight to keep what is ours. If it means we must destroy them in the process, then we destroy them.'

'Like this!' Sticks squawked. His limbs struck out, flailing in all directions.

'Not exactly like that,' Pan said. Leaning closer to Cale, he whispered, 'He is much more dangerous than he appears ... I think.'

Cale nodded.

Pan tilted his head, considering Cale from a different angle. 'Do you think you could do it?'

'What? Me? Kill pirates?'

Pan nodded.

'Like, for real?'

Another nod.

Cale forced out a laugh and shook his head. 'I don't know.'

'Sticks,' Pan called out, 'give him Touch.'

The short piece of wood was tossed from the tree-house. The splinter spun wildly. Cale reached out and pulled back as it flicked past him to land behind.

'Careful with that thing,' Pan said. 'If you do not control it, it will slice through you like running through water. It is a Never thing, and more solid than anything you know of.'

Cale stared at the timber shard resting amongst the leaves. It did not look sharp. It was just an old, dirty splinter of wood. Decorating the rounded end were small runes, its deep etchings filled with reddish black grime. He spotted a crown, a rooster, a bow and arrow, a top hat. Others were too encrusted to make out.

'Take it.'

Cale stood unmoving. Each symbol was simple in its design. Yet the more he stared at them, the greater depth and detail they revealed. There was complex history hidden within each image.

'You need to hold it, Cale.'

With eyes locked upon the wooden shard, he reached down and placed three fingers upon the flattened end. It squirmed beneath his touch, and growled, sending a droning tremor into his fingers, up through his arm and into his head. He heard it, like the speech of the ocean. It spoke in something like a sliding whisper. Pictures formed out of the vibration in his head, images of enormous jungles, ancient and everlasting, white-sanded beaches with crystal waters, and savannahs of wildflowers, patterned over the land in all the colours he knew.

He heard the voices, countless voices; those who were lost. There they were – boys, just like himself, hundreds and hundreds of them. Some were in darkness, some in light. There were smiles and laughter and teeth and dirty feet, the jungle plants peeling around their leaping and racing, and lifting painted faces to the sunbeams striking through.

There were runners and swimmers, the water exploding around their legs and arms; and climbers and hunters, peering out from the tops of trees across the plains; and the warriors, the water-wolves, heads lifted to the skies as they howled to the horizons.

Then the golden sun set and the pink skies grew dim. Cold fell and there were streaks of red and slicing light, the broken bodies layered upon the rotting jungle floor and the white sands bleeding; and the darkness, the swelling darkness that grew larger and larger until it towered over head and threatened to break upon the world, drowned it all in oblivion.

Cale fell backwards, his hand clutched protectively in the other. He sucked air into his lungs, seeing that nothing had changed around him.

A hand reached down and pulled him to his feet. 'What do you think?'

Cale could only breathe, waiting for the images and sounds to seep down into his mind until they no longer flooded the surface. 'Strange. All this is strange.'

'Do you like it?'

'I don't know,' he mumbled, into his chest. 'Yes. Maybe.'

'Would you fight for it?'

Cale turned his questioning eyes up to Pan.

'Would you rule it and die for it?'

A pressure fell upon him, a weight that filtered through his limbs, wanting to plant him into the ground, push him down through the earth, setting him amongst the buried boulders and fuse him to the foundations of the world. 'I have to go,' he said, his legs quivering. 'My sister's waiting for me.'

'Alright. Go, then.'

Pan and Sticks's expressions hardened. Cale felt like an intruder under their combined gazes. He turned, confused and exhausted. With the light at his back, he was drawn to the surrounding night. As he reached the distinctive line where the amber illumination halted, he turned, and said, 'I'd like to come back.'

After a long moment, Pan said, 'We will have some fun together.'

Cale nodded, turned and stepped into the night. He fell into a light jog through gnarled shadows, refusing to glance behind. He was afraid to see that nothing was there.

14.

DROWNING PLATES

The kitchen window was fogged by the steaming water. The young woman appeared as a smudged silhouette as she hung her head above the rising wisps of steam. She felt them brush her face, small condoling caresses from fairy-like creatures. Her hands soaked in the hot water of the kitchen sink. She watched them drift amongst the plates and cutlery, savouring the warmth the rest of the house was denied.

'*Another beer* …' his habitual demand staggered through the small rooms of the house.

He was a creature from a more primitive time, she thought, an early design for a human being that consisted primarily of basic instincts.

She hissed through her teeth and threw more plates into the bubbly scum water, holding them on the bottom, waiting until they ran out of breath and drowned.

'I heard you, love,' the drawn-faced woman returned.

'Don't call him *love*, mum,' she said, as the woman entered the kitchen. 'It's bloody sickening,' she said, adding as much disgust to the words as possible.

The mother looked up. 'Don't be such a square, Tara.'

Tara looked into the depths of the sink, the plates now dead. 'You're embarrassing our whole gender. And setting women's lib back at least sixty years. And nobody says *square* anymore.'

'Come on, Tara.' Her mother peeked over her shoulder, and then stepped closer to her daughter. 'Larry's a good man. Better than Jack. You'd have to agree with that, wouldn't you?'

'*Where's that beer, Sal!?*'

'They're both as bad as each other. Larry's just got more money.'

'Tara, do you seriously think I'm dating Larry because of his money?'

'God, no. He's almost as poor as us.' Tara grabbed a few more utensils and drowned them, too. After watching their death, she said, 'I think you're dating that dirtbag because you're weak.'

The hurt on the mother's face swamped the look of insult.

'Hey!' Larry barked, lurching into the kitchen and slumping against the wall. 'You brewing that beer yourself, woman? C'mon, I'm dehydrating in there.'

'Just a sec, Larry.'

'Get your own fucken beer,' Tara said, spinning, flinging the scum water across the room.

Larry twisted his lips, disfiguring his ugly man-face further.

'And besides the fact that it's mum's beer – she paid for it – alcohol is a prime cause of dehydration, moron. It doesn't prevent it.'

'Watch your tone, missy.' Larry ground the words with his teeth, moving forward to grip her upper arm and squeeze hard to draw a wince in her expression. 'I don't take no shit from some wannabe dyke.'

'Double negative,' Tara grunted, through her clenched teeth.

'Larry!' her mother yapped. 'I've told you a thousand times. Do not touch her.'

'Or what?'

Her mother stared at him, the fury forced into her expression weakening with each beat. When her face fell she shook her head, saying, 'You're a real bastard sometimes.' She turned and left the room.

Larry threw away Tara's arm like a petulant child. He chuckled a few breathy notes in her face, and said, 'ah, you women need to lighten up,' before collecting a beer from the fridge. Cracking the top with a chicken flap of his arms, he downed the can in front of her.

When Tara was much younger she had believed that it was her mother's bad taste in men that produced an endless parade of losers and deadbeats along the peripheries of her home life. She now understood that all men are dirtbags. Even the nice ones. They were just dirtbags too gutless to show women what they are really like on the inside.

And women, with their pathological need to love and be loved, so afraid of being alone … They all disgusted her.

After Larry released his resonating belch and went for another can, Tara left the room. Her mother was lying on the couch, staring ahead to the glow of the television. The drawn-faced woman did not glance at her daughter. Tara looked down on her with a twist of distaste to her lips, hoping it did not resemble Larry in any way.

*

The sky grumbled and groaned as Alley counted her way across the common grounds. She eyed the churning mass of grey, pleading with them to hold out until nightfall.

'Hey, Alley-cat,' Megan sang.

'Hi,' Alley returned, throwing down her bag and taking a seat on the opposite side of the wooden table.

The rising of Taz's brow in greeting was just visible behind her large sunnies. 'What's new?'

Alley shrugged, feeling her stomach growling, staring at her bag, but not wanting to fish out the sandwich inside it.

'Hey,' Megan said, tapping her hands on the mildewy timber between them. 'Here's some good goss. I saw Romina and Trent in town yesterday, sucking each other's face back to the bone.'

Alley watched the dance of Megan's hands. 'I didn't know they were together.'

'Of course they're not,' Taz said, leaning on the table. 'They're both just being sluts. Who cares anyway? Manicured airheads getting ready to spawn the next generation of superficial morons, good for nothing besides making tanning salons a billion dollar industry, and filling the Net with all the need-to-know facts about their lives, like all the exotic types of venereal disease they contracted last week and how shiny their hair is.'

'Wow, Taz,' Megan breathed. 'You certainly had a nice, heaping bowl of bitch before you came to school this morning.'

Taz tilted back. 'Just calling it how I see it.'

'Hey, what happened to your arm?' Megan said, sliding up Taz's sleeve to reveal the inky bruises from a tight grip.

'It's nothing,' Taz said, pulling away.

'You been rumbling again?' Megan asked, with a cluck-cluck of her tongue.

'You should see the other guy.'

Megan placed an arm around Taz's back and shimmied closer.

'Enough affection for one day, Barnacle Bob,' Taz said, shrugging her off.

'Whatever,' Megan returned, looking back to Alley.

'I saw Milly,' Alley said.

Taz dropped her sunnies to the end of her nose. 'I haven't seen that chick in ages. Still alive?'

'Barely. She's not looking well. I've never seen her so thin.'

'Man! She still not eating properly?' Megan said. 'I thought she'd grow out of it.'

'You should've seen her. It was awful. I think she needs help.'

Taz looked to Alley with an are-you-serious stare.

'Still …'

'What? So you want to go to the cops or something? Report her for not finishing her vegies? That chick's in her own little world.'

'It's probably going to kill her, Taz.'

'Maybe,' Taz shrugged.

'Her mum should be doing something about it,' Megan said.

'Ha!' Taz burst. 'That meth-head's more off the planet than Milly is. Hear what she did with those guys out the back of O'Reilley's the other weekend? She's the one who's sending Milly delusional anyway.'

'And Lukey,' Alley said.

'Yeah, Lukey; *how to raise a future druggo* … The best thing that could happen to that kid is if his mum OD's and dies.'

'Tara,' Megan gushed beneath her breath, as though Alley could not hear.

Taz swallowed the remaining words and turned her attention to the furore of the common grounds. 'Sorry, Alley,' she murmured. 'I didn't mean …'

'No. It's alright,' Alley said, nibbling on her thumb nail.

'Hey, hey,' Megan said, slapping the table. 'Lookey over there. The new kid. Wait. He's coming over here?'

Alley turned on her seat to see Pan striding through the scattered groups of students in their direction.

'I can see why I'm slipping on skank drool in the halls,' Taz said, with wry smirk. 'A boy like that could even turn a girl straight.'

'Hey, shut-up, ho,' Megan said, giving Taz a solid punch to her arm.

'Don't worry. I know he's just a regular dirtbag underneath.'

'Whatever.'

Taz turned to Pan as he came to a stop before their table. 'You lost, pretty boy?'

'No,' Pan returned.

'This corner is the upper-class shit of the school. It doesn't accept sightseers. And there's a heavy toll for passing through. How much money you got?'

'None.'

'That's not near enough. Piss-off before I take your shoes as payment.'

'Taz,' Alley reprimanded the girl with a quiet breath.

Pan looked to Alley and held out his hand. He showed her a black and white photograph. It was of a bay, taken from a nearby cliff.

'Hey, that's mine,' Alley said. 'I mean, it's a photo from the classroom.'

'I know. There is a whole wall of them.'

'You stole it.'

'No. I just wanted to ask you about it. It reminds me of someplace I know. Where is it?'

'Give back her picture,' Taz sighed, rising to her feet.

'Taz, it's alright,' Alley said. 'It's near the beach,' she said to Pan, accepting the photo from him. 'It's hard to get to. You have to follow the cliff tracks.'

Pan nodded. 'I want to see it. Take me there sometime.'

Before he received any response, Pan turned and wandered back into depths of the common grounds.

As with most of her contacts with Pan, Alley was left with confusion and an unfamiliar lightness to her body. There was an urge within to trail after him, not to engage him in conversation, just to be near him.

She turned back to the girls to see their brows sitting high above open eyes. They looked to each other before turning back to Alley and bursting into laughter.

15

THE ANCHORS DESCEND

The streets were darkening. Alley's bag was only mildly heavier from the food within it. The measly government assistance payments never went far.

The sky above rumbled. A few drops fell, exploding upon her unprotected hair.

She passed beside the reeking stream, aptly named Turpentine Creek. Its thin flow of rainbow water navigated itself around shopping trolleys, garbage bins, broken outdoor furniture, and a store's decapitated mannequin frozen in the motion of clawing its way from the muck.

The air shook as trucks ran over the approaching bridge.

Finishing the count on a measured set of steps, she raised her head and found a group of three people a short distance away, disguised by the shadows of the tunnel.

Alley groaned as she noticed one was Bryce. His little lapdog, Jarod, was at his side. The other, a lopsided, scraggly man, she did not recognise. This was the reason shortcuts were not main thoroughfares.

Her jerking stop drew their attention, but they did not stop their business.

Staring at her with a sadistic grin, Bryce fished in his pocket and retrieved a wad of cash. Within the guise of a sociable handshake, the exchange was awkwardly apparent, and the black anchor tattooed on the back of the vendor's hand was like a blare-horn.

Alley stepped back, *three*, and spun. She was confronted by a fourth man. He was tall and thin, and stood with a curve as though his rubber bones were unable to keep his stretched body erect.

His scrawniness and vacant expression contradicted the man's vigour. As though he was an emaciated gym-junkie, the thin stretch of muscle over his skeleton quivered and pulsed under his skin.

'Come meet my new friends, Alley,' Bryce called behind.

The guy before Alley pushed her back with a hand weighted by an anchor tattoo. She stumbled deeper into the thick gloom of the underpass. The numbers running through her head filled every part of her mind. They softened her fear, stitched her body together to keep her from falling apart.

Alley was turned to face Bryce.

'Met these lads, yet, Alley? A very motivated collection of gentlemen.'

Alley glanced to the two Anchors. They stared at her with dead expressions. Jarod stood to the side, holding his hands before himself. His eyes flickered between all persons present.

'Hold her still,' Bryce said

Another eighteen-wheeler rumbled overhead, shaking the scene.

Alley felt a hand latch onto her arm and squeeze. Her eyes shot to the wall of dull light at the end of the tunnel. Nothing moved. It was only a still image, a photograph of another world.

'Let me get that for you. It looks heavy.' Bryce removed the bag from her shoulder. It skidded across the ground when he attempted to punt it into Turpentine Creek. Vegetables, food cans and bread scattered themselves amongst the dirt and grass. Two bright specks joined the tumble, continued rolling when the tomatoes stopped nearby, and escaped within a tall cluster of weeds.

'Leave me alone, Bryce,' Alley stammered, attempting to jerk away from the hand that held her.

Bryce stood back and studied her. 'It doesn't work like that, you see? This is how it is.'

'What? No. Just let me go.'

'I can't,' he said. 'You're you. I'm me.' His beady eyes darted around and located something exciting. 'You understand that? You are your brother's sister. And I … I'm many things.'

Alley tried to turn to follow Bryce as he walked around her. She was held still.

Bryce returned, one hand slathered in dripping grime. 'Fate is what they call it. You're bound to your path, Alley. And I'm bound to mine. We are products of those paths, nothing more, fated to what we are.' He glanced to the Anchors. 'And sometimes fate is bloody hilarious to watch.' With a torturous slowness he reached for Alley's face.

'No,' she breathed, already feeling the filth soaking deep down into her body. 'Don't, please,' she whimpered, the mud already filling her lungs, drowning her.

All colour drained from the world. All sound muted. She struggled against the one that held her. Sparks of light were frantic, darting around the edges of the scene, scouring the cracks in the walls for help.

'C'mon, Bryce,' Jarod chuckled. 'Give her a break. She's messed up enough as it is.'

As the mud was about to touch and engulf her, she fell. Landing on her knees, still trembling, Alley looked up to those that surrounded.

Bryce and the two thugs were staring down one end of the tunnel. In the dull light of the afternoon, Pan stood, hands on hips, calmly watching the scene.

'Just the guy I wanted to see,' Bryce nodded. 'Fate …' he mused.

'No such thing,' Pan grinned.

Bryce turned to the Anchors around him. 'I have another proposition for you guys.'

The two Anchors did not acknowledge him. They glanced to each other, smiles turning their mouths. The muscle bound skeleton glided forward as an angular gust. Pan slid to the side, ducked, weaved, came up under the savage hack of jagged knuckles and elbows. Pan struck once, twice, paused, set his feet and struck a third time. The Anchor collapsed.

Pan stepped back, arms hanging loose.

The second Anchor lunged; a wall of pumping fists. The form of Pan smeared. It was not a smudge of shadow, but a glimmer of many movements. The second Anchor convulsed and toppled to the side.

'Holy shit,' Jarod gushed. 'D'you see that, Bryce!? Holy shit. Let's get outta here, man.' Jarod jogged backwards, enticing an inert Bryce with a waving hand. 'Holy shit,' he chanted one final time and fled.

Pan strolled over to the scrawny Anchor and sat upon his chest. He considered the man beneath him with a tilted head, sighed, before collecting his tattered shirt in a tight scrunch. He raised a fist high above the Anchor's twitching face.

There were no lights now, only threads of darkness. The tendrils crawled in from the shadows, their vaporous ends snapping forward as though hunting by scent. They flowed towards the prostrate Anchor with curious eagerness and layered themselves upon his body.

Dark ribbons wove themselves in a misty haze around Pan's knuckles and wrapped around his rigid arm. They reached forward, stretching towards the strips of darkness on the Anchor. They connected and drew taut.

'Pan, don't,' Alley breathed, from her position on the ground.

Pan held himself steady. The ribbons of night, connecting his fist to the Anchor, strained. He released the ball of his hand and lowered his arm. The dark threads snapped without sound. Pushing upon the Anchor, drawing a gurgling grunt from the man, Pan got to his feet. Alley watched the dark ribbons slither in retreat and merge with the bordering shadows.

The two crippled Anchors stirred. In a gangling heave, one climbed erect. He dragged his unresponsive limbs to his colleague. Collecting him in a knot of arms, they aimed their tangled bodies for the exit opposite to Pan.

Bryce, his aloneness luminescent in the gloom, warped his open mouth into a snarl. 'What kind of freak are you?' he growled at Pan.

Pan's tepid smile was enough to send Bryce backing away with a disgusted shake to his head.

Alley climbed to her feet, examining her arms, the creases of her palms and running fingers over the contours of her face. There was no mud. She was clean, but she still felt dirty.

After her thorough examination, she tuned a hard stare on Pan. 'You were just going to watch all that?'

'I was.'

Alley swallowed the uncomfortable lumps in her throat and chest, gulping them down to somewhere deep. 'What's wrong with you?'

'Nothing.' Pan paused. With a low voice, he asked, 'You wanted me to save you?'

His question was serious. Moving to the scattered produce, she recollected all the items and returned them to her bag. Her hands shook enough to threaten her grip on each item.

Pan waited.

When she was finished, Alley stood, refused to look at Pan and strode away. Pan's footsteps were heard behind. 'What are you doing?' she breathed, dismayed.

'Walking with you.'

'I don't need your protection now, Pan.'

'I was not thinking of that. My home is near yours.'

'I don't get you.'

'I do not get you either,' Pan said.

Turpentine Creek slipped away as their feet found the asphalt of the road. The solid, dense structures of town lumbered upon their path. The night had submerged the streets. Beneath lamp posts and shop fronts, small bubbles of light were suspended in the murky flood.

'When can you take me to the lagoon?' Pan asked.

Alley looked at him, mouth agape. 'I don't know.'

'I would really like to see it.'

'I said, I don't know.'

They walked on in silence. Kensington Park unfolded beside them. Alley maintained intent on her stride. She did not think she could stomach the sight of any more dying things.

Pan yawned, stretching his arms wide. 'Alright, I will take you to see my home if you take me to see the lagoon.'

'I don't want to see your home.'

'It is good. Your brother likes it.'

'He'd rather be swimming.'

'Why does he like swimming so much?'

'It's the water.'

'He likes the water?' Pan questioned.

'I think he's afraid of it.'

'I do not understand.'

'Neither do I,' Alley replied, and stopped.

He turned to her. 'What is it?'

'Why do I tell you these things?'

Pan raised his brow.

'I can't stop it. Whatever comes into my brain slips right out my mouth. It's not like me.' Alley looked down at the gnawed nails on the ends of her fingers. 'It's like dreaming.'

'Dreaming?'

'Yeah. You know, like there's no filter between what you are, and the rest of the dream world. You can't hide anything of yourself in a dream.'

His eyes made tiny adjustments as they switched between each one of Alley's.

'It's terrible,' she mumbled.

'Dreams?'

She placed a fingernail to her lips. 'You think I'm crazy.'

Pan shrugged.

'I don't know what my brain's doing half the time.'

'I know what you are talking about,' he said.

'You do?'

'Dreams. I know what a dream is like,' Pan stated.

Alley lowered her fingers from her mouth.

'Come,' Pan said, collecting her hand and tugging her in the direction of the park.

Her protest dissolved as she found her stride falling into rhythm with Pan's.

The paths were made of a loose, grey aggregate. Many had burst from their frames, spreading themselves into the surrounding dirt. Their feet made polite munching sounds as they chewed the path with each step.

A few melancholy lamp posts stood in the distance, inclining their heads in a contemplative way. Their glowing amber gems – those having avoided all the well-aimed stones and airborne beer bottles – shoved against the night that held the estate.

'Where are we going?' she asked, hoping Pan was not paying attention to the slickness of her palm.

'There,' he said, pointing to the large, ornate gazebo sitting as the hollow, white heart of the park.

Alley was unable to slow Pan's pace.

'Coming to the gazebo tonight ...?'

'Yeah, just drinking at the gazebo again ...'

'I've seriously never seen so much vomit ... the gazebo was painted in it ...'

The gazebo regularly popped up in hushed conversations in the middle of class. This was a place of privilege.

Alley scanned the area. No one could be seen.

'What are we doing?' she asked, letting Pan pull her up the stairs.

Pan released her. She stood in the centre, not wanting to move and somehow desecrate the structure.

Graffiti and the names of previous visitors decorated most surfaces. They were documented in indelible marker or carved into the timber. Two adjoining sides of the eight were charred by a fire that lacked enough motivation to level the construction.

What was the big deal, she wondered, scrubbing the warped decking with her feet. This place did not look that special. But she supposed, like Mystics Bay, she was just unable to see it.

'Pan, what are we doing?'

'You like to count steps ...'

'I don't like to.'

Pan bounded to a seat and up to the rail. He spun on a toe, jumped and caught the edge of the roofing. Swinging twice, he disappeared above.

With a tentative step, listening for his movements on the roofing, Alley walked over to the rail. She peered upward into the night sky and a beaming face popped into her view. The clouds parted and stars formed a scintillating halo around his head.

Pan extended an open hand. 'Come.'

'If you think I'm going up there, you're crazier than I am.'

Pan grinned and stretched towards her.

Alley bit at her thumb nail. 'No chance, Pan.'

Pan stretched further.

'You're going to fall.'

He slid off to his stomach, his fingers wriggling for her.

'Alright, alright.'

Alley assessed the obstacle; the seat and the rail; just two large steps; ONE and TWO.

Athletic ability had never been one of her greater traits. She demonstrated the fact quite well as she clambered onto the rail. Rising, her hand snapped upward and clutched Pan's, stabilising herself as she began to tilt.

With a smooth movement, Alley's feet left the rail and she was drawn upward. There was little strain on her shoulder. It was more like floating, a balloon of helium lifting into the ether, to be gently placed upon the corrugated iron roofing of the gazebo.

Pan released her and turned to the view.

It seemed a different town, standing four metres above it. Upon the cliffs, looking down, Coalcliff was a small place, alone and afraid, cowering within a dent in the forested climbs. In the streets, the grime and grey cloaked any possible splendour trying to make itself known.

Here, afloat on the sea of Coalcliff, Alley heard the wandering breeze drone with a soft melody as it moved through the park. The resilient trees, retaining their crumbling crowns, whispered along with the tune.

Up here she was free from Coalcliff's seeping darkness, yet, close enough to feel the life of the town – as wayward as it was.

Pan lowered himself to the night-chilled metal and lay on his back. Alley did the same. The storm clouds were racing each other to the horizons. They left behind a glittering trail of night sky.

'I almost forgot how many stars there are,' Pan murmured. 'There's not many left in the sky where I come from.'

'Light pollution?'

'More like dark pollution.'

There was quiet between them. Alley heard Pan whispering numbers.

'When I was little, I taught myself to count,' she said.

Pan's counting stopped.

'I got so good from counting my mother's steps. She wasn't right in the head … Clinical depression. When my father died she got worse. She'd just sleep. All the time. A friend of the family, Mrs Duhent, used to look in on me and Cale, make sure we were fed. I don't even know how I felt about it; my mother always sleeping. I just remember feeling terrified when she was up and about, wandering the house after I was in bed. That's when she'd drink. Drinking made it worse. She'd try to hurt herself. I caught her a few times. All I remember is the blood. It looked like she was covered in it, like it was pouring from her. I was so scared. So, whenever I was in bed, I used to stay awake and listen. It took her eighteen steps to move from her bedroom to the kitchen cupboard where all the alcohol was kept. I did it every night, listen and count, waiting for her steps to fill the numbers. Soon I was counting other people's steps, my teacher, kids in the playground. I didn't even know I was doing it. When people started to realise I couldn't stop, I was sent to counsellors. They were worried my mother's illness was affecting me. I trained myself to count silently, only focusing on my own steps. I didn't want my mother to be taken away. I've been doing it ever since.'

The night sky shimmered. 'I don't think I'm totally crazy,' Alley said, to the twinkling dots. 'It's like there's a puzzle in my head, or a riddle that I'm trying to work out. Sometimes I'm so lost in it that I don't even notice what's going on around me. But the problem is; I don't even know what the puzzle is about. I strain my brain to figure out answers I haven't got the questions for.'

Pan shifted. 'I am sure that once you figure out the answers the questions will be easy to find.'

Alley laughed. 'Yeah, maybe. It's like the other girls spend all their time concentrating on the rotation of their wardrobe and the state of their hair. And I have to spend all my time concentrating on hiding how crazy I really am.'

'Perhaps. But maybe all the other girls are doing the same thing.'

'I doubt it. I'm sure I would've noticed something.'

'I think, on some level, they do. On some level everyone does.'

Alley sat up and looked down on him.

His gaze stopped its wandering of the heavens and turned to her.

'I always thought you had the maturity of a toddler. But sometimes you sound like a wise old man, like you're a hundred years old.'

'I have been around a long time, Alley.'

'Really?' Her eyes fell from his eyes to his lips.

'I am forever.'

Sporadic bursts of laughter ricocheted through the park. Alley turned to see a collection of shadowed forms drifting between the trees. With excited yelps and squeals they moved towards the gazebo.

As the group neared and gained definition Alley hung her head. Pan rose to his feet.

'Hey, check that out,' one released, with an inebriated slur.

'Pan,' Romina said in a sliding tone. 'Hey, come have a drink with us.' She swung a bottle before herself like a pendulum able to hypnotise.

Alley noticed Trent standing at the rear, arms folded, looking up with a level stare.

'Shut up, Romi,' one said, between gulps of his drink. 'That's the guy that messed up Bryce. I should punch him in the face.'

'Good luck with that, you gromit,' Romina returned, maintaining her eyes on Pan.

One of the girls stepped to the side as though dodging unseen projectiles. 'Where's Bryce, anyways? He's supposed to be hooking us up.' She lowered herself to the steady ground and held on tight.

Pan strode forward. Stepping from the gazebo roof and into the air, he dropped and landed as though the ground had risen to meet him.

'Whoa. See that? What a bloody maniac!?' one gushed.

Turning his back on the crew, Pan held his hand up to Alley. She moved to the edge.

'Oh my god,' Romina laughed. 'Check this out. She's gonna stack it. Get your phone out.'

Alley stepped back.

Pan reached his hand a fraction higher.

Alley felt the drop tugging her, the roof sloping a little further. Her toes were shimmied to the edge. She stiffened. Her heart was thumping hard enough to knock her forwards.

Pan looked up with no concern in his smooth expression. 'Just fall,' he said.

Keeping her eyes on his, Alley jumped. Panic seized her limbs as she became weightless. Pan's hands were around her, directing her to the ground with a steady softness. Her landing was no more than an amiable meeting of her feet and ground.

'Damn it,' Romina said. 'I would've paid anything to see her face plant.'

Pan and Alley walked past them.

'Bryce has got your number, boy,' one of the guys said under his breath.

Moving past Trent, Alley noticed him watching her.

The high-pitched jabber of Romina and her friends reignited as Alley moved amongst the trees. When they reached the street, Alley turned her attention to the sky and said, 'I'm not counting, Pan.'

She saw Pan nodding sombrely, as though he had some idea on the significance of what she said.

16.

A STRIKE FROM THE NEVER ONE

The smell of morning was thickening by the time Pan entered Tree-home. Not much progress had been made on the construction. A heap of timber planks were scattered in a rough circle amongst the leaves. Pan imagined Sticks attempting to transport the bunch under his arms to the heights of the home, and losing his hold halfway up.

All lights were absent. The place was dark and lifeless.

'Sticks,' Pan hollered, searching the decks and levels layered in the tree. There was no response.

Touch had been driven into the tree trunk. Its wooden blade was embedded deep. A rivulet of white sap ran along the underside of the weapon, releasing lethargic drops that blobbed onto the golden leaves beneath.

Was it one of his games?

Listening to the gooey splatter of dripping sap, Pan backed towards the edge of the clearing. The gentle murmurings of the stream beckoned. Obscured by the bordering murk was a small body sprawled in the silt of the stream's bank.

'Sticks!' Pan dashed towards the child. He took Sticks in his arms and peered into his face. It was pale and slack, and his body was cold. 'Sticks, wake up.' Grime clung to the child's face and clothes as though he had been recovered from a shallow grave.

A breathy groan crawled from the little throat. Sticks's eyes fluttered and pried themselves open.

'You okay, kid?'

'Sleepy.'

'Have you been eating the food? Drinking the water?'

Sticks nodded and squirmed his way from Pan's hands. He collapsed in the mud and plunged his face into the slow moving water. His chest heaved as he drew the water into his body with massive gulps.

'That is enough, Sticks,' Pan said, rising to his feet.

Sticks continued to drink.

'Enough!'

Sticks sucked at the river, wanting to drain it of every last drop.

Pan collected the scruff of the boy's neck, hauling him from the water and tossing him onto his back. 'I said that is enough.'

Sticks stared upward, panting.

'You will drown yourself, drinking that much,' Pan grimaced, feeling the cold of the closing night.

'I'm thirsty. I'm always thirsty.' Sticks released a burp that brought a rush of water up from his gut. His angled head was not enough to keep the regurgitated river water from pouring down his shirt and into his lap.

Pan protected himself from the cold with a swathe of arms. 'Where are the lights, Sticks?'

Sticks peered through the surroundings. 'There are no lights.'

Pan watched as the boy, the only survivor of all the lost, stared through the world. 'Sticks, what about Vinny?'

'No lights.'

'Remember him … Vinny boy? Back home?'

'There's only dark.'

'Sticks! Listen to me. Vinny boy! Wanna go on a hunt with him? Find an adventure with Vinny? You remember Vinny boy, Sticks?'

Sticks blinked at the words.

It was not a good sign. Sticks's regression was much faster than he anticipated.

Sticks rolled to his side and crawled towards the river. 'Thirsty,' he breathed.

Pan pushed him back with his foot. The child landed on his back, eyes closed and drawing the air with short breaths as though it were poisoned.

'Alright!' Pan crowed, compelling Sticks's attention. 'We will make our move. We will have our home back.'

'Home?'

'Yes. I will force that damn crown on his head and the dark can feed on the king at last.'

'Crown the king … How?'

'With blood, of course.'

'Of course.'

'One true strike from his hand will be enough.'

Sticks sat up. '… In the name of the Never.'

'Exactly.'

'Pirates?'

'I found two today. But there are many more.'

'True?' Sticks yelped, his face awakening. 'How they get here?'

'I do not know. The thing they follow might be closer than we thought. So, do you wish to come? Are you fit for an adventure?'

Sticks drew an imaginary sword from behind his back and held it high.

Pan nodded. 'The waking hour is soon.'

'We'll be quick.' Sticks pushed himself to his feet, careful not to dirty his invisible weapon in the mud. 'We'll run to them. Run all the way,' he grinned, and drew his blade across his neck.

*

Cale shivered and shifted and buried himself deeper in the foam. The dreams lingered, waiting for his return. As he settled he fell and was resubmerged in the wet. It was the stuff of nightmares; so deep beneath the surface that it was a voyage of days to the air above. He was unafraid. These were the pleasant dreams; his lungs capable of drawing air from the water that held him, and the weeping woman with flowing dark hair somewhere at his back, never able to be seen, with one hand around his ankle to hold him down and another upon his belly to keep him afloat.

He breathed the water, drifting, until a heavy hand was placed over his mouth and two small fingers pinched his nose.

A subtle pain bled through his body, creeping outwards from his chest. It ignited, like a flame put to spilled fuel. His body buckled. His scream caught in his throat.

I'm awake. But I'm drowning … Am I awake?

When his mind was filled by a desperate howl he was unable to release, Cale was dragged to the surface.

Chilled darkness encased his body.

Am I dead?

'No.'

The night bulged and two figures materialised before him. He knew them; Pan and his little brother, Sticks. Had they found their way into his dreams?

An earthy brown paint was smeared in a thick line across the width of their faces, over their eyes. The sky-blue sheen in Pan's orbs and grassy green tint in Sticks's shone within the face paint.

'Am I still sleeping?' Cale heard his voice say, unsure if he initiated the words or not.

'Let us say you are dreaming,' Pan replied.

'Is there a difference?'

'There is.'

Sticks held an edged piece of timber above his head, posing in triumph. 'We hunt the pirates.'

'Pirates?' Cale laughed, a sound that echoed into the depths of the surrounding dark. 'Sounds fun.'

Pan's face peeled back as he grinned. He stepped away, moving at a march, arms swinging wide and knees reaching high. A beaming Sticks fell in behind like an obedient soldier. Cale found himself at Sticks's back. He could not feel his limbs swinging in time with the others. He was afraid to search for his feet and find them still, his body hovering, drawn along in the two's wake.

The wind breathed around them, strewing Sticks's humming tune. The insistent pressures of the breeze could not find Cale. Or perhaps they did, and only passed through his nothingness.

The darkness shimmered. Stars blurred above and, like splattered milk, ran down the sky, leaving thin streaks that shone on the black backdrop.

Cale blinked slowly and revealed familiar streets, the salt-washed homes of Coalcliff and the coastal pines amongst them. On closer inspection he saw they were artificial. They would fall forwards and land flat like two-dimensional objects, cardboard cut-outs on the uneven stage of some primary school production.

This is Coalcliff, Cale thought, hearing the indistinct cheer of a hidden crowd. It was the sound of the ocean, its endless bleeding upon the land, and he knew it as well as he knew the beating of his heart.

The waters spread before their jovial march, scintillating with bits of fallen stars. Lights of anchored ships bobbed on the surface. They clustered together until the wind collected them and threw them into the air like confetti.

Tree-home, Cale thought, that's what this feels like.

'Kind of,' Pan said.

Two words popped into Cale's mind; the Never.

'Almost. We are about halfway between your home and mine, upon the back road of all that we know of, the path that follows the edge of death.'

'Death?'

'See ...'

Cale's awareness was drawn to the distant waters. There, galloping on the midnight sea, a large creature could be seen. It ripped the ocean into clouds of spray, its furry coat lunging in time with its powerful bound. 'It's a wolf.'

'A Great Wolf.'

'I want to meet it.'

'No, Cale. The thing is dead. And it is wise not to wander here. Death and madness await those who stray.'

But this is my dream, Cale thought, raising his head. He drew a breath and howled to the skies.

'Cale, no!'

But the distant wolf planted its paws in the water, sliding to a stop. Cale was forced to raise his arms, protect himself from the wave of water rushing upon him. When the spray eased, Cale blinked his eyes clear and lifted his head. Dominating the view before him was a black and grey mane of fur, thick and bristling. The solid snout was angled towards the sky with dignity. The wolf's steady yellow eyes watched him curiously. There was knowledge in its penetrating gaze, and an ageless might.

Speak your peace, boy. There is much distance still before me.

The wolf's jaws did not open to release the words. They appeared in Cale's mind, growled through his thoughts to shake his body. He was awed to stillness.

I said, speak.

'I, um… I want to help you.'

Help? Me, a Wolf of the First Pack? The wolf's eyes glistened as a rumble of gentle laughter filtered through Cale's head. *You are courageous. Or mad. In what way do I require your help, boy?*

Cale felt tiny under the wolf's yellow stare, no more than a quick snack for the massive creature. 'I don't know. They say you're dead, that all of you are dead. That doesn't seem right.'

Again, rumbling humour shook his mind.

Compassion, also … But do not mourn for us, boy. Death is an unavoidable step we all must tread. I lost my brothers and sisters as the great night descended. The wolf shifted and displayed a small body draped over its back. *I broke from our final run to retrieve this water-wolf from the dying jungle. Once, beneath a summer moon, I ran at his side. His howl was a cheerful song, I recall. I believe his brothers knew him as Vinny.*

Cale saw the coating of dried blood on the body. 'Is he dead?'

He is.

'What happened to you all?'

Ahhh, death finds us all so easily. And its only tactic is its patience. But there are some stubborn beings, the wolf turned to the side, its eyes thinning, *where death must shred entire worlds in order to claim what it is owed. But this boy across my back may be saved. His life was lost in place of another. He may live upon another shore. But a shore I am unable to find. You,* the yellow of the wolf's eyes flooded upon Cale, *perhaps you can find a new shore for this fallen water-wolf.*

'I don't think I can. I mean, where would I start looking?'

Save him or not, boy. Such choices are yours and yours alone. Remember that. The wolf glanced over its bulking shoulder. *Look, boy, the ones of light come. Beware. Their minds have gone to the abyss. And the dark will not be far behind them. I must depart. I must find my family before the endless night spreads its final blanket. And together we shall see the end of the tale of the First Pack … together we shall rest.*

The water detonated as the wolf pounced into the air, over Cale, and continued with its gallop. The rainbow charge of light became noticeable as the water settled, racing towards him on the path of the wolf. Cale could see the frenzy of the approaching storm, the fear churning within it.

'Pan, where are you?' Cale searched the surrounds. Dark water stretched to the horizons in every direction. No land could be seen, not even beneath his feet. He returned to the rippling mass of colour to see it had gained definition. It was a herd of people, running, or fleeing, towards him. They each emitted a glowing light from their bodies. All varied in shade, with some sputtering as though their light were a candle flame about to go out.

They were tall and muscular, both men and women, wearing simple clothes and no footwear. Sweeping around Cale, many paid him little notice. Their faces were contorted with fear, stretched wide and twisted in a gruesome way.

'Pan, help!'

As the name was released, a few slowed and turned vacant stares on Cale. A woman shedding a tawny gleam, brown hair matted across her face with sweat, dove at him. She latched onto his arm and tugged him into their flight.

'Stop!' Cale cried, as his body stiffened. His failing strength attacked her grip to no effect. 'Pan!'

'Come, child,' the women whimpered. 'Come. You must hurry. The dark follows.'

Cale was unable to move. The immobilising terror spread through his body from her touch. He felt his body being hoisted into the air in the embrace of strong arms and carried into their run.

'Enough!' came the word of command. The group stumbled to a stop.

Cale felt a small tussle over his body and was pulled from the embrace of the stranger, onto his own feet. He looked to see Pan and Sticks before him.

The glowing flock shifted nearer Pan, whispering and fidgeting, the looks of terror in their expressions unwavering.

'Calm yourselves,' Pan said, heavily. 'Where are you running to? This place is too dangerous to be running around like that.'

'We run away,' said a young man, wearing a soft green glow. 'Away from the endless night.'

'We cannot defeat it,' said another, no glow visible, his skin dark and lifeless. 'We must flee our home. We must flee for our lives.'

Pan threw his head from side to side. 'No. I need you to gather the rest of your tribe.'

'We cannot,' many cried together.

'Find your others. Our home needs you. Remember who you are.'

'We are forgotten relics,' one spat. 'Nothing more.'

'No. You are the spirit of the land; its rocks, its trees, its mountains. You are the embodiment of its strength, damn it!' Pan beat his fists on his thighs. 'How long do you think it will last without your tribe?'

Another lightless man gripped the sides of his head. 'Our chief has fallen. Our fight was futile. And our princess has abandoned us.' He displayed his arms in dismay. 'Look. Look, King. My light. I have lost my light. What does it mean? Tell me!'

Moans of woe swam through the group. 'We are lost. We are ended. Our princess… the Tiger abandoned us.'

'I know,' Pan breathed, 'I know of the Tiger. But she still lives. She is lost, but she is not dead. You need to rally. You need to stay strong. You need to win me more time.'

'Not possible,' a handful cried and broke into a sprint for the surrounding dark.

'Stop,' Pan released, without conviction.

The light of a woman flickered and disappeared. 'The Tiger has forsaken us, forsaken her tribe. She has forsaken our home. There is no tribe without her. There is no fight left. It is all over.'

'It is over,' they repeated, turned together and fell into a run away from Pan, Sticks and Cale.

'This is some messed up dream,' Cale murmured. Watching the rainbow shades of the group dissolve into the dark, he asked, 'What were they?'

'Forget about them,' Pan returned, stepping forward to place his foot on solid ground.

'But they were so strange. And scared.'

'Forget them, Cale,' Pan grunted. 'We have a task. Come. We are on a hunt.'

Cale felt his body being tugged along behind the two. The hazy dreamscape swayed, flowing as Sticks reignited his lively hum. Listening and drifting, Cale's anxiety dissipated. His eyes settled on the shifting of Pan's shoulders, and any thought other than the awaiting steps, became a mere draft tickling the hair on the back of his neck.

Sticks's wandering tune halted, halting their movement. 'Pirates,' he whispered, and lowered his small body.

Upon a stretch of blue-black grass were a scattered group of people. Rough words and grinding laughter filled the spaces between them.

'They're the pirates?' Cale questioned, his voice travelling outwards in ripples.

'You can call them Anchors if you like,' Pan said.

'Anchors?'

'They are the bad guys, Cale. But there is one bigger and badder than all the rest.'

'Who's he?'

'It is the end.'

'Huh?'

'It is an enemy.'

'What's he look like?'

'Well, it is like the night-time for the night. It travels as a massive dark ocean, I am told, rising up and falling down to drown anything that It does not like ... which is everything I know. It is an anchor, the greatest of them all ... the Dark Anchor.'

Cale turned to the sway of pirates before them.

'These guys are filled with the Dark Anchor. They're Dark Anchors on a small scale, destroying things and ending things.'

'Why?'

'Who knows? Some people like to build and create. Others like to tear down and erase.'

After a moment of pirate observation, Cale said, 'You know what?'

'What?'

'I think they're scared of the Dark Anchor, too.'

'You think?'

Cale shrugged. 'It's not so scary when you turn into the things that you're scared of.'

The pirates' eyes were glazed, their jaws slack. Every now and again one would point in a direction, indicating some wonder unseen. Others were interacting with objects or living things that Cale could not see. It was as though he was only seeing half the picture. He knew all this would make sense if only he was able to see what was being denied to his sight.

'Pan,' Cale said.

'Yes?'

'Is it me not really here or everything else?'

'Both.'

'So, what is here?'

'I am,' Pan replied, and strode towards the pirates.

Wearing his stretched smile, Sticks moved to Cale. 'He's here forever. Everything else isn't. He's the best Never One.'

The collection of pirates noticed Pan's approach. Their swinging limbs were steadied. They pushed themselves from invisible walls and rose from invisible seats, and assembled themselves together.

'You,' one growled.

'Yeah, me,' Pan replied.

Their voices echoed through the area, doubling upon themselves and rolling back on the following sentences.

'Why fight It?' a pirate scoffed.

'Because I can win.'

'Not forever.'

'I am forever.'

The pirate sneered. 'Embrace It. It is terrible and beautiful.'

'I will take your word for it.'

'It is a different kind of freedom. A superior one. A different kind of eternity.'

'I like mine better.'

'There is no fear once you accept It.'

'Ha! I do not fear anything.'

'Bah! There is an end for us all, boy.'

'Not me. Not the Never.'

'It's already ours.'

'If it was, I would not be here.'

'You won't be when It comes.'

Pan stood back, lifted his head and laughed. 'You will have to catch me first.'

The pirates advanced.

Cale stepped forward. Sticks held out his hand, stopping him. 'Pan has first fun.'

The pirates rushed, falling upon the space that Pan occupied with driving legs and arms snapping forward. Pan ducked, weaved, stepped to the side, he crowed to the sky and evaded again.

The pirates were a writhing mass of spearing limbs, buzzing as they cut through the air. Pan flowed around the strikes, laughing, unable to be struck. The swarm morphed in response. It stepped back, encircled and came upon Pan like a tightening noose of barbed wire.

Pan shimmered; movements too fast for the eye to register. Attacks punctured his light to hit only air.

The pirates hissed and roared and became frenzied. Pan solidified, deflected a storm of attacks, struck with his fist and followed through with an elbow.

Streams of darkness whipped amongst the thrashing bodies.

The head of a pirate snapped back and he dropped. Pan dove over the falling body and into a roll. He stood, flickered through movements and was shrouded by a haze of blood and thin dark streamers.

The remaining pirates dashed in a momentary retreat, disoriented.

Cale looked up into a red-eyed glare. A glinting blade slithered forward below his sight, trailing a dark wake.

'No!' Pan cried. 'He is mine.'

The armed pirate collapsed. Before a toothy grin, Sticks's wooden sword retreated with a bright red coating.

There was a pause to the mayhem. Cale found the remaining pirates looking to him. They turned questioning glances to each other. One shrugged. 'Tell the others,' said another. One fled.

'Sticks!' Pan hollered.

Giggling, Sticks ran after the fleeing pirate only to be booted off his feet.

Pan threw his weight behind a fist, shattered the shield of a forearm and landed knuckles on a jaw with a resonating thud and muffled crack. He spun, lowered his body, struck with the outer edge of his foot. It connected with a tattooed leg, snapping the ankle and sending the pirate to the ground. The cry of agony was silenced as Pan stomped on the chest.

The dark streamers, blowing in the wind, festooned the whole area in macabre celebration.

'What is he?' the final pirate said with a flick of his head towards Cale, arms raised in surrender.

Pan lunged, caught a wrist and twisted hard. The pirate buckled to his knees with a yelp. Pan raised his free hand into the air, a guillotine's blade ready to fall. With a snap, he struck the back of the pirate's neck, released him and watched the body land heavily on the ground.

The scene became still, Pan's smile the loudest thing in this echoing pocket of night.

Cale returned to himself. He had been absent during the entire brawl, the horrific images playing on a screen to the vacant theatre of his mind. Now it flooded upon him. 'Are they dead?'

Pan glanced around. 'Except that one,' he indicated with a finger. 'He is alive.'

It's only a dream … Cale forced his eyes to search the battlefield. *It's only a dream* … A pirate was trembling, his arms clutching his left thigh. His entire leg was in a sharp zigzag, bone protruding at each corner. *It's only a dream* … Cale felt his head spin.

Pan strolled to the crippled pirate.

'Can I have him, Pan? Can I, please?' Sticks asked, bouncing on his feet, displaying his timber shard.

'No. You have already had one,' Pan said, collecting the pirate by the scruff of his collar.

'I want another, Pan. I said, please.'

'No. You let your other one get away.'

'Aww.'

Pan dragged the groaning pirate nearer Cale. 'And this one is for him.'

Sticks huffed and stared at Cale as the pirate was dropped at his feet.

'Kill him, Cale,' Pan said.

'Huh?'

'Kill him.'

'Kill him?'

'You heard me.'

'But … I …'

'Cale, this guy is a pirate. He is one of the ones that takes, takes away everything that you are. You know these types of people. You know they must be stopped.' Pan turned to Sticks. 'Give him Touch.' Sticks obeyed.

The wooden blade was placed in Cale's hand. The wood was sticky with blood, trembling in the hand that held it.

A gentle arm wrapped around Cale's shoulders and a hand directed his shaking arm towards the pirate. The edge of the timber was placed on the throat of the man.

Cale looked into a set of moist eyes. He saw a mixture of restrained pain, fear and defiance.

'He is the one who takes away everything you are. You can stop him. Judge him, strike true and take his life. You will rise and we will bow.'

Cale imagined himself in the water, struggling against its lack of substance, its ability to drown, to kill. He applied pressure and felt the timber separate the skin of the throat. His eyes filled with water, blurring the image of the man.

Dark tendrils slithered in along the ground. They reached towards the pirate, stroked the skin as though testing the authenticity of the body.

Something deep inside prevented Cale from movement.

Pan placed his fists on his hips. 'Kill the pirate.'

'I don't know if I can.'

'Kill him!'

Cale closed his eyes, gripped the sword and tossed it aside. 'I don't want to.'

'You know these people!' Pan yelled. 'I have told you. They are the ones who take. It is a mercy to kill them.'

'Well, then we just have to hold on tighter,' Cale returned, feeling an anger rise up in him.

'You know it does not work like that. You need to be strong enough to kill, Cale. It is the only way to protect. The water-wolves killed to protect. They had the strength. They were not cowards. It is what made them great.'

'The king kills,' Sticks squawked.

Cale turned to the boy, unsure what he heard.

'Look, I'll show you how,' Sticks said and rushed in. His little body slipped around Pan. Collecting the wooden shard from the ground, he toppled forward. The blade sunk into the centre of the pirate's chest.

'Sticks!' Pan barked.

The pirate buckled. His face lit up with surprise, as though surfacing from a deep dive, searching above to find that there was no air up here either. His mouth gaped and his eyes bulged. Everything about him strained and then relaxed as his life was taken from him.

Dark streamers crept up into the pirate's mouth and nose, worked their way around the eyeballs into the back of the sockets and disappeared within the man's head.

'Sticks,' Pan said again.

The boy retrieved his weapon, the blade sliding from the body with a soft whisper. Sticks danced backwards, hooting, 'We win this one, ha ha!' swinging his sword high above his head.

Blood was flung in arcs across the night. A splatter landed cold against Cale's face. *It's just a dream …* He felt his head spin with greater speed and the dark world rushed around him. The ground sucked his body downwards. Cale offered no resistance to the fall. He collided with the earth and everything shattered, their tiny pieces scattering into the nothingness. He was glad this was only a dream.

17.

CRY HAVOC

Mr Kemp tapped his scribbles on the white board. 'Metal corrosion,' he said, excited by the topic. 'Cathode protection, ladies and gentlemen. Can anyone give some forms of cathode protection …? And, yes, this was in last night's readings … Miss Sandon?'

'*What the hell is cathode?*' Cale heard Lisa Sandon whisper nearby.

He chewed on the end of his pen, his eyes following the frantic path of a fly at his side. Small tic-tic-tics were heard as it battered itself against the glass of the window, desperate for escape. There was clearly none. That did not deter the fly from running headlong into the glass, stopping for short moments on the window sill, recuperating, before making another futile attempt. Would it ever give up?

'Cathode protection? Mr Lebani …? No? Mr Amir? Ah, Miss Biermann, don't let me down …'

'Sacrificial anodes, sir.'

'Very good, Miss Biermann. I am glad at least one person could be bothered with the homework. Now, a sacrificial anode, also known as a galvanic anode, is used as a …'

Cale did not like Mr Kemp's class. Mr Kemp had an awful habit of calling on students to give answers. There were a few tactics Cale employed to avoid being called upon. The first was not to sit in the back. The students occupying the back seats were usually Mr Kemp's first targets. The first few rows were also a dangerous hot spot. When Mr Kemp was getting desperate for participation, he tended to look upon the eager faces closest to the board. The safest place was the neutral zone, the middle of the room, close to the side, preferably not right against the wall.

When Mr Kemp's eyes scoured the room for his victims, Cale's head went down. He buried his face in his textbook, flipping through the pages, searching for answers he usually did not hear the questions to.

The fly landed on the sill and scratched its head, considering the predicament from a different angle. It rolled its shoulders and stretched its wings. After wiping the sweat from its brow, it took to the glass once again.

Just give up already …

Tic-tic-tic …

It was too stupid to quit, or too oblivious to the uselessness of its struggle. It would never win. Cale considered squashing the thing, finishing its fight for it. It would be a mercy, wouldn't it?

'You see,' Mr Kemp's voice droned on in the background, 'these sacrificial anodes are positively charged metals—'

'*Aluminium!*'

'Correct. Aluminium is one.'

'*Bingo!*'

'Calm down, please. Now, these metals are attached to other metals that have a higher import, such as the hulls of ships. In these cases, the corroding effects of sea water will concentrate on the sacrificial anode, and ignore the ship's hull. Sacrificial anodes are essentially destroyed in order to prolong the life of more valuable metals.'

'That's cruel, sir,' Lisa called out.

Cale, with hand raised towards the window, redirected his attention from the fly to Lisa, and on to the teacher.

Mr Kemp tilted his head. 'I understand your qualms, Miss Sandon, but cruelty is a human construct. There are forces out there beyond such trifling human concerns. In these worlds fairness is irrelevant. The lesser is sacrificed for the more valuable. That is how it must be. Now, we have aluminium as an effective sacrificial anode, what else makes a good sacrifice?'

Mr Kemp's sight was drawn towards Cale. He dove into his textbook and threw his eyeballs from one side of the page to the other.

'Mr Creed?'

Cale lowered his head further and furrowed his brow ... and squinted.

'Mr Creed, can you tell us what else makes good sacrificial material?'

Cale, lips moving, raised a finger and sent it running up and down the pages, apparently reading at a savant's pace.

'Mr Cale Creed, can you enlighten us?'

The air thickened and staled. The scene was solidifying. He felt eyes turning and latching onto him, holding him. He felt himself begin to freeze. His arm locked, unable to turn to the next page. His airway tightened, only allowing short, quick breaths to pass through.

'Cale ... Cale, are you alright?'

Let me go ...

The door swung inwards, shattering the static situation. All eyes released Cale and turned to see wild hair exploding above a glistening run of teeth.

The hushed exclamations bubbled up from below and fizzed upon the surface of the student's heads.

'*Check it out. Pan.*'

'*That's the one Jarod said.*'

'*Yeah. Took down two of 'em.*'

Mr Kemp glanced to the students' animation before turning to the bright figure in the doorway. 'Well, well, if it isn't the newest addition to our wonderful scholastic community. What brings you to our learned classroom, Mr ... Pan?'

He lifted one arm, extended a finger on a limp hand and targeted the far side of the classroom. Cale straightened.

'Mr Creed? And what will you be requiring of Mr Creed today?'

'Just him,' Pan replied.

'And for how long?'

Pan scanned the open stares of the students.

Mr Kemp glanced the time. 'There are still twenty minutes left of his class, Mr Pan.'

Pan stared at the teacher, his grin unwavering.

'Very well,' Mr Kemp said, looking to Cale. 'Mr Creed, you may go. Tonight's revision is pages thirty through to forty-five in your reading block. The corresponding activities will be done in tomorrow's class.'

Cale nodded, despite his reading block having been thrown into the ocean many months ago after one swim practice.

Manoeuvring through the desks, the room was absent of the usual petitions and complaints. In its place was a reverent hush. The wide eyes of the room, hanging on Pan, shifted to Cale. He did not find these stares compressive. They seemed to make him move straighter and with a more secure step.

Pan directed Cale down the hall and out into the gloom of the day.

'What are we doing?' Cale questioned, peering out from beneath his brow, still expecting some form of authority to put a halt to this scam.

'There might be a bit of trouble around.'

'There's always trouble around.'

'I want to make sure you get home alright.'

'Really?'

'Yes.'

'Hey,' a voice called out.

They both turned to see Alley walking across the grounds, camera being tucked away beneath her windbreaker.

'What are you two doing?'

Cale raised himself on his toes. 'Pan got me out of class early.'

Alley looked to Pan. 'Why?'

Pan smiled.

'I don't—'

'What are you doing out here?' Cale leapt in.

'I have a free. I'm supposed to be studying for my finals.'

'Why aren't you?'

Alley raised a fingernail to her teeth. 'I can't concentrate. There're too many distractions in the library.'

Cale watched Alley. She looked over Pan's shoulder, eyes darting back and forth as though she followed the flight of a dragonfly only she could see. Alley flinched and dropped her hand from her mouth, preparing to swat at some invisible insect.

Glad to see Pan's attention was elsewhere, Cale dropped his head and said, 'C'mon, Pan, quick,' and trudged away from his sister.

Pan paused, looked to Alley, and said, 'Coming?'

Cale drew a long breath through his teeth, holding back a groan as his sister nodded.

Together, they headed out of the school grounds, Cale watching Alley from the corner of his sight. There was something off about her. He noticed she was not counting her steps. What did that mean? Was she not being crazy as normal? She looked much crazier than normal, he thought. He did not want to ask her if anything was wrong, just in case she answered him.

'It feels like something's going to happen,' Alley said, searching the lumbering storm clouds above.

'What makes you think that?' Pan said.

Alley wrapped her arms around her middle. She glanced around herself before closing her eyes, walking alongside them blindly.

'Hey, Pan, when can I check out Tree-home again?' Cale questioned.

'You wish to come back?'

'Yeah.'

'Whenever you want, kid.'

'Awesome.'

Cale continued to call out to Pan whenever it looked like his sister was gathering herself together to say something. He directed Pan's attention to the opposite side of the street, pointing out interesting objects far from his sister's position.

As they reached the brown estate that was Kensington Park, Alley lurched to a stop. She retrieved her camera and fired off five shots in quick succession, towards the concrete at her feet.

Cale watched Pan watching his sister with a heavy brow. 'Hey, Pan, look over there. That's Beanie Lady,' he said, indicating the hunched form located in the shadows of two buildings. 'She's not right in the head.' He inspected his sister from the corner of his eye. 'I mean, like in a bad sort of way.'

'There is no need to be afraid of her,' Pan returned.

'I'm not afraid. Everyone makes fun of her. She probably shouldn't be in this town.'

Beanie Lady shuffled out from the shadows, inching to one of the street garbage bins. Huddling over the receptacle, she sifted through its contents with a vacant expression.

'You may be right,' Pan said. 'She might not belong here.'

'She probably belongs in Deep Moss,' Cale said, viewing the cliffs that walled the town. 'She looks like a mental patient.'

'She looks powerful to me,' Pan said.

'You sure?'

'I am. She reminds me of someone from a time long ago.'

Cale dropped his sight and studied the large woman.

'A warrior.'

'What? Beanie Lady?'

'A warrior with an entire family as strong and true as she was.'

Cale imagined the woman, stripped of her rags and acquired clothing, now adorned in a warrior's garb of stitched leather and chainmail. She stood upon a rise, head raised and one foot before the other. The rubbish she retrieved from the bin and held up to the light was actually her fist being lifted into the air, her family at her back, fierce and unafraid. She roared to the skies and led the charge against a seething, dark swarm of enemies.

Beanie Lady's family disappeared in a puff. She crumpled into herself, becoming small, as the town of Coalcliff pushed upon her. The grey buildings surrounded her, looked upon her with disdain and let slip darkly dressed figures from its shadowed holes and fissures.

'We must leave this place,' Pan said.

'What's happening?' Cale murmured, watching the gang of Anchors spill from lanes and backstreets. Their black tattoos, on the backs of their hands, were vivid within the gloom, like small patches of a black-hole sown to their skin.

Alley picked at the nails on her fingers, fingernails nibbling fingernails. 'I've never seen so many of them together before.'

A woman, towing a small child, found herself engulfed. She drew the child near as the Anchors moved around her. An Anchor, striding with a distant purpose, shoved the obstruction from his path. The woman and child toppled, each with a squeal.

'Hey, you!' an elderly man yelled, striding towards the Anchor. A rush of white knuckles collected the old man in the jaw, sending him to the ground.

The attacking Anchor did not turn his scorn upon the fallen man. He stepped on and over the body without slowing his stride.

Bewildered, the old man cradled his face, searching the streets for witnesses to the attack. Those nearby shuffled back from the icy waters of the dark tide.

'There's Ryan's brother,' Cale said, indicating a scattered few in the shadow of the herd. 'He's in the grade below you,' he said to his sister.

'And Chris from my year,' Alley added. 'And look, Bryce and Jarod.'

Cale ducked his head, searching for Mitch and Gavin in their ranks. He stepped back, allowing Alley to take the lead.

The Anchor's objective became clear. Nearing Beanie Lady, they restructured their swarm to surround her in a clutter of tense muscle and tight fists.

Words were thrown at the large woman. Beanie Lady lurched away, eyes strict and upon the ground. Attempting to manoeuvre herself through the first ring of Anchors, she met a wall of shoving hands. She retreated a step and released a breath that seemed to deflate her form.

'Why are they doing this to her?' Alley mumbled. 'She hasn't hurt anybody.'

More words were hurled. An Anchor stepped in, swung a leg to collide with Beanie Lady's side. She bent, but did not fall.

Onlookers had taken positions at a safe distance. Phones had been retrieved and were held to the ears of worried faces or sat at the end of extended arms, capturing the assault in high pixelated detail.

'If she's so powerful why doesn't she fight them?' Cale said.

'I do not know. She might not have any fight left in her.' Pan moved away. 'We have to get out of here.'

'Pan,' Alley said, with a shake to her head. 'What about that lady? She may be strange, but she doesn't deserve this. We have to help her.'

'This is not my battle.'

'You shouldn't be so quick to wash your hands of this,' a voice said behind.

Pan turned to Eran. They squared themselves against each other. The smouldering collection of violence beyond became an indistinct backdrop to the silence between the two.

Cale and Alley shared a glance.

'Do not put this on me,' Pan said, matching Eran's stare.

'And who should we put it on?'

'I am the one trying to fix all this?'

'No, you are not,' Eran returned. 'You're just trying to save your own hide.'

Pan released a snort of humour. 'Is there a difference?'

'What are you two on about?' Alley called out, attempting to break the tension between them.

Eran turned to Beanie Lady. 'This woman is going to be slaughtered on these streets.'

'What do you mean? Why?'

Studying Pan's even expression, Eran said, 'It's war. Lives will be taken.'

'Eran, they're not going to murder somebody in broad daylight.'

'They will. They no longer care. This town is almost theirs.'

'But the police …'

'They'll kill them, too.'

'Eran,' Alley said, stumbling against his solemnity.

Pan neared the young man. 'I must get these two away from here.'

'You won't help her?'

'I have bigger concerns than this,' Pan said.

Eran turned his grave eyes on Alley and Cale. His brow furrowed. 'What are these two to you?' he asked.

A commotion shook the throng of Anchors. An Anchor charged, grunted a few concealed words and shoved Beanie Lady from her feet to her back. It was a heavy fall.

Shouts of condemnation were launched from the distant edges of the scene.

Eran stepped towards the confrontation.

Pan held out his arm. 'You think you can take them all?'

'Croco knows what's happening,' Eran said, flexing his fingers.

Pan laughed. 'And?'

Eran opened his expression.

'Do not look at me, you blind, little tribesman,' Pan said, holding a hand up against Eran's gaze. 'This,' he directed a rigid finger at the mass of Anchors, 'this is not my fight.'

An Anchor drove a foot into Beanie Lady as she struggle to her feet. She took the strike without a sound.

'It is, Pan. This is your fight. This is all because of you, because you won't accept.'

'I do not have to.'

Eran turned from him. 'If that's what you believe, then run.'

Pan chewed the inside of his mouth.

'Run. Go on and flee. Extend your life by just that little bit longer.'

'That is not what this is about.'

'Then prove it, Pan. Show her that all her efforts have not been in vain.'

Pan shook his head and rolled his eyes to the sky. 'Just be sure not to slow me down.'

'You also.'

'Ha.'

'What are you two doing?' Alley said, in her loudest voice that entered the world as a squeak.

'You do not want to see this, Alley. Get Cale out of here,' Pan said, half turned. 'Keep him safe. Please.'

'You two can't be serious,' Alley murmured, reaching for Cale's hand. He pulled back.

'No,' he said. 'I want to see it.'

She retracted her hand, startled by the grimness in his words.

Pan glanced to Cale before nodding to Eran. The two tilted forward and sprung into a dash. Cries of warning erupted from the Anchors. With a reckless speed, the two leapt and dove into the dark horde. The area exploded into mayhem. Anchors tore towards the attacking two. Many others rushed outwards, randomly striking dazed pedestrians to the ground or throwing loose objects through shop windows. The bystanders screamed their alarm and fled. A few of the more courageous took up posts further back, continuing to document the violence, or howling for police they knew would not arrive until the hostility had expended itself, or lay crippled upon the asphalt.

Alley was held by the sight, her hand frozen in the motion of reaching for her little brother. Eran was right. This was war.

Bodies were flung into the air, or tossed, flailing madly, into the swarm. Roars of pain rumbled through the streets. Curses lashed out as though they could strip the skin from the two. Pan and Eran were a blur amongst them, concentrated tornadoes of lancing limbs. Anchors crumpled around their position until there was a writhing carpet of darkly adorned people at their feet.

Alley searched the scene, hunting for some indicator of reality. She found Bryce at the rear of the battlefield. His wandering, open eyes found her. He blinked at her, his jaw hanging loose.

A momentary stillness travelled through the mass of Anchors. They gathered into small units and shifted their chaos into an ordered structure.

An icicle of dread pierced Alley's shock. She watched misty threads of darkness flow towards Pan and Eran. Slithering amongst the churn of bodies, the inky ribbons struck for the two. Sparks of light darted out from hidden places. They collided with the lashing threads, detonating with small flares and showers of ash.

Alley protected her eyes, fearing, as in the library a few hours before, one of those specks of light to attack her.

Pan and Eran were drowning in the dark multitude. Pan was struck in the back. He stumbled and received a blow to the head. Blood ran and Pan fell. Eran was swept from his legs, disappearing beneath a rain of stomping feet.

The ribbons of night arched high into the air and dove into the fray, squirming between the thrashing Anchors, hungry. Alley held herself, numbering the steps of feet as they bounced on the road. Cale cried out Pan's name as though it might lift him clear from the beating.

A small hill of bronzed rock strolled into the streets. It swayed into the battle, its two short chains of boulders swinging wide from its body.

The Anchors paused within the shadow of Croco. His lips pulled apart, displaying his run of small teeth, 'Howdy, fellas,' and the Anchors poured upon him.

Croco swung his arms as though his fists weighed a tonne. They swept up nearby Anchors, scattering them into those surrounding. Clearing a tight cluster of the gang, Croco revealed two buckled forms. Hauling them to their feet, Pan and Eran wobbled, steadied, and broke into frenzy. The three flowed around each other, precise and perceptive. They protected each other's blindsides and doubled up on each other's attacks to lay down the Anchors with efficiency.

By the time they reached Beanie Lady's position, many of the Anchors were fleeing, carrying crippled companions back into the shadows.

As the drowsy whine of police sirens rolled in from the surrounding streets, the remaining Anchors scattered. Pan, Eran and Croco were left sucking at the air, at Beanie Lady's side.

On her knees, arms at her sides, palms to the heavens, Beanie Lady looked up to the three. Eran extended his hand towards her.

With a hardening of her expression, she turned to the concrete beside her. 'I did not ask for your help,' she said. Climbing to her feet, Beanie Lady shuffled away without a glance in their direction.

Eran lowered his eyes and watched his arms as they tied a knot across his chest.

The first patrol car rolled into the street and was rushed by the plucky pedestrians that remained. It offered Pan, Eran and the others time to make a casual escape.

Entering a deserted street, Pan lifted the collar of his shirt to wipe the blood from his brow. He laughed, 'Just like old times, ay?'

Croco halted his huge body with a suddenness that drew them all to a stop. He looked down on Pan with frown. 'They know you're up to something.'

'So?' Pan returned, grinning through his bruises.

Croco's small eyes shifted to Cale for a beat. 'She got hurt because of it.'

'And like you care about that, crocodile.'

Croco stepped towards Pan, showing his teeth. Eran's eyes switched between the two.

'I should just eat you and be done with it,' Croco grunted.

Pan smiled back, planted his fists on hips, and said, 'Try it.'

18

THE CRUELTY OF THE LIGHT

'Oh my. Alley. Cale. You look troubled, my darlings. Whatever is the matter?'

'Hello, Mrs Duhent,' Alley and Cale said in unison.

Mrs Duhent clasped Alley's shoulders and peered into her with a stern grimace. Releasing Alley, she turned to Cale.

'Some people were causing trouble in town,' Alley said, regathering Mrs Duhent's attention as Cale shifted nearer Pan, his eyes on the elderly woman's large hands.

'Ruffians and scoundrels; terribly, the town has been infested.' Mrs Duhent hummed, and coughed, and braced herself against the side of the house. 'It's not like it once was, children. Ah, to retrieve the old days …' The distant edges of her grimace lifted as she found Pan. 'Come. Come for some green tea and biscuits. It will calm you, and strengthen your heart. And you can introduce me to your new friend.'

'I've got swimming on,' Cale said.

Pan straightened. 'I will come with you.'

'No, no, no, you poor boy,' Mrs Duhent said, latching onto Pan's arm. 'Look at you. You are hurt. You must sit and drink tea with

133

me. It will help those bruises. And it is not every day fortune gifts this poor old woman with the presence of handsome young men. Come, come.'

Alley watched Pan as Pan watched Cale take off at a jog. Behind his level expression was a hint of fever.

Coerced into the Duhent's home, Pan stopped his wriggling as he found himself amongst a rainfall of suspended stars, sparkling tapestries of astrology charts, and panoramic images of misty jungles and crystallised coastal waters.

'What is this place?' Pan said, running light fingers along the webs of dreamcatchers and over large hunks of gemstone on display.

'This is my home, young ...'

'Pan,' Alley offered, standing with her back against the sensibleness of the kitchen behind.

'Pan,' Mrs Duhent nodded, 'this is where I meditate upon the deeper, unseen forces of life.'

Pan reached up and sent a mobile of gilded stars into a spin. They caught the synthetic kitchen light, broke it, coloured it gold, and cast it across the room in glittering fragments.

'Do you believe in the eternal forces that defy both time and space and structure all that we think to be true, young Pan?'

Alley searched her fingernails for any that were in need of a thorough nibbling.

'It is the only thing I believe in, old lady,' Pan said, his title for Mrs Duhent delivered with such lightness her stretched lips curled a little higher at each edge.

Alley lowered her hands from her mouth.

'Ah, souls of the kindred kind, I think.'

Pan looked at a run of books on Angel lore, Demonology, Wicca practice and various other esoteric topics. His hand collected a small black book.

Mrs Duhent bent her squat little body to read the title. 'Ah, Milton ... an interesting man. There is no pearl more precious than a poet's heart ...'

'*And no story sweeter than that of a devil's redemption,*' Pan returned, flipping through the book.

Mrs Duhent's brow knuckled. 'Milton's words?'

'No. Maidens of the sea.'

'I have never read it.'

'It is a *them*. They are people I know.'

'Beautiful ... *For who would lose, though full of pain, this intellectual being ...?*

Pan replaced the book. '*Those thoughts that wander through eternity,*' he said, fingering through other titles, '*to perish rather, swallowed up and lost, in the wide womb of uncreated night ...*'

Mrs Duhent did not share Alley's surprise. She looked satisfied. 'You are familiar with Milton's book?'

'I am familiar with most stories.'

'Most, you say. That is an achievement for one so young. You must have much time on your hands, young Pan.'

The growing smile on Pan's face fell. He straightened from the shelf of books and looked to the front door.

'Come,' Mrs Duhent said, collecting Pan's elbow and ushering him into the kitchen. 'The tea I promised.'

Again, Pan's squirming ceased as he located the spread of cards on the kitchen table.

'Ah, the tarots. Little windows that allow one to read the details of the human soul. Are you familiar?'

'Little windows?' Pan said.

'Yes, yes. Here, let me show you.'

With a small smile, Alley watched Pan's interest as Mrs Duhent collected the spread of cards into a pile. A speck of bleached light peeked over his shoulder, glinting as it considered the cards below.

Alley retreated towards the shadows of the adjoining room, her wary stare watching as the speck rose like a compacted dawn over the grey-shirted mount. The depths of the shadows she hid herself within were not enough to stem the attack. Her right eye was caught and held and squeezed with a torturer's cruelty. Rumbles of pain struck out from the epicentre. Ache shouldered its way through her mind, stomping around her brain in a tantrum.

In rhythm to the movements of the speck, her pain followed the small light as it dropped to the ground and darted along the floor to the room at her back. It leapt onto the couch and burrowed its way amongst the assortment of cushions stacked in a sloppy pyramid on the seat.

Pain continued to thud against the inside of her skull. It was not going to release her. Covering her right eye, Alley stumbled to the couch. She sat down and pulled up each cushion, searching for the bright culprit to the pain in her head. Each cushion was turned over in her hands three times and then placed upon the ground. When they were all inspected and removed, Alley had only found gloom.

'Alley …'

She pushed her hand down between the padding of the couch, searching for anything. She wondered what a ball of light would feel like. Would its bite hurt as much as the ache it caused behind her eye?

'Alley …'

And what would she do with it when she caught it? Could she strangle a reason from it, or threaten it to leave her alone?

She dug deep, her fingers probing every inch of the couch's depths. Lowering herself to her stomach, Alley pushed down further, scouring the hidden reaches, those places never explored by human hands.

It must be here somewhere. She lowered her head, shoved her face into the separations of the padding, peering into the lightless crevices.

'Alley!'

Alley started and raised herself. She found Mrs Duhent and Pan standing nearby.

'Whatever are you doing, my darling?'

'I thought I saw something,' she replied, the pain subsiding and leaving a hum of confusion in her head.

'Oh? What was this something, dear?'

'It was … something. Like a light, maybe.'

'Coming from the couch, darling?'

'No.' Alley rubbed her head, unable to understand the shapes shifting in her mind. Remnants of the light blurred the edges of each thought, mashing them together. 'It escaped into the couch. Hiding, I think.'

Mrs Duhent turned a quizzical look on Pan. 'This house is a very spiritual place.' He watched the movement of his tattered runners as he tapped them on the floor.

'This is interesting,' Mrs Duhent murmured, turning to her shelf of books. 'Have you seen this type of thing before, child?'

'I don't know. Maybe. When I was younger.'

Mrs Duhent nodded ponderously, looking through the titles of the books. She withdrew one from the run, entitled *The Spiritual Medium*. Returning to the kitchen, she took a seat at the table and raced through the pages. 'Moving lights … And when you were younger …'

'I guess. But not like this though. It's hurting my head. Like a migraine. It's so sore.'

With a jerk, the elderly woman sat back and stared at the wall for a beat before turning to Alley.

Alley dropped her hands from her face. She saw that Pan had disappeared. All that seemed to remain in the room was Mrs Duhent's grimace. It reached from ear to ear, like an elegant frog in fearful silence.

*

The elderly woman closed the medical pamphlets and pushed herself from the table, feeling the weight of her years pressing upon her shoulders, coercing her back to the chair. She shuffled to the window and stared out at the rear of the property. The small construction that housed the children stood with a slight lean. It was odd. She had never noticed the terrible dilapidation of the building before.

Returning to the table, she found her medication in her hand. She had not realised she had grabbed the expensive placebo, its only use to appease her husband and doctors.

The sight of the small container twisted her lips. The constant nausea and lethargy it had introduced to her life was resting at the moment, buried beneath heavy thoughts. Her husband, a rarely seen visitor in her mind, was sitting obtrusive and large.

She knew she was waiting for that old fool to die. Only then could she lay herself down and drift away from this mortal plane, shed this struggle and gain the rest she deserved, joining with those she has spent every waking hour yearning to hold. Not until he was beyond the reach of sorrow and loneliness and all other human conditions could she depart herself.

And the children … She felt her heart drop a few feet. Would they be alright?

The pamphlets before her had been left by customers who came for spiritual healing, those she had met at the hospital, others with terminal illnesses. They came to her with small voices and a restrained pleading in their eyes. They spoke of their afflictions and their personal research into alternative medicines. That was where she had heard those symptoms; the bursts of light in the vision, the muddled thoughts, the migraines.

Her eyes moved from the medical pamphlets to a book; *The Spiritual Medium*. The cards, used to divine future events and the human soul, were spread beneath it in an incomprehensible mess. She placed her hand upon the lot, feeling the edges and corners and cool, smooth surfaces, and watched her arm as she wiped it all to the floor.

19

WORLDS APART

The air was a chemical soup. Cale hung his head, feeling the chlorine corrode his eyes and lungs. Hardened to the sting of salt, chlorinated water was an alien substance, noxious to his coastal being. The boys either side of him adjusted their swimming goggles. His only pair was adrift on the ocean currents, sent sailing by Gavin's hand. He had not bothered to scrounge for another pair.

The marshal gestured to the eight boys. Cale stood and looked down the line to Mitch. His eyes were secured on the far end of the pool.

They stepped to the starting blocks. The schools of their region formed a dense wall of deafening cheers and waving banners. It seemed to rise into the sky, tower overhead, enclose them in an airtight container.

The seven other boys jiggled their hands and feet, loosening their limbs. The rumble of the crowd shook Cale's ribs, rattling his heart. The rest of him was still.

'*Positions!*'

Cale's guts squeezed themselves as thin as a piece of paper as he climbed onto the eighth block. The coloured flags of the turn indicator above whipped violently, threatening to tear themselves from the wire. He continued to swallow the taste in his mouth, trying hold down what wanted to come up.

The first chime was sounded. Lowering himself, he felt the cheers and hollering calls rush around him, avoiding his position to find the other swimmers. The blast of the second chime dominated for a brief moment. This was their world, up here with all the animated faces and mighty voices. The final chime sang, passing through his bones and muscles, releasing him from their world and into his own.

The crowd was non-existent down here in the quiet wet. The other swimmers were only concepts.

Cale's strokes were fluid, an extension of the water itself. He felt weightless, free, striking away from physical restrictions and nearing that impossible moment where he would be capable of flight.

He could not imagine a hand strong enough to hold him here. It would slide from his slick skin, his body slipping through the water with too much speed to be caught and held.

His turn was executed in his mind. His body followed in perfect reflection. The water seemed to pulse and draw him onwards, and, much sooner than he expected, Cale found his hand against the wall. He gripped the edge and peered through a chlorinated haze to the clock. The cheering of the crowd had escalated. The previous record was almost eleven and half seconds behind him.

The following moments were framed in a fog that had nothing to do with the chlorine. He climbed from the pool when the others had finished and collected his towel. Mr Lowen and the girl's swim coach, Mrs Tindell, walked over and congratulated him with words he nodded to, but did not hear.

The noise of the crowd had eased back. When his name reverberated through the air, along with his time, it reignited in its hysteria. When he was asked to stand and be acknowledged, Cale placed his towel around his neck, held its tattered ends and stood from his seat. He could not prevent the corners of his mouth from lifting.

When Mitch wandered nearby and said, 'I should wipe that smirk off your face,' Cale placed his fists on his hips, smiled wider and said, 'Try it.'

*

Carla and Maria readjusted the barstool in the warped shadows of the paperbark. Taking a few large steps rearward, Carla peered through the eye of her camera, 'Just tilt the bottom side left-ways a bit.'

Maria looked up from her crouch with a blank face.

Dropping her camera with a huff, Carla looked to Alley and Taz at the table. '*Quiet words before the dawn* … That's what I'm going to call it. It's about the negative impact of technology on individual thought. It'll get me top marks, for sure.'

Alley nodded, thinking back to Carla's last project; *Spoken thoughts in the dark*, jumbled dinner settings in dappled light. And, the one before that; *Whispers upon the night*, piles of books positioned in the raised arms of Maria's shadow.

Asking if they were a part of a themed collection, Carla had answered with an emphatic, 'No, of course they're not.' They were individual pieces, each with their own unique story and life.

'What's your final project on?' Taz asked.

Alley spun back and said, 'I haven't chosen a subject yet.'

'Cutting it fine.'

Alley shrugged.

'I know,' Taz said, removing her sunnies, 'put a shoe in a hat, balance it on a bicycle, and call it *The resurgence of communism in democratic states*. They'll call it *avant-garde* and give you an A.'

'Put that in the maybe pile.'

'Or a bit of delicious irony,' Taz continued, with a louder voice. 'Take a photo of yourself banging your head against the wall and call it *Emotional breakdown induced by pointless activity*.'

Alley attempted to share her laughter with the two behind. Carla's pouting scowl returned her to Taz. 'I thought it was funny.'

Taz flicked her brow, taking a sip of her coffee. 'I hit too close to home.'

Alley smirked. 'So, no chemistry today?'

'There is. I'm on a field experiment,' she said, lifting her coffee cup from the table. 'It's my ninth double espresso in two hours. I'm peeing every ten minutes and I'm so jittery I can't read my own handwriting.' She took another sip, smacking her lips together. 'It's bloody awesome.'

'Alley!' a voice called out.

'Well, well,' Taz said, twisting in her seat, 'our glorious vice-captain has come to let us bask in his wonderful glow. Greetings, powerless figurehead,' she said to Trent, as he stopped beside the table.

'Taz,' Trent greeted, with a straight face, before looking to Alley. 'We just got word from the swim meet.'

Alley could feel the heartbeat in her fingers and toes.

'Your brother absolutely killed it. Broke six records. Smashed them.'

'Really?'

Trent nodded, his rosy lips exposing his faultless run of teeth. 'Not bad, yeah?'

Taz nodded her approval. 'What a little champ.'

Alley reigned in her grin, trying not to look like an idiot before Trent. She became conscious of the small sum of money in her bag and knew exactly what she would do with it.

20.

THE FIGHT OF A WARRIOR

Alley exited the store, turned down the side street and came to a stop, watching the bottle wobble in its flight. It caught specks of sunlight, storing them as it arched downwards. The large woman – all gnashing teeth, frenzied howls and clawing fingers – bobbed to the side. The bottle collided with the brick wall and shattered, scattering its collected bits of light.

The group of boys laughed and taunted her, dancing back as the woman rushed towards them, throwing her large fists before herself and screaming through her frothing mouth, 'Stand and fight!'

Alley, her courage bolstered by the lack of tattooed insignia on their hands, dropped her bag and rushed into the clash. 'Get away from her!' she screamed.

The boys, projectiles in hand and ready to launch, paused to watch Alley's flailing-arms approach.

'Whoa, hold up, Alley,' one of the boys said, his face tight with excitement. 'It's just Beanie Lady.'

Beanie Lady stomped at the ground, tearing at the clothing on her front and throwing her fist into the solid wall at her back. She set her head back and wailed to the sky with all the abandon of a doomed creature, 'Stand and fight!'

'What have you done to her?' Alley breathed.

'What we always do to her,' came the reply. 'But she's never done this before.'

'It's great,' said another. 'We found her Godzilla mode.'

'Just go,' Alley said. The boys remained. 'Go!' she screamed, into their haughty expressions. 'She doesn't deserve this,' Alley called out after them, as they wandered away with amused shakes to their heads and words of insult under their breath.

The woman continued to storm, secured in her rage. The blood from her knuckles lined her hands and wrists, and speckled the brick wall that was now cracked and concaved.

Alley approached her, pushing through the rending cries. She stood before Beanie Lady as the woman's crimson fists swung at her. 'Wait. Please. You know me. You spoke to me. Remember?'

With fists raised and ready to fall, the large woman turned unfocused eyes on the small body below. The violence possessing her waned. Her soiled expression sagged. She stumbled back, clutching her face as moisture in her eyes condensed and ran down her cheeks. As her back found the wall, she sunk to the pavement.

Alley inched closer. 'Do you remember me?'

'Poor sufferer,' Beanie Lady mumbled, letting her head rest against the bricks.

'They're gone now. Are you okay?'

'I do not even know where I am,' the woman whispered to herself.

'You're on Kensington Street, near the park. Do you want some help for those cuts? What's your name?'

Beanie Lady's dark eyes turned to her. 'Name?' Something like amusement hardened her visage for a moment. 'I have no name in this place.'

'No name?'

'I am a detached shadow. A ghost in penance.'

Alley lifted her thumbnail to her teeth, ignoring the bewildered stares of a couple walking nearby. 'You don't remember your name?'

'My name was forsaken, along with my home.' Beanie Lady attempted to push her large form onto her feet. Drained of all strength, her arms wobbled and gave way.

'Here,' Alley said. As though aiding Mrs Duhent, she manoeuvred herself beneath the lady's arm and hauled her erect.

Beanie Lady pushed away and caught herself on the wall. 'I cannot accept your help.'

'It's alright.'

'No. I must stand unaided. It is all I have left. I am a fighter.'

'I'm not sure I …'

The woman's head drifted to the side. 'A failed fighter,' she added.

'Failed? Because of those jerks?'

'No.'

'The Anchors the other day?'

'No. They are no more than mockery to my failure.'

'Then why have you failed?'

Beanie Lady shook her head with small movements of disbelief. 'How do you fight that which cannot be fought?' she said quietly, seeming to direct the question only to herself. 'How!?' The bottom of her fist was thrown against the bricks.

'I don't know,' Alley said, into the following silence.

'What am I? What is it to be destined for defeat? What do I do if I cannot fight?'

Alley looked to the ends of each of her fingers, to the point where the nail joined the skin, the glowing inflammation and the constant rawness. 'I guess, you just fight anyway.'

Beanie Lady looked down upon her.

'When everyone knows you can't win – and even if you know it yourself – you fight anyway. There's some kind of victory in doing that. There must be.'

Beanie Lady's head nodded forward, resting her chin upon her chest. 'Perhaps,' she mumbled.

Retrieving her camera, Alley viewed the woman through its little window. She saw the dirt upon her, the grime that this town coated upon beautiful things, and the multihued aura of the woman attempting to shine through.

Firing off a few shots, Alley knew this to be the final statement she would leave within her photography class.

When Beanie Lady broke into her bent shuffle, a voice snorted, causing Alley to start. She turned to the shadows to find Croco.

He stood with a slight sway. His usual, unshaved surfer veneer looked more dishevelled than ruggedly masculine today. From two fingers, a half depleted bottle of whiskey dangled.

'How long have you been there?' she questioned.

'Long enough,' he grunted.

'You could've helped her.'

'No,' he sneered. 'No, I couldn't have, little girl. The last thing she needs is a knight in shining armour.'

'What do you mean?'

'But you …' he said, his finger pointing towards her, drifting left and right. 'Words of a warrior …'

Alley watched his bleary gaze. 'What's happening around here, Croco?'

Croco dropped his arm, lifted his head and took a swig from his bottle. 'Do you really want to know, little girl?'

After a pause, Alley nodded.

He staggered forward. 'What happens when an unstoppable force meets an immoveable object?'

Alley had heard this riddle before. It was a paradox.

'Or,' he continued, whiskey trickling through his beard, 'when an undying life squares himself against death …?' With a wobble, he raised his arms and, after the third try, brought the points of his two index fingers against each other. '… Two timeless entities crossing swords?'

'I don't know,' Alley replied, quietly.

Croco let his arms fall and shrugged. 'I do, little girl.' He took another drink, and said, 'The destruction of everything you know.'

21.

CHALLENGE

Cale's brief glimpses at the world as he turned his head for a breath showed the others a distance behind. He dropped a leg, hung his stroke. His smooth glide wrenched as though a tether around his middle had snapped taut.

He listened to the smacking slosh of the others as they powered through the final lap.

'Cale,' Mr Lowen said, standing above his lane as he hung onto the edge. 'I thought we found a swimming superman the other day. What's wrong with you?'

'Nothing,' Cale murmured, focusing on the concrete lip as he hauled himself from the water.

'Mitch, good work. Not your best time. But you came first.'

Mitch spread his grin around the area.

Passing Cale as they moved to their gear, Gavin scrunched his nose and called out, 'It smells like piss around here, Mr Lowen.'

'Hey. Watch your language.' Mr Lowen sniffed the air. 'It smells the same as usual.'

Cale removed his new pair of goggles and headed to his new towel. Collecting one end, he whipped out the length of the bright material, cleaning away any possible sand particles with a flourish.

Mitch and Gavin watched him.

'It still stinks like piss,' Gavin hollered, above the chatter and grumblings of the ocean.

'Enough, Gavin. Practice is over, everyone. Head home and I'll see you all next week.'

Cale took his time, gathering his belongings for his walk home. Mitch and his friends lingered, but made no move when he fell into his homeward trudge. With his new towel in hand and the results of the regionals continuing to pop up in quiet conversations in his classes, Cale felt a howl stirring in his chest. The whirl of wheels and click of pedals diced up the thought. Mitch and co. angled their bikes around him and skidded to a stop before his path.

'What now?' Cale breathed.

Gavin shook his head in mock commiseration. 'You think winning a few races and a new towel's gonna make you less of a loser?'

Cale gathered his towel into his arms.

'Where the hell d'you get a new towel anyway?' Gavin laughed.

'It was a gift?'

'Yeah, right. Who'd wanna give anything to you?'

'It was from my sister.'

Gavin shook his head again. 'From your freak of a sister? A freak of a present, given from a freak to a freak.'

'She's not, you asshole,' Cale growled. 'You're more of a freak than she is.' He stepped forward, hands scrunching into tight balls.

Mitch dropped his bike, compelling the other three to do the same. 'C'mon, man, don't try it. You'll only get yourself hurt again.'

Cale felt a hot churning inflating within him, urging him onward.

'Let's get the towel,' Gavin said, and led two of the boys forward. There was a brief tug-o-war, concluding with Cale being pulled from his feet.

'Piss on it,' Mitch nodded.

The towel was thrown to the ground between the feet of the three boys. Cale clambered upright. His mind swirled, his thoughts frenzied and his breathing tight. He could not take down all four of them. He did not need to.

Cale charged, pushed all his weight behind his fist and drove it into Mitch's stomach. The boy doubled forward, the air rushing from him with a loud woof. Cale dropped his arm, brought it up, smacked his knuckles into Mitch's lowered face.

A rush of movement came in from the side. Cale thought of Pan. He weaved, sidestepped the punch, struck forward with his foot and sent the boy onto his back.

Turning, Cale found Mitch charging, fists swinging. They caught each other, held each other close with one hand as they attacked with the other. It was a hectic muddle of two fists, two snarls and two sets of eyes catching glimpses of a face almost as familiar as their own, now masked in violent splatterings of red.

An arm around Cale's throat yanked him from the brawl. He was held back, his airway restricted, as Mitch recovered. Cale kicked and thrashed, unable to break the hold. Mitch advanced, fist rising.

'This is it, isn't it!?' Cale screamed, through a constricted throat. The dam within him, stable and fortified for all these years, sprung a leak. 'This is what you wanted all along!'

Mitch paused, his arm ready to unleash. 'What are you on about?'

'You wanted me to attack you!'

'What? You've lost it, man.'

'No. I'm right. You wanted me to hurt you. You wanted a reason to hate me.' The hold around his throat loosened. Cale wriggled free and stood before Mitch, ignoring the blood dripping from his face. 'You needed something to hate me for, didn't you? So you could take away the one thing I have. The only thing I have left since it happened.'

Mitch dropped his arm. His sight shifted to his friends. They turned awkward looks towards each other.

'What are you on about?' Mitch grunted.

The dam inside him broke. The memory it had been constraining charged with no hope to recall it. 'The fact that it wasn't my bloody fault,' Cale gushed. It poured out of him, tugging the words along with it. 'That's the only thing I have; the fact I didn't do anything wrong. And you want to take it away from me, don't you? You need a reason to treat me like this. You want to hate me, when it was him. It was him. Not me. I couldn't have stopped what happened to us. How could I?'

One of the boys picked up his bike, jumped on and pedalled away.

Mitch strode forward, threatened Cale with another punch. 'Don't you say that. Nothing happened to me. It was just you.' He looked to Gavin, and scoffed, 'What a freak.'

Cale ignored the fist hovering in the air. He wiped his eyes and collected his towel.

'That's it,' Mitch huffed. 'I can't look at your face anymore. I'm done with you on this team.'

'I'm not leaving,' Cale returned, shaking the dirt from his towel. 'Neither am I.'

'Race for it,' Gavin said. 'You'll kick his ass, Mitch.'

'Yeah. Let's do it,' Mitch nodded. 'Whoever wins is the one who deserves a spot on the team.'

'Fine,' Cale said, wiping the blood from his face with his shirt.

'Here. Tomorrow. We'll sort it out then.'

'What about around the headlands?' Cale sniffed. 'The point at Deep Moss?'

'You're on. We'll start on the beach. First one to swim around the rocks wins.'

'Friday.'

Mitch lowered his brow. 'Friday? The swells …'

'Afraid?'

Glancing to Gavin with a chuckle, Mitch replied, 'Friday, then.'

When they had ridden away, the churning heat within Cale grew cold.

What have I done!?

*

Stupid idiot. Stupid idiot … The words repeated in Cale's mind.

What was he thinking? There was no victory in this. Even if he won the race, the hell Mitch and his friends would have waiting would be meticulous and absolute.

The night was closing in. He tried not to think of his mother. The light of Mr Duhent's garage glowed in the gloom. Cale's steps were light as he travelled across the yard. Mr Duhent was not in there.

He missed the smell of the garage and all the interesting shapes and complex objects that comprised the workshop. It was an unfamiliar, but relaxing feeling he had when he was slathered in grease, hunched over a motor, following Mr Duhent's systematic instructions, as the old man watched on at a safe distance.

Cale did not know why he wanted to avoid Mr Duhent these last few months.

The dusty grime sat thick on the concrete floor. He drew rings with the toe of his shoe. Nothing had changed. Not that he was expecting it would. Still, there was a niggling in the back of his mind that told him it was all different now.

Mr Duhent would be back soon. Then he would have to chat to him, answer questions on school … and friends … and which girls were chasing after him. Before he turned and ran for his shed, Cale found himself at the end of the garage, eyes raised to the roof, staring at a plank of timber running along the top of the brick wall. Behind it sat Mr Duhent's rifle.

It was only a year or two ago when Mr Duhent used to let him fire it. They shot at wind-chimes hanging on a distant tree at the rear of the property. When Mrs Duhent caught them, she blew her top.

'What are you doing!? What are you doing!?' she screamed at her husband.

'It okay. It okay. I buy better wind-chime,' he replied, with a cocky smile.

'I don't care about the wind-chimes, you old fool,' she repeated over and over, whacking him over the head with a rolled up newspaper as he skulked back to the garage.

Cale remembered the time when Mr Duhent caught sight of the fox. Cale liked the look of it, the orange and black of it.

Moving on the fringes of the forest, it froze as it caught sight of them also. Its beady eyes peered at them with curiosity, maybe a questioning of friendship.

Cale watched as Mr Duhent raised the rifle, took aim and squeezed the trigger. He could not remember the sound of the discharge. He only remembered the fox dropping to the ground. On its side, its legs skipped, believing it was still able to get away, escape the bullet that exploded its little fox insides.

'Hmmph,' Duhent had said.

And that was all that was said.

Cale was silent. He had never seen an animal shot before. It seemed easy, terribly easy.

He went back to his shed that afternoon and lay on the couch. When darkness fell and Alley was asleep in her room, he got up and slipped out into the night. It was freezing, he remembered. Trudging through frosted grass he headed towards the forest. After scouring the scrub and through the thick tufts he found the body. He fell to his knees and placed his hand on the furry neck of the fox. As though it had absorbed the chilly, stilled night, the fox was cold and stiff.

Mr Duhent did not like foxes. They attacked his hens, back when he had hens. He wanted the fox dead, erased from his life. And now it was, just with the simple movement of one finger.

Cale stared at the butt of the rifle, visible behind the timber. He imagined himself climbing onto the bench, retrieving the weapon, collecting the shells from the tin on the window sill and holding the loaded rifle in his hands. He was unsure where exactly he would aim the thing. He assumed that knowledge would only be gained when the rifle was held and was ready to release its command of ending.

*

There were no drapes on the window. There was only an unobstructed view of the two figures as they growled and shoved at one another.

A large young man toppled over the kitchen table, sending it juddering across the floor with a groan. He clambered through a broken chair and caught the table's edge, staring at the old man before him.

'Worthless mongrel,' the old man slurred.

The young man pulled back. He had never accustomed himself to the rancid smell of scotch whiskey and stale beer that issued from the man in a toxic cloud.

The old man swayed in an elliptical orbit around his own feet. 'Can't even protect your own little brother, you worthless mongrel.'

'Give me a break,' the young man returned, head lowered, feeling like a wild beast. He could tear this frail old drunk's limbs off, tear them clean from his rotting body, if he wanted, and beat him to death with them. 'He just got himself into a scuffle. It's fine.'

'It's fine …' the old man repeated. 'Mitch,' he called out, 'Mitch, come show Bryce how fine you are.'

Mitch remained hidden. He knew better than to step into the suffocating ash and heated flow of these eruptions.

'You mongrel dog, Bryce … What's the point of ya? Can't take care of him. Can't protect him. Your own blood.' His bloodshot eyes drifted around the space the young man occupied.

'I can't be around Mitch all the fucken time, can I? I'm not fucken omnipresent.'

'Don't you curse at me,' the old man growled, each word sent in time with his staggered stride. His backhand collected the young man precisely. No matter the inebriation, the old man was accurate to the point of a marksman.

Bryce accepted the strike. Ever since he was small, his old man had challenged him like this, dared him to strike back. With alcohol liquefying the old man's bones, dissolving him from the inside out, this deteriorating old thing before him would crumple at his touch.

'I'm not afraid of you,' Bryce sneered. 'You're no more than a walking corpse.'

They stepped towards each other. Sighting Mitch in the doorway, face looking like a lumpy plum of worry, Bryce lowered his arms. He accepted another solid backhand across his face, turned and left the house.

22.

TO KILL THE BEAST

Cale balled himself up small in the corner of the couch. There was a distant drone of words when Alley came home. He acknowledged them with a lifting of his brow. The swollen bruises around his eyes prevented him from raising it too far. When she entered her bedroom silence fell. Climbing to his feet, he staggered to the light switch and made everything disappear. He lay back down, held himself and waited for the blankness to fill him.

In his dreams he was drifting down deep. No matter the direction he turned his body he could not quite see the woman with dark hair, the woman with one hand on his ankle to keep him down, and one hand on his belly to keep him afloat. He did not care that her hand on his ankle was stronger than her other. He just wanted to see her and let her see him.

The murmurs of ache in his chest grew to a blazing pain. His body bucked, the final throes of a drowning man, and Cale found himself on his feet, night wrapping around him, a figure at his side.

'Pan?' Cale's voice echoed through the empty world around them.

'Hi, kid.'

'Another adventure?'

'Yes.'

'Where's Sticks?'

'This one is just for you, Cale.'

The nothingness they existed within shifted. Cale understood they were moving. Similar to his previous dream of Pan, he held no sensation of his body, could not feel the swing of his legs or arms, or the impact of his feet on the ground. But, he supposed, this was what all dreams were like.

The encompassing black, at times, seemed so close, Cale was afraid of colliding with it. Other times, its depth was so profound the sensation of it made him nauseous. He was glad when shapes materialised at their sides, offering something substantial on which to rest his eyes.

Concentrating on the angular silhouettes, Cale could just make them out; houses, perhaps, shop fronts and park benches. But then he would focus a little too far and the forms would blur and melt away.

'Where are we going?' Cale's voice said, a moment before the sentence appeared in his mind.

'I found a pirate.'

'We're hunting more pirates?'

'This is a different kind of pirate, one of the more horrible ones. It is a beast. We must hunt it down and kill it … Here.'

Cale looked down to see a rifle being handed to him. 'What am I supposed to do with this?'

'Just hold onto it.'

A twinge in his guts made Cale hold the rifle a short distance from his body. He listened for the gentle call of the ocean. There was only silence. Cale shivered. They were not in Coalcliff.

'Where are we, Pan?'

'Close.' Pan's hand seemed luminescent in the gloom as it waved towards Cale, signalling him to lower himself into a furtive scamper. 'Over here. The cave of the beast.'

Cale peered at a colourless mass, a hole deeper than the nothingness around them. 'Is this it?'

Squinting helped. Contours and outlines appeared. Some looked like trees, fence palings, garbage bins. To his side, Cale thought he was looking at a mailbox.

As he mapped out the area, Cale felt as though he was sinking. 'Pan, where are we?' It reminded him of a place he knew, a place from many years ago, around the time of his mother's death, when he was forced to live with that man. 'Where are we, Pan? I want to see where we are.'

Pan searched the blankness at their feet, retrieved an object. He stood, retracted his arm and launched it forward. The sound of something hard colliding with solid timber rang out in the abyss.

A rectangular panel of light appeared on the cave wall. It spread a warped, orange patch on the dark world at their feet.

Held by the light pouring through the cave window, Cale watched a massive hand, covered in scales and hair, reach through the curtains. With long, probing fingers and nails like eagle talons it clutched the thick partition and drew it slowly to the side.

'Do not run.'

The sight of the horrid thing was immobilising. How could he possibly run?

The curtains were released. A lock clunked as it was turned, the sound toppling over itself as it spread.

'Remember the gun.'

Cale looked to the rifle in his hands. It felt weightless, a thing filled with air, as he raised it and took aim.

There was a splinter of light. It widened, became a doorway. A set of glowing, red eyes, deep within a tangled forest of oily fur, peeked around the edge.

'Are you scared, Cale?'

No, he was petrified.

'You can end this thing. Call it out, Cale. Kill it and you will be crowned a great king.'

The trigger was cool and responsive, eager to retract, nudge the firing pin to nod its grave consent to the bullet.

'Call it out, Cale.'

'What's its name?'

'I do not know. But you do.'

Cale raised the rifle as Mr Duhent had taught him, butt against his shoulder, his grip on the stock firm. He tilted his head and looked down the sights. His finger twitched and his arm trembled.

Lowering the gun, Cale let the thing drop from his hands. He turned and ran for the awaiting nothing. The blaring echo of the rifle, as it collided with the ground, gave pursuit, calling out to him with one word, *coward*.

23.

LIVES SOWN WITH
THE DARK TENDRILS

T he window was polished to a jeweller's standard. The alcoholic wipes left no streaks. Within, she stood, twisting this way and that, before the panels of her built-in wardrobe, the sliding doors fashioned into floor-to-ceiling mirrors.

The knocking at her door was frail, but persistent. It reached her as a distant thrum. The view before her consumed her senses, the chunky curves of hips, the fat stores in her ankles, upper arms and wrists … the ugliness of it all.

Her phone buzzed. Checking the screen she saw it was Tanner. He was such a sleazy bastard, the type of guy who can make groping a girl in a club look as appropriate and expected as shaking the hands of a client.

GLAZE TONITE??? his message said. *IM STOCKED UP!!!*

The phone was thrown to her bed. It was a tempting offer. It was amazing what some booze and a few small pills were capable of. She could cleanse the world with one of those cocktails; make everything clean and shiny and perfect. Even if it was only for one night, all the ugliness could be shed and she could fool herself into believing that beauty was a possibility.

But, no, she could not handle it again tonight. She needed a break. Her body was not acting right; the exhaustion and nausea and everything out of time, and the blackouts happening with a worrying frequency.

'Milly,' the croaking call crept into the room, defiling the sanctity of her space like a stalker.

The girl spun, vertigo shouldered her. Her sight managed to catch a bony hand clutching her doorframe.

'Mum!' she condemned the woman with a yelp. 'I told you a thousand times not to come in here.'

Her mother stood clutching the doorframe as though the grave would claim her if she released her grip on the world.

'Get out!' the girl said, indicating the hand that was polluting her room.

Her mother's lips worked through soundless words as they always did when she was out of it.

'I'm … just checking in …' her mother breathed.

'Get out, mum. I'm busy.' Milly walked over and pushed on the door, forcing her mother to withdraw her hand.

The woman lingered in the hall, breathing heavily, before shuffling away.

Milly stood there, hands to her stomach, feeling itchy with no place to scratch. She retrieved her phone and replied to Tanner, placing her order for the night.

Collecting the container of alcoholic wipes, she spent some time scrubbing away the stains of her mother's hand. She then withdrew another wipe, placed it over her nose and mouth and breathed deeply.

*

Alley did not care what she looked like. She retrieved her windbreaker and wrapped herself in warmth and comfort. Whether the other students were aware of what happened or even cared, they kept their distance all the same. Alley accepted their radiating disregard as a mercy, preferring that than their taunts and droopy-eyed stares of pity.

The calls of Megan and Taz were ignored as she left the school grounds. Moving through the streets, the rain came down. Alley removed her windbreaker, lowered her head and spread her arms, allowing the crisp, clean pricks of water to pepper her body.

The charcoal day fell deeper into its gloom, colouring the world in monochrome as she reached the forested cliffs. The murmurs of the ocean could be heard through the trees, their whispers just beyond Alley's understanding. Maybe they were warning the cliffs of her approach, or, perhaps, ushering her towards the edge.

Why am I the one always left alive?

She quickened her stride, tried to be nimble and light over the sodden forest floor, untouchable. A log snagged her foot, sent her falling forward. The mud of the ground rose up before her, threatened to swallow and drown her. A tree was close enough for her to catch. She stared down at the mud, considering letting go. The thought seemed tempting; losing herself in those dark depths never to resurface.

The insane mechanisms of her mind held her back. She knew she could never bring herself to do it.

Gulping down some chilled air, Alley broke into a run. The forest lashed at her with thin switches, nipping her legs and leaving a sting.

Through gaps in the trees she saw the immense wall of churning grey that was the sea and sky. She increased her pace, feeling the edge of the cliffs rushing to meet her.

As the last few branches whipped her body the forest gave way and the ocean spread outwards, racing the sky to the horizon. Alley steadied her arms and stumbled to a stop just before the drop. The sight below reeled and she felt herself tilt forward. Stepping back, breathing hard, she felt her heart bash itself against the cage of her ribs.

'You can fly?'

Alley jumped and turned. Pan stood a short distance away, his scruffy shards of hair resisting the rain as it attempted to plaster it to his scalp. 'What are you doing here?'

He turned his attention to the distant beach, no more than a thin, yellow divider from where they stood. 'You think you can fly?'

'No.'

'You would fall then.'

'Probably.'

The oceans had roughened. The dark spread was a nonsensical thrust of jags and points; a prelude to the storm swells.

'What are you doing here, Pan?'

'You come here a lot. Is the lagoon nearby?'

Alley levelled Pan with a stare, a corridor for everything she felt within. 'My friend died last night.'

Pan nodded.

'They just told me. She's dead.' Did he hear what she was saying? 'She was out at a club. She took something. They couldn't revive her. She's dead. She's only my age and now she's dead.'

Her words collided with Pan's indifference, fell to the floor and lay lifeless.

'Did you hear me?'

'I did.'

'Do you care?'

'Am I supposed to?'

Alley released a long, aching breath. Turning to the town, the view was smudged by the layers of rain. Soft steps brought Pan up alongside her.

They stood together, studying the details of Coalcliff below as though they were its woeful creators.

'It hurts when something precious is taken for no good reason,' he said.

She looked to him, watched his eyes as they travelled across rooftops, fell into the streets and wandered amongst the buildings. He turned to her after a while and matched her stare. Alley lent towards him, parting her lips, aiming them for his.

Pan shirked. 'What are you doing?'

Alley looked to the ocean, feeling her face flush. She placed her thumb nail between her teeth and bit down hard. 'I don't know,' she mumbled. 'I don't know anymore.'

'You tried to kiss me.'

'I know, Pan.'

'You want me to be with you?'

'I don't know. Maybe. I just know that it's easier when you're near. Even when you infuriate me … the times when you're not around are worse. I know I'm not normal. But when I'm with you, I know it doesn't matter.'

'Alley …'

She forced herself to look at him. His arms were folded and his head was low. She had never seen him stand so small.

'I am sorry. I am not here to save you.'

Her embarrassment settled. 'What do I need saving from?'

Pan shrugged. 'Something. Your ending.'

'My ending? You make no sense sometimes. What do you mean my ending?'

'I do not think it is going to be a happy one.'

She searched the stones at her feet. 'Sometimes there are no happy endings.' Lowering herself, she placed her hands on the rock. It was cold and lifeless, as she expected. 'That's the way of the world, isn't it?'

'Well, for some, perhaps.'

'For me?'

Pan reached for her arm.

Without looking to him, Alley dodged his touch, stood and headed south. Pan followed.

'There you go,' she said, into the wind. 'Mystics Bay.'

'This is it,' he stated. 'A Water-home.'

The waters were dark and broken, murky jags prickling the surface. Two small figures rocked back and forth as they awaited the oncoming swells.

'Eran and Croco …' Alley said. 'They shouldn't be out there this week.'

Pan moved nearer the precipice.

'You know them, don't you? That fight in town …'

'I do know them,' Pan confirmed, eyes locked on the distant two. 'They come from where I come from.'

'Where?'

'The Never.'

The world grumbled. Alley's questions were forgotten as she watched the horizon bulge, the waves gorging themselves on motion as they swelled forward. The small figures stuttered, propelling themselves for the shore, finding position. The lead wave rose up, collected them, sent them sliding along its wall. Eran and Croco wove between each other, more fluid and structured than the thing that held them. Alley was reminded of their harmonised brutality against the Anchors.

They stitched two white lines across the face, holding the wave together as it sucked and spat. It was not enough. The wave hesitated, drew up, and broke completely in one final lunge. The little bodies were cast into the roaring maw of the ocean, chewed and ground along the reef.

'I hate that part,' Alley said, unable to remove her eyes from the frothy aftermath. The little figures popped up; two dots on the white foam. 'It's like they're punishing themselves.'

'They are,' Pan returned. He spun and leapt for the path snaking its way down the cliff to the bay. Alley was drawn along behind.

The path was thin, no more than a dirt depression dug by the shuffling of feet over many years. Pan leaned into the decline, taking the turns without slowing. Alley needed far greater concentration to negotiate the track.

Reaching the rock-shelf, Pan glided over crevices and rock-pools as though he was intimately aware of these sharpened, fissured platforms.

Alley called out to him. 'It's too big out here. You'll get washed in.'

The ocean released its roaring detonations. She exchanged her view from the torment at her feet to the charging monsters moving across the ocean's top. Waves dove at the rocks, exploding, sending up clouds of heavy sea water to bolster the light rainfall.

Needing her arms for balance, Alley was forced to accept the downpours of chill and salt as she travelled after Pan.

News stories of fishermen being swept off these rocks blipped in her mind. Images of waterlogged corpses being dragged roughly from the grip of the water merged with the view before her. The ashen shade of the scene became the decaying grey of lifeless skin.

'Pan,' she called out again. 'Come back.'

Pan raced, heading towards the edge. Before leaping into the ocean, he came to a dead stop.

A distance behind, Alley found herself still also. A wave was building in the distance. Its mounting approach was, at first, a caution. It gradually drew up the ocean before it, building itself into a rippling threat, intimidating the coastal land with sheer enormity.

Alley looked from the far left to the far right. The wave covered the entire length of Mystics. It climbed into the sky, preparing to haul itself onto the cliff tops surrounding. It was now a declaration, guaranteeing that those small bits of mortality below would be tested.

'Pan!' Alley screamed. 'Get away from the edge.' Staring upward, she could see no distance would be far enough.

The wave towered and paused, as though such immensity needed a moment of reverence before unleashing. Pan stood, fists planted on hips, head back, studying the frothing lip far above with a detached interest. Then it fell. With a shearing howl, the ocean threw the size of itself at Pan and the rock beneath his feet.

As light was taken from the world, Alley's muscles twitched and collapsed her into a ball. Her arms swathed her head in a feeble protection. Darkness and the ocean's roar swamped her a moment before the blow hit.

Her body was jarred and jolted, shaken by the hands of a violent earthquake. She expected to be thrown into the churn, scrubbed across the rocks, her skin peeled from her bones. But she remained attached to the stone beneath her. The frenzied rush of water was unable to wrench her into the roiling madness.

The rough jostling from side to side eased. Her chest ached to draw breath. The water around her became still, changed direction, and retreated with a smooth urgency. It was then that Alley noticed the two hands holding her upon the rock.

The fizz of sea foam tickled her skin, an apology for the ferocious outburst. Returned to the world of calm air, Alley snatched a massive breath and let Pan lift her to her feet.

The frothy tail of the wave slipped back into the ocean and, as though it had been its intention, two dark lumps had been deposited on the edge of the rock shelf.

Alley wiped the sting of saltwater from her eyes. Her clothes were now weighted with a good portion of the sea. Eran and

Croco climbed from their stoops, bringing their boards to stand erect beside them, poised like flattened spears.

'So, this is it,' Pan stated.

Eran and Croco stood steady. The ocean had calmed at their backs. Mystics had regained its tranquil air.

Pan inspected the cove. 'I was wondering how everyone got here.' He shook his head, laughing under his breath. 'I should have guessed … the maidens of the sea … trouble makers.' He turned to Croco. 'I never believed that I would see the day when you would give yourself to protecting a Water-home.'

'You hard of hearing?' Croco said. 'The reasons I do what I do, are mine alone.'

'And you,' Pan said, looking to Eran. 'Do you forget how many of your tribe the maidens have brought to harm in their mischief?'

'It's different now,' Eran returned. 'They're aware of what's happening. They gave us an escape.'

'Escape? There was no need,' Pan said.

Eran glanced to Alley.

Croco rolled his neck, growling. 'You lost even before it began. And you can't see it. Now this town's done for … 'cause of you.' He tilted his board forward, targeted Pan's chest with its point. 'It was *you* who brought *them* here.'

Pan shrugged. 'It is not my intention to save this town.'

'You little grub. You've existed for too long. Time has blinded you. You can't see it. And you can't accept it.'

'Can you?'

'Can I? Of course I can. And I'm as much the Never as you are.'

Pan lifted his head and laughed. 'Do not compare, crocodile.'

Displaying his teeth, Croco lurched forward, turned and leapt from the rock. Getting his board beneath him, he landed upon it and skimmed the surface. 'You're right, Never One,' he called over his shoulder, his strong voice bouncing across the waves, 'I shouldn't have left,' and paddled out into the bay. 'I'm also the Never, dead king. And I'll do what you cannot.'

'Croco …' Eran shouted.

'Do not do it, you stubborn old creature,' Pan hollered, with tired disapproval. 'Come back.'

Croco's industrial sized arms continued to pump, thrusting him further from the rocks. Eran's brow was high, his eyes wide, as he looked to Pan.

'Croco!' Pan said, stepping forward, his voice tightening. 'Croco, do not go back.' He took another step. 'Croco … If you go back there … I do not know if I can find you when it is over.'

'It is over!' Croco's voice echoed into the shadowed extents of Mystics.

Reaching the centre of the bay, Croco raised himself, pushed down on the board, dived and disappeared beneath the water. The rain smothered the ripples of his entry.

Alley scanned the surface. 'What's he doing?'

Eran placed his board to the side and sat down on the rock, staring out across the ocean.

'Eran?' Alley questioned. He brought his knees and arms to his chest and buried his head. She turned to Pan. 'What's happening? I don't understand.'

Pan spun, his face hardened, and returned back across the rock shelf.

Offering Eran one last look, Alley hopped after Pan. 'Talk to me. Tell me what's going on. What happened to Croco? Where did he go?'

'He went back home,' Pan grunted, not turning to face her.

'Home? Why?'

'He went back home to die with the rest of it.'

24.

THOSE WHO REMAIN

The cliff edge was hidden in the solid night. Pan strode along the precipice as though offering challenge to the drop. He located the large figure before him, black hair flowing beneath a set of tight, woollen caps.

'You heard about the croc?' Pan asked, drawing up alongside her. He took her silence as confirmation and shared her view of the Water-home far below. It was too dim to see if Eran remained at the water's edge.

Pan shook his head. 'He was a stubborn creature.'

The large woman tilted towards him. 'Creatures of the Never usually are.'

When the humour dissolved into the nothingness of night, he said, 'I heard you hunted down the dark thing.'

'Yes.'

'It did not end well.'

'No.'

'You survived.'

The woman shrunk into herself. 'I fled.'

'You survived. Many did not.'

'I should have fallen at their sides. I was their leader.'

'No. You did what you had to. This thing would have taken more than just your life.'

'I know.' The woman scanned the surrounding black, scouting. 'We first saw It in our dreams. Every night we slept, It consumed a little more of our minds. Many were falling to madness. My father was the first to resist. He was the first to fight It in those intangible realms. He was the first not to wake.'

'The Panther was a great chief.'

'With the tribe in my hands, I led them across the land, hunting It. We went to the boundaries and beyond. There were great trials, great battles and great losses. We broke through the limits of what we are and we found It.'

'And?'

The woman drew in a few deep breaths, before answering, 'We were humbled.'

'Croco said It cannot be fought. He said It is not an enemy.'

A rumbling moan came from the woman as she lowered herself to the rock. 'He is correct,' she sighed.

'Tell me then, Tiger. What is It? What did you learn? Give me something.'

'This thing is beyond us. It is timeless. And It is necessary. And It comes for all.'

'It hunts?'

'No. It is only life's shadow, always in its wake as life journeys on. No being can exist without drawing It closer with each breath.'

The night moved around them, shifting, forming momentary shapes that melted back into the blankness.

'It will not catch me, Tiger.'

'You cannot outrun it.'

'I will defeat it.'

'The boy?'

Pan straightened. 'You know of him?'

'The first time I saw the child, I could see the weight of the town upon his back. I know the town weakens him. And I know the Never draws him towards its eternity. He senses the pull, feels the freedom the further from the town he steps. I understand now why the maidens open windows upon such places. I understand now why the slithering fingers of the endless night wriggle towards this town. The child is so lost, and so in search of dreamful worlds, he is a raw element, an element upon which the foundations of the Never are created.'

'No,' Pan said, quietly, 'he is not completely lost. He binds himself to this place. His memories bind him. It makes him fragile.'

'Well then, Never King,' she twisted and looked up to Pan from her seat, 'is it that you desire the child as an ally, or as bait?'

Pan stared at the Water-home and visualised what lay beyond, decaying, awaiting his return. 'The fear within him, his memories … He cannot join with the Never, only defend its life.'

'… Defend *your* life, Never King. Your life.' The large woman regained her feet with another breathy rumble. 'I have called for the maidens.'

'Why? What for?'

'I have asked them to reopen the window of their Water-home.'

'You're following the croc? Not you, too. There is nothing to be gained.'

She lifted her arms, pulled back the material cover and displayed her skin. 'Where is my light? Where?'

Pan blinked at her. 'It is this town. It is …'

'This is not me. That is the reason. I am back in the Never, fighting as I was born to do. That is who I am.'

'Croco said … *You* said It cannot be fought.'

'It cannot,' she returned, shuffling away. 'But that should not be a reason to stop me.'

*

The stale air-conditioned air flowed into Alley's body to chafe her throat and lungs. The bouquets and wreaths of flowers sat garish against the off-white walls. The decorating seemed only half done, as though it was not worth putting in too much effort, for soon it would be over and everyone could go and get on with their lives.

Milly's mother, Mrs Greene, sat in one of the front corners. Her remaining child, Luke, sat at her side, sharing the same look of numb detachment as the woman alongside him.

Mrs Greene would frequently flinch, sit up and scan the room. When her eyes found Alley, Megan and Taz, her anaemic lips would curl up into her cheeks.

Alley placed the nail of her index finger between her teeth, preventing a return smile from forming.

The friends and family of Milly entered with probing gazes. They searched the room, locking eyes with everybody as though they were all allies, living collaborators against the ubiquitous hand of death.

What would they think if she released the scream building in her chest? Started smacking the frilly decorations from the walls and out of the vases?

When the eulogy began, in all its flowery unoriginality, Alley slipped outside. Megan and Taz did not follow.

Framing the funeral home was a garden. Small plants, pruned into balls, sat above a spread of red, volcanic rock mulch. The plants were arranged to be as unremarkable as a garden could be. Near the doors sat a magnificent chunk of coloured sandstone, defaced by tacky, metal letters spelling the name of the owners of the home.

From a distance the red of the mulch, orange and greens of the plants, and the yellows and pinks of the sandstone, almost made the building attractive. Standing closer, Alley was able to see the dense scattering of cigarette butts through the mulch.

She lifted her camera from her hip and targeted a tight collection of discarded cigarettes. These are the things that she wanted to remember; the grimy details, the things that are disregarded in reminiscence.

A speck of light, structured like a knitting needle, struck her eye and pushed through into her brain. Alley dropped to her knees. She accepted the spreading ache, lacking strength to resist it. She did not bother to search for the perpetrator.

When the pain subsided she cleared her vision and collected her camera from the ground. Rising, she found Eran strolling towards her.

'Hello, Alley.'

'Ah, hi.'

Eran watched her.

'Ummm ...' Alley's hum petered out before she could find something to say.

'You're not inside?' he asked, after listening to her monotone tune.

She lowered herself and took a seat on the garden's concrete edge. 'Why should I? Why should any of them bother? How does this help Milly? How does any of it fix anything?'

'It isn't for Milly,' Eran said, taking a seat next to her. 'Funerals aren't for the dead. Funerals are for the living.'

Alley nodded and drew a slow breath. 'I didn't know you knew Milly.'

'I know her as much as I know anybody.'

Alley looked to him, wondering how long she had known Eran. It could have been a few weeks, or since her first day of school. Both possibilities seemed undeniable.

She placed her fingertips to her eye. It seemed these lights were incinerating her thoughts and memory. Her head was such a mess. Everything was so confusing. The thought of a two and a half hour exam was enough to fill her brain with an empty drone.

Alley shifted. The concrete edge of the garden was not a comfortable seat. 'So, did you come here for her?'

'In a way,' Eran replied, after a moment of serious thought. He stood and studied the ground before him. 'This is only the beginning.'

'The beginning of what?'

'Endings. Death,' he shrugged. 'It's coming here, to this town. Maybe Croco was right. It's all going to end, one piece at a time.'

'It feels like it sometimes.'

In silence, Alley and Eran remained beyond the walls of the funeral home, waiting as the final chapter of Milly's story was written and her book closed. Everybody was invited back to Milly's Aunt Mary's place. It was an understandable venue compared to the alternative. Alley accepted the invitation, agreeing to a lift in Megan's bubble of rust and grinding parts. Eran declined.

Mary's house was a cottage sitting on the coast side of Coalcliff. Inside was a clutter of objects. Figurines and decorative plates covered all surfaces, each enthroned on an embroidered doily.

Moving through the hall, Alley ran her fingers across the head of an androgynous child, encased in porcelain, casting a fishing line into a pond of twisted blue pyramids. Each room she was ushered through was densely populated with patterns and polished creatures and tiny, frozen people. There was nowhere clear to look. Even the ceiling was a mass of angles and objects, the moulded edges working their way towards the elaborate central light.

Alley assumed this woman was afraid of contemplation. It was as though every shift of her eye needed to find an innocuous little distraction lest her mind be ensnared by its own thoughts and self-destruct.

Megan and Taz sat side-by-side on the lounge, nuzzling as they peered through Megan's phone. Alley left them to their closeness and moved through the rest of the house. Everyone was now settled in their positions, nibbling on finger-sized portions of food. No one offered her a second glance as they exchanged hushed words as though this was now a house of stiffly flowing secrets.

The guests seemed cautious of themselves, wary of sound and large movement. Alley considered taking a photo, seeing if she could capture the sense of constraint that filled each room. She decided against it.

In the kitchen, Alley found herself alone. She moved to the window and peered out into the backyard. Reflecting the innards of the house, the yard was a thick tangle of wild plants ballooning around garden gnomes, birdbaths and stone statues of native fauna in startled poses.

Beneath her was a crawling black line of ants moving along the inner sill, down the wall and along the stainless steel sink. The tiny scavengers had invaded and now swarmed upon a half-eaten sugar biscuit, crumbling in a pool of spilled coffee.

Raising her camera, Alley lowered it again when quiet voices were heard from the adjoining laundry. Creeping closer, the smell of damp clothes and mildew filled her sinuses like gunk. It was Mrs Greene and her sister.

'*…Just for one night?*'
'*No, no. I need to be in my own home,*' Mrs Greene replied.
'*You shouldn't be alone.*'
'*You don't know what I need, Mary.*'
There was a long pause before Mary said, '*I could stay at yours?*'
'*No, no. You don't get it. I need to be by myself.*'
'*So, Luke?*'

'*Yeah, I dunno, just a couple of days.*'

'*A couple of days? What am I supposed to do with a four-year-old for a couple of bloody days?*'

'*I don't bloody know. Figure it out.*'

'*Geeze. You really going to do this? The boy's just lost his bloody sister.*'

'*And I've just lost my bloody daughter.*'

Another pause.

'*Alright. A couple of days.*'

Alley returned to the lounge room and took a seat next Megan and Taz. She relayed what she heard coming from the laundry.

'She's probably going to score and waste herself,' Megan whispered.

'Probably!?' Taz scoffed. 'There's no probably about it.'

They all knew it to be true. That would be Mrs Greene's first priority; jump into the oblivion of temporary death.

'It's not good,' Taz continued, 'when she wakes up she's gonna find Milly still gone and the world just the same putrid grey it always is.'

'And I bet she'll just go score again.'

'Yep. She'll try to fall deeper and deeper. But she'll just keep on floating up to the surface. And then she'll just keep scrambling further and further down, taking longer and longer to come up. Then, one time, she won't resurface at all. And that'll be that.'

Alley was almost at the front door when she was confronted by Luke's expression of curious awe. An action figure hero dangled from his hand. An arm and leg were missing from the plastic man's right side, leaving the mightily moulded chest and abs a little less imposing.

She stood before the boy, looking down on him as though she was peering through the small window of her camera.

She was thirteen when her mother threw herself from the cliffs of Deep Moss. Upon hearing the news, something big and dark grew within her. It now sat like an ancient pyramid, unyielding and everlasting. Although it felt like decay, it would never crumble. A savage thing it was, resting in the background of the twisted jungle of who she was. It was so integrated with her being that it was hard to distinguish its separateness sometimes. And, when she focused on that monolithic mass, she could see that it dominated the entire vista.

She turned her back on the boy and left the house. What else could she do? When Luke had his own dark structure within him, that was when he would need her sympathy.

25.

MAIDENS OF THE SEA

Where was he?

Alley sat on the edge of the Duhent's property, waiting for Cale. Her feet scrubbed the loose asphalt of the road. She did not have anything to say to him, she just wanted him nearby.

It was Friday. There was no swim practice. Night had fallen. He should be home.

No specks of light had attacked since earlier that day. It seemed that nightfall had sent them into hiding. Alley could understand their reaction. She felt unsafe sitting out in the deepening dark.

'Hi.'

Alley let loose a small squeal of fright. 'Shit, Pan. You scared me half to death.'

He nodded, not restraining his amusement. 'I am looking for your brother.'

'Yeah, me too. He should be home now.' Alley examined the surrounding dark. 'What do you want him for?'

'I am going to see something at the lagoon. He should come with me.'

'I don't know where he is. What's over there?'

'It is hard to describe,' he replied, turning away.

'Can you wait with me?' Alley yelped, before cringing at the desperation in her words.

Pan hesitated. 'Come with me.'

'But Cale …'

'Okay,' he said, dissolving into the night.

Alley inspected the night. It was a darkness that seethed. 'Pan,' she called out, jumping to her feet, 'wait up.'

The shadows of the streets were being compressed, as though storing energy in preparation to launch. Alley walked nearer Pan. 'The night feels … wrong.'

'It is becoming stronger.'

Reaching the headlands and moving through trees Alley paused. 'It's so quiet.'

Pan looked to her.

'I don't hear the ocean,' Alley said, lowering her sound as she searched for any noise other than their own. Moving amongst the trees towards the precipice, Alley believed she would be looking out across a desert, or a barren wasteland, something that was unable to produce anything but silence.

The ocean was there. It was a sheet of mirror, moulded against the coastline, reflecting the black filtering down from above.

'Look at it,' Alley breathed, as though her voice was capable of fracturing the polished surface. 'There's not even a ripple.'

She followed Pan to the winding track leading down to Mystics Bay. There, she came to a sudden stop. The waters of Mystics were alive with a subtle blue glow.

'Is this real?' she asked.

In the surrounding dimness, Mystics was an azure gem maintaining its hold on daylight.

'Over there,' Pan said, directing Alley's attention to a specific point in the waters.

Near the rocky shore was a blemish of movement in the blue crystal. Alley watched three large fish swimming amongst themselves, trailing each other and zipping in retreat as though absorbed in a game of tag.

As one drew near the surface she saw limbs. 'It's not fish!' she laughed, the sight surprising her. 'It's divers. Wait …' A head broke the surface. An arm stroked the air. There was no neoprene wetsuit painting the bare skin, no breathing apparatus, or even a snorkel. 'They're just swimming,' she said, seeing the other two emerge.

They bobbed in the water and lazily sculled in small circles. Their distant chatter reached the two above as a soft patter. It was broken by chortling laughter that swept across the smooth surface of the cove.

'Closer,' Pan whispered.

In a low scuttle they moved down the path.

'They're old women,' Alley gushed, coming to a stop in her crouch, watching their smooth, playful swim around each other.

The movements of their legs were gentle. The rising and falling of their arms from the water were soft. They cast no ripples across the surface, their body parts seeming to merge with the water rather than break through it.

Something tight collected her upper arm and tugged. Alley looked to see Pan's hand holding onto her. She noticed she had descended more of the path. Her shoes and socks had been removed and lay like a crumb trail behind her. Looking to her bare feet, she found her hands at her jeans, halfway through the unbuttoning. 'I, um …' she stammered, resecuring the buttons and slinking back for her shoes and socks.

'The water looks so good,' Alley mumbled.

Pan was not fazed by her behaviour. He had taken to a knee behind a small rise in the slope.

Ensuring no muck had found the soles of her feet, Alley replaced her shoes and socks and re-joined him. 'It would make a beautiful photo.' She grimaced, remembering her camera was back home, before she saw one of the women roll over and perform a few backstrokes. 'Oh my god, they're skinny dipping.' Her humour disappeared as she turned to Pan. He peered at the three wrinkled bodies with a small grin. 'What the hell are you doing?'

'Watching,' Pan said, his bright eyes not moving from the elderly women.

'You're sick, Pan.' She grabbed his shirt and yanked him away from the edge.

'Hey,' he grunted in annoyance, swatting at her hand. 'Listen.'

'No. This is …' she trailed off as she heard a faint rolling melody, drifting upwards to hang above the bay. It was as restful as a serenade. One of the ladies was humming. Alley forgot the creeping chill over her skin. The ominous presence of the surrounding dark faded from her thoughts. 'Can you hear that?' There were words being sung, possibly in another, more sinuous language.

Esteem and wealth and a loving breath, Alley believed she heard, *all holds naught to a grip on death* …

'Do you hear it?' she asked.

Pan shifted back. 'They know I am here.'

'How?'

'They are mocking me.'

The three women had moved nearer the rocky shore. They targeted a dark form moving through the shadows. It moved with a slow, unstable lurch. It was not a sinister shape. It looked sad and broken.

'Beanie Lady?' Alley stated, as the large woman emerged timidly into the blue glow of the cove. 'What's she doing here?'

With head lowered and hands twisting around themselves like those of a bashful child, Beanie Lady moved towards the water's edge. The three ladies, faces sharing the strange luminosity of the water, beamed up at Beanie Lady as she came to a stop above them.

Lowering the bulk of her size, Beanie Lady removed the boot and collection of socks from her feet. With a tentative shuffle, she moved into the water. With each step, Beanie Lady shed the tattered pieces of clothing and material from her body.

The three elderly swimmers drifted back in time with the woman, their arms outstretched and giggling mouths spread wide. There was no ridicule or embarrassment in the merriment of the elderly women. It was welcoming and Alley found herself smiling along with them.

Soon Beanie Lady was submerged up to her chest, wearing nothing but the hats atop her head. The three women flowed towards her. They took the hands of the dark-skinned woman and led her deeper. The elderly ladies dropped below the surface, their forms blurring into indistinctness. Beanie Lady's collection of beanies came free from her head as she sunk and disappeared beneath the water. The woollen hats drifted on the surface, absorbing water until they were heavy enough to sink to the depths with the woman who once wore them.

Alley knew that no matter how long she waited, the four women would not resurface. 'The Never?'

Pan nodded. 'Home.'

'Who were the three women?'

'Acquaintances. This is a window of their Water-home, a window that looks upon your town.'

Alley peered down into the water as though she might see some wondrous thing on the other side.

'Not without the maidens,' Pan said, softly, watching her. 'Croco can slip through its gaps. He knows this water well. But most need the maidens to slide it open.'

'Can you open it?' Alley whispered, unable to remove her eyes from the glow.

'Ha. I could if I wanted to. But there is no need. Light is the fastest path to the Never.'

'Light?' Alley turned to Pan to see a speck of bright weaving an elongated figure-eight through the dark space at his back. 'Is all this real?'

'For some, it is.'

The glow faded from the cove, leaving the waters looking dead. The ocean roused from its slumber, shifted itself and sent waves rolling inwards.

'Will she be happy?' Alley asked.

'Happy?' Pan searched the cove. 'Who?'

'Beanie Lady.'

'Oh. Well, she is going back to disappear.'

Alley nodded.

'But, yes, she is happy, I think.'

26.

THE HUNGRY WATERS

The sea was wild. It bucked and thrashed, clawed the sky with mighty jags, frothing white foam like a rabid beast.

Cale dug his feet into the sand and peered up at the storm clouds churning and charging, interlocking to form a tighter net over the world. Behind him were Mitch and his friends.

'*He's gonna wimp out!*'

'*Look at him. He's gonna piss his pants.*'

Cale felt a small rock slam into his shoulder blade.

'*Don't be so mean,*' one of the girls could be heard whining, as though they were tormenting a stray dog.

'*He won't do it. He's scared out of his mind.*'

Cale was scared out of his mind. But he was always scared out of his mind.

Mitch walked up and took a position beside him. They shared a view of the raging thing growling and salivating at their feet.

'Pretty rough out there,' Mitch said.

The wind whipped around them, attacking them from all directions.

'You gonna chicken out?' Mitch asked.

'No.'

'Have you ever swum in anything like this before?'

'I don't think anyone has.'

Mitch huffed; a sound close to a laugh. 'Probably. There's gotta be a first time for everything, hey?'

Cale raised his head and straightened his shoulders. He looked to the point beneath Deep Moss Heights. The sharp piles of dark water rushed upon the rocks like kamikaze pilots, disintegrating themselves in massive explosions.

'How you gonna tackle it?'

Cale glanced to the boy next to him. 'Dunno. Sticking close to the rocks,' he nodded in their direction, 'will probably get us swept into them. But it's a lot longer if we swim out around them.'

'The waves are dumping out there. I've never seen them dump out there before.'

'A big one'll scrub us along the reef.'

'How deep is it out there?'

Cale shrugged. ''Bout two metres at the moment. Only one in some places.'

'You sure you don't want to back out? You won't make it around the point. I don't even know if I can,' Mitch chuckled.

Cale wondered if Mitch could see his chest being charged by his thumping heart.

'I can't,' Mitch muttered.

'What?'

'I can't back out.'

'And I won't.'

'I can't let you beat me. They'll never let me hear the end of it.'

Cale saw Mitch reading things in the sand. He was breathing hard.

'I have to beat you,' Mitch said, through his teeth, looking to him.

'You don't.'

'It's your fault.'

'What is?'

'Everything ... All those times I stayed at yours ... at his place.'

Cale looked away.

'How could you let me stay over?' Mitch's voice rose higher.

'I don't know,' Cale returned. 'I didn't know what was happening back then. I was scared.'

Mitch's face twisted with disgust. 'But how could you? You were supposed to be my bloody friend.'

'I don't know!' Cale cried out.

They both fell silent and looked to those behind.

'What are yous waiting for?' Gavin yelled his annoyance.

'I'm giving him a chance to back out!' Mitch called back and tossed up a few notes of laughter. He returned his hard stare to the water.

After a moment of quiet, Cale asked, 'Did he ever do anything to you?'

Mitch turned and shoved him. He raised an arm, preparing to throw a punch. A few encouraging cheers were cast from those behind.

'Don't you ever say that,' Mitch growled. 'It wasn't me he messed with. Only you,' he spat and dropped his arm.

'It was just me, wasn't it?' Cale returned. 'And it will only be me the rest of my shit life.'

Mitch dropped his gaze. He drew a long breath, shaking his head. 'When the police spoke to dad about what happened and what they suspected,' he swallowed, 'about me, he went ballistic. I told him that nothing happened to me, but he still got drunk and trashed the house. I thought he was going to kill me, as though it was my fault. He kicked the shit outta Bryce. Dad said he should've been looking out for me. Bryce had to miss a few days of school. Dad said I'd cop it too, if I ever mentioned your uncle's name again … or yours.'

Cale looked to Mitch. 'Holy shit. That's true.'

'What is?'

'I haven't heard you use my name since it happened.'

Mitch shrugged. 'My old man …'

'And he wasn't my uncle.'

'Whatever. I thought my old man would leave it at that. But then I got to school. They found out what was written on the blog. I heard what everyone was calling you.'

'I did nothing wrong,' Cale said mechanically, the memory triggering the automated response wired into his brain by his councillor.

'They were calling you a freak. That you were probably into that kind of shit. I knew it was going to get back to dad.'

'I did nothing wrong.'

'Like it matters. Everyone in class knew that I crashed at yours.'

'What the hell are you two doing? Get on with it!'

Mitch half turned. 'Shut the hell up!' He looked to Cale. 'I had to side with them. You get that, don't you? My old man woulda murdered me.'

Cale stared at his feet. 'What's the point of two people being destroyed, yeah?'

Mitch drew a deep breath, the tail end trembling. 'It sucks what happened.'

'Yeah?'

'Yeah. All of it … But mainly for you.'

Cale nodded.

'And Gavin … he's a bloody dickhead.'

Cale laughed. 'Yeah. He is a dickhead.'

Mitch rolled his shoulders. 'But I can't back out.'

'And I won't.'

'I know.'

They both moved into the water, the chill shock attacking like electricity, up through the legs and into the body. The ocean water always seemed colder than the pool water. Icicles formed and condensed in the lungs, preventing adequate breath.

The small crowd of spectators clapped and cheered and cried Mitch's name.

'You know,' Mitch said, the waves charging their stomachs and chests in provocation, 'if you do, by some miracle, beat me, they'll respect you for it. They probably won't like you still, but they'll respect you at least.'

'What will you do if I do beat you?'

'Dunno. Basketball, maybe.'

'You never know, it could be a tie.'

Mitch smirked in a way that reminded Cale of when they were younger, and said, 'Yeah, you're right. It could be a tie.'

Raising his arms above his head, forming a spear point, Mitch dove beneath a roll of whitewash. Cale followed and the stormy world around him transformed into a muffled physical fight in liquid space.

Despite the lack of visibility, Cale knew he had a better chance of gaining distance under the water rather than upon it. He propelled himself with strong, even strokes, visualising his position to the rocks and the reef break beyond. The underwater currents harried his flow, jostling him off course, nudging him towards the rocks.

When his lungs ignited he struck upward. Breaking the surface, he opened his mouth to the air only to receive a solid blow that shoved him back into the depths. Cale scrambled upward in a frenzy, his lungs burning. He broke the surface with a wild heave and sucked a mouthful of air before another wave dropped. He stabilised himself from the tumble, kicked in a presumed direction and made a little progress. He repeated the pattern.

Regaining the surface once again, Cale shot a few glances around. The rock shelf was a comfortable distance away. The audience could be seen following near the cliffs, pointing and jumping. The billowing sprays kept them at bay. He followed their excited gestures to find a dark ball being dunked by the rolling sets. Mitch was closer to the rocks, slapping at the water with large, wasteful strokes.

Cale dove, thrust, glided. Finding a calm pocket, he went up for air and crawled a distance across the heaving surface. Glimpsing the collapse of an approaching wave sent him back down. Again he flew. He could keep this up for the length of the swim … further even. Maybe he would not stop.

A roiling surge tossed him. He protected his arms, swam clear when the surge slowed. His fear was fading.

Gathering fresh supplies of oxygen, Cale viewed his remaining distance. After another few dives he would find himself in deeper, calmer water. Beyond that, the rock shelf gave way to the stone shore. A wave would carry him to the finish at that point, hoisting him upon its shoulders in triumph. He had this won.

Perhaps, he would wait in the shallows; let everyone see who the greater swimmer was, and then exit with Mitch at his side. Offering half the victory to Mitch would give him the opportunity to remain on the team. How could they disapprove? The perfect display of strength and humility …

Cale ducked another wave, surfaced and searched the waters behind. He found Mitch had made similar progress. But, in his grapple for distance, he had sacrificed his clearance of the rocks. Perilously close, Mitch now battled the waves for the horizon, striking for escape. Each rolling charge positioned him inches deeper into the slopping jaws of the awaiting rocks.

Cale looked to the open waters ahead of him, studied the finish line of the stony shore in the distance. The escalating roar of another set of waves caused Cale to draw a breath and sink as a mass of foam and water rumbled over his head. He swam with the turbulence, utilised it. As it eased he turned upright and pushed at the water.

'Mitch!' Cale cried out, a short distance before him.

Mitch's expression was divided; his eyes opening in terror, his mouth snarling with a feral determination. He shook his head and stabbed a finger to the ocean beyond.

Cale swivelled and was met by a looming wall of darkness. It was a mountain, snow-capped and steaming, racing to fall upon them, crush them, and hold them beneath its incredible weight.

Distant screams and hollers of alarm punctured the roaring charge of the beast. Cale was held. Hands were upon him. He was frozen, a feeble victim lying down to be taken and devoured.

'Cale!'

He was physically spun.

'Cale!' Mitch shouted into his face. 'C'mon!' He dove for the rocks.

Cale aimed himself for Mitch's wake. He saw the blanket of shadow fall upon them and stopped. For a brief moment all sound disappeared, as though it too was being sucked up into the lip of the wave with the rest of the ocean. When the dark mass fell, it came down with a shrieking howl and everything became chaos.

His first memories were of being held in a full embrace of water. Or he believed they were his first memories. They could not have been simple imaginings. He knew the water too well. It was a memory, his truth. And the women with the dark hair, standing above, with one hand to hold him down, so the other could keep him afloat … He had been shown this struggle in order to overcome it.

Cale kicked and thrust, attacked the water that attacked him. It held him tight, threw him in every direction, except towards the surface. It spun him, flipped him and sent him careening into the sea bed. Dull thumps travelled through his body. Only part of his mind registered that he was being scrubbed along the reef.

Slowing, he thrust out his arms, grabbed rock. He twisted, planted his feet and pushed. He broke the surface with a roaring gulp of air and found himself in darkness. The second mountain in the set collapsed upon the world.

His sense of himself was ravaged in the madness. His body thrashed, aching for air.

Where was she now? How could he ever beat such things? For this was the true nature of water; to hold him utterly, working its way into and around all parts of his body, probing, taking. He knew these things were beyond his strength.

27.

NEVER ONE

The torment seemed endless. But the building agony in his chest assured Cale there was an end. He waited, enduring as though it was a muscular reflex, and the churn eased and released a semblance of control to his body.

Cale broke the surface and drew air. The third monster in the set lumbered forward. A mindless grip on life was no defence against such an untamed force. The rocks were his only chance.

Driven near the shelf, he dove, powered through the remaining distance and caught hold of rock. The stone was slick, unhelpful. He clutched it, held his face to the dripping solidness and sucked air. Hushed, desperate cries reached his ears. He raised his head. The small group was a bundle of dampened screams, jumping bodies and pointing arms. Cale looked behind and saw only the frothy wall of the approaching wave, its eagerness to wrap up every inch of his body.

He dragged his weight upwards, barnacles and oyster shells sliding through him painlessly. Diluted streams of red patterned his skin. He reached level rock and sprung to his feet. The rushing roar of the wave pressed upon his back as he hobbled at a run across the rock towards the small crowd. The wave fell and exploded. He felt a charge of wind and sea spray slam him from behind. He maintained his feet and continued to run.

He slowed as he saw the faces before him.

'Mitch!' one of the boys yelled. 'Get Mitch!'

'He's still in there!' another hollered.

Cale halted, stuck, pressed between two ghastly walls.

'Mitch!' one girl screamed, her hands pressing into her cheeks, her face tight with weeping. 'Mitch hasn't come up.'

Cale turned and saw another dark set rolling in. He looked back to them.

'Go get him!'

'Get him out!'

Cale felt himself trying to speak. Only rasping breaths made it from his throat. His head trembled in a side to side motion.

'Mitch!' another girl wailed, collapsing into a crouch, wrapping her arms around her legs.

Gavin stepped before the group. 'This is your fault!' he yelled. 'Go get him!'

That liquid mass was waiting to re-secure him in its grip. 'I …' Cale breathed. 'I can't go back in there.'

The couple who ran to the surf club returned with two large men and their boards.

The world slid back, compressed and became a two dimensional plane upon which figures and shapes went through their movements. Cale retreated until the stone of the towering cliffs stopped him. Numb, he collapsed and watched the images shift back and forth; two men diving into the rough water, the crazed motions of the others, the violent form of the ocean.

Two more men and a woman arrived, taut, stiff necks craned back like small prey searching for unseen dangers. There was a purr of a four-wheeler, the undulating call of an ambulance, a faint strobe of emergency lights pulsing through the dusk.

The search continued. The girl's screams had faded into sobs. The boys stomped across the rocks, hands atop their heads.

Only when one of the paramedics placed a hand on Cale did he remember he was there. Hands travelled his body, addressing his wounds. He accepted the touch, savoured the immobilising poison. It was when they attempted to lift him and direct him away that he broke through the restriction. With a cry he knocked away the hands, punched and kicked and threw as many vicious words as he had stored away.

Night seeped in and, like mockery, the ocean smoothed and calmed, flattened like a mirror.

When night fell soft arguments broke out between the adults. As the majority turned their backs the call came. A few more jumped in the water and Mitch was lifted onto the rocks. Everyone gathered. Cale stood. The scratches on his arms and leg and chest and stomach looked like his, both battle scarred by the same savage combat. Mitch was calm now that the fight was over, resting.

'Wake him,' Cale breathed, his words so far from everybody.

The paramedics ran their hands around Mitch's body, prodding and feeling. Cale wanted to scream. They stopped and sat back and the adults ushered the younger ones away in all their tears and scrunched faces and head holding.

Cale felt the night reach him. He looked behind himself, south, across the ocean and towards the opposing cliffs that curved away, disappearing as they travelled in towards Mystics Bay. There, bleeding out into the still sea, was a cerulean shine.

Mitch was loaded upon the four-wheeler and transported to the awaiting ambulance, no one seeming to notice the blue tinge to Mitch beginning to glow bright. With Mitch inside, the ambulance drove away, the two dark rear windows gleaming with a blue light from within.

Cale stood where he was, ignoring the gentle requests of the adults.

'*It should have been you,*' Gavin mouthed words. They reached Cale as clearly as though he had shouted them.

He stood dumbly, receiving the glares of the others. They spoke to him, saying, *You thought you knew suffering before …*

He ran.

It should have been you.

His eruption of movement lasted until he was hidden from sight. Then he dissipated and sifted through the streets like a small puff of fog. He was a ghost amongst the items that made the town. He was a nonentity, except for the giant inside. It was now armed, and it hacked and slashed and tore at his insides.

'Little one. Little one.'

Never one, was what Cale heard. *Never one.*

He staggered around the house, ignoring the plodding stride of Mr Duhent. The steps stopped and something heavy fell and Cale moved to the little forgotten shack in the far corner of the property. He slipped up the steps and opened the door and felt the two sets of eyes on him like sunburn.

'Oh my god, Cale.' Alley's voice pushed through the fog that he was. 'What happened to you?'

What happened to me?

'Cale, what happened?'

'Are you serious?' he whispered. 'What happened to me? Who cares!?' he screamed, to the limits of tearing his throat. 'Who cares what happened to me? It doesn't matter. I'm nothing!' He kicked the wall, puncturing the plasterboard.

'Cale …' Alley gushed.

'No,' he said, warning her with a finger. 'We're nothing. We. Are. Nothing!'

She gaped. Pan was straight-faced and still.

'We should die,' Cale said, feeling every breath as though it was wrong. 'It should be us.'

'Cale?'

'She should've done it,' Cale nodded to himself. He felt like a transcended savage, beyond moral constraints. 'She should've killed us back then.'

'Cale …' Alley gushed again.

'But she messed it up, didn't she?'

Pan straightened. His hands fell from his hips.

'Don't you say that,' Alley said, her shock removing all her volume.

'Everyone hates us. Everyone wants us to die. They're right. Mum knew it. That's why she tried to kill us, wasn't it?' Tears rolled down his cheeks and he scratched at them roughly, threatening to claw the eyes from his head.

'Cale!' Alley shouted. 'Stop this!'

'No. She knew it. We're nothing but hurt. Never. Never anything but that.'

He turned and tore back through the door and into the darkness. 'Come on, do it,' he grunted, through his breaths, 'Come on,' praying that this the building force within would explode him into the tiniest of pieces.

The body, dead on the ground, was just that; another dead body.

*

Pan moved through the darkened woods. He entered the copper sheen of Tree-home and left the cold, lightless town behind. There was no movement. A gentle whimper drew his attention to the shadowed depths of the tree roots.

Sticks was limp, his head resting at an awkward angle on the leaves. His eyes split open as Pan approached. 'Home yet?'

Pan surveyed the darkness pushing upon their light. Cale was now completely lost, but only halfway to the Never. His peculiar affinity for the water was the leash. But it was a tenuous connection. If he could be coerced to take up the sword and strike without fear, he would rise to be a mighty king of the Never. In its blind, natural hunger, the Dark Anchor would consume him without question. The end of the king would occur, and Pan would live. The Never would remain, ready for the return of its true, eternal owner.

Pan nodded his reply to the boy. This is how it must be, because forever is not meant to come to end.

28.

AND THEY FALL
LIKE AUTUMN LEAVES

The hospital was dotted with a thousand windows, a thousand little portals. Through one was an old man. He lay on the bed, tethered like a prisoner, serving sentence for a crime he had not committed.

He could not remember how he had arrived. His thoughts had been jumbled, soaked and squashed into a large wad. Bits of information could be gleaned from the pulpy mess; of the little one walking with such sorrow; of the trail of misty dark threads that followed him; and of falling.

Within these sterilised smells and bleached white surfaces he felt his life draining away. This could not be it. He wanted to be around the browns of wood and rust, the slimy spread of grease and the cold reliability of steel. That was who he was. When his life left his body, those were the substances that he wanted it to leach into.

A draining, that is what this was, like the thin pillar of oil running from engines when he bled them. The light was draining from his sight, the breath draining from his lungs, the sound from his ears. The feel of that hand in his was draining, too. Draining was the vision of that frog-mouthed woman, that beautiful frog-mouth he had not kissed enough.

He watched misty snakes as black as pitch make their way across the pale linoleum. They raised their heads and sniffed. Slithering through the air, they crept over his body, wrapped themselves around him and tunnelled their way into his chest.

There was no pain. It was just an emptying onto these surfaces, the final drops dripping onto these strange smells and bright lights.

*

Alley watched the tears fall from Mrs Duhent.

'So sudden,' Mrs Duhent said, her voice restrained. She dabbed her eyes with a scrunched up tissue.

Unable to think of anything to say, Alley sat and stared into her weeping face.

'It's so hard to believe, my darling. It was so quick. My whole life I had known that man. The things we had faced together … And now,' she threw her hands up and let them drop, 'poof. Gone. Like it never was.'

'I know,' Alley returned. She resisted the urge to delve into an attentive session of nail biting. 'I mean, you have a lifetime of memories with Mr Duhent.'

Mrs Duhent grimaced as fresh tears filled the runnels down her cheeks. 'We weren't speaking. What stubborn old fools we are. And he left me. They all leave me.'

'He knew how you felt, Mrs Duhent. I'm sure of it.'

'Yes, yes, my darling. But to look at each other, see each other, and reaffirm what you are to each other … it strengthens the spirit, the love.' Her head swivelled from side to side as it lowered. 'To see him one last time …'

'But you'll find each other again … in the next life?'

Mrs Duhent pushed herself up from the table, releasing a groan and a sob together. She waddled to the kitchen counter and collected another tissue. 'Alley?'

'Yes, Mrs Duhent.'

'Promise me, darling,' she said, gazing out the window, 'you'll look after this home when I go.'

'Mrs Duhent,' Alley said, turning her sight to the side.

'You must. I am already making the arrangements. It will all be yours.'

'No. Don't say that. This is your place.'

'No, my darling. This old crone is tired. This sickness … it will take me now. I have decided. I don't want to fight anymore.'

'Mrs Duhent …'

'And you,' she said, not turning, 'you must go to the hospital, see a doctor.'

Alley straightened in her seat. 'Why?'

'The lights. The confusion. The pains in the head. These are symptoms I have heard before. Patients at the hospital speak of them. They may be the ill effects of a head sickness. You must—'

'Mrs Duhent,' Alley said, pushing herself from the table. 'Head sickness? What are you saying?'

'Alley, my darling.'

'No. Wait. I thought you didn't believe in all that stuff, doctors and hospitals. None of it's real.'

'Please, Alley. It explains—'

'What? Why I'm insane?'

'Alley, you must see a doctor. Your mother … a similar condition, I believe. If they had helped her in time …'

'You think I'm crazy like my mother? You think I'm going to try and drown two children then throw myself off a cliff? You think that's how messed up I am, Mrs Duhent? My mother's daughter, is that it?'

'Please, Alley. I am only concerned for you.'

'I'm not my mother, Mrs Duhent,' she said, backing towards the rear exit.

'Sit, darling, sit. I'll make some more tea.'

'No. I have to go. I'm sorry about Mr Duhent, but I have to go study for exams.'

'Very well. I have said all I could say. And goodbye, my darling.'

The words were too thick to ignore. Alley stopped at the door. 'Mrs Duhent, please don't say it like that.'

'No. Do not, child. Leave. Just go. I have had enough and my husband has left me with our love severed. Our connection is lost because this world is a foul thing and bleeds foulness into us all.' She slapped the counter top painfully hard. 'Save your own life or not, child. That is now your choice. There is no room for everlasting love anymore. This world has grown dark.'

'Mrs Duhent ...'

'Leave me, child! Now!' She slapped the counter once again.

Alley stumbled through the back door and out into the yard. As though it had been lying in ambush, a bright speck attacked. Collecting herself from the dirt, Alley searched the surrounds for an indicator of where, and who she was.

29.

THE ULTIMATE ACTS

The storm had fractured. Light and sky crawled between the cracks. The clouds ignited, burning in orange, pink, and soft red as dying sunlight touched them.

The house was a simple, weatherboard construction, the sight typical enough to be dreary. The dilapidation set it apart from the others, as well as the fact it had not housed a human soul in over a decade.

'What is this place?' Pan asked, just behind her shoulder.

'Just an old house now,' Alley replied.

'Does anyone live here?'

'No. Not in many years.'

'Why? Houses need people to live in them. That is their purpose.'

'It feels wrong. I guess the owner felt it as well. That might be why he didn't sell it. What do you think?'

Pan studied the details of the ruin. 'Something happened here.'

'It did.'

They moved down the front lawn. It was bare, the grass patchy and yellowing off. The house seemed to swell as they approached, glowering upon their intrusion. Its windows had been shattered some time ago, a few of the apertures still dangling transparent fangs. The front door was sitting askew, clinging to the doorframe by its lower hinge. It was ajar enough to admit a body.

The innards of the house were colourless, a more desolate shade than the familiar grey pall of Coalcliff. The smell was thick. As though the house was a corpse, the reek of mildew and rot and charred timber rose in its decomposition.

Rubbish littered the floors and hall; junk food wrappers, aerosol cans, tattered magazines, soiled pieces of clothing. The discarded spread complimented the variety of stains that had been sprayed across or oozed down the walls.

'This was my room,' Alley said, stepping through the doorway, absent the door. It had been removed from its hinges, broken into pieces and fed to a fire that had been lit in the centre. The fire was now a pile of cold chunks of charcoal, fossilised remains of combustible bits of the house.

Alley stepped around the room, looking at nothing. She stopped before a large spray-painted mural, reading, *DINKO WAS ERE '13*.

'… Just announcing to the world they exist,' Pan said.

They left the room, the sliding of their steps crying out in the quiet. It was as though this house existed in its own dimension, one without time, sound and life.

Alley reached the back room. It had been stripped bare, skinned of its flooring and plasterboard to leave the wooden bones exposed. 'I loved the rain as a kid.' The lack of time in this place leaked inertia, slowing her as she headed for the rear window. 'I loved jumping around in the puddles,' she said, eyes fixed on the view of the backyard. 'I used to beg my mother to go outside and play in it.' Alley was transfixed by the sight. Her memory held every detail without flaw.

'What is out there?'

'Just a memory now.'

'Show me.'

Pan led her to the opening, collected her hand in his and placed it on the remaining shards of the windowpane.

The window was whole once again, bearing the lingering, foggy smudges of a little face and two little hands. The drapes were unsoiled and held back with her mother's lace. The rain was silent as it fell outside. The poor drainage of the yard caused a large pool of water to collect in the middle. That is where she played, the little girl with a wild flow of black hair. She looked to be no more than six. She jumped around in the pond, trying to cause bigger and bigger splashes, each foot a diving meteor crashing into the ocean. It became a thick, murky slop as she stomped and jumped around in its depths, laughing and holding her arms out to the rain, the skin of her face spattered with muck.

Just within view, the back door swung open. The little girl was too engrossed to notice the slack figure in the white nightgown. The rain plastered the thin material to the woman's thin limbs. She drifted through the rain with a lurch, each step seeming to be disconnected from the previous.

The little girl stilled when two hands were placed upon her shoulders and turned to face the woman. Her little lips worked up and down, forming the single syllable. A cautious excitement was worn. It tightened into confusion as the woman forced the little girl onto her knees. The girl's lips moved quick, sending questions, as the water held her up to her waist. The woman was blank, not seeming to hear and her eyes not seeming to see. But tears did stream down the limp expression, as though somewhere within, buried beneath the countless layers of darkness, was the mother of this child.

The girl's little hands rushed up and caught the woman's wrists as she was bowed forward, head first into the mud. It was as gentle as baptism. The woman stared down at the submerged child as it thrashed its little arms, her face calm and absent of any living twitch, tears distinct amongst the raindrops.

When the little girl became motionless the woman rose and lifted her arms to the rain and methodically washed the mud from her hands.

Alley was unsure who pulled back first. They stood a distance from the window. It was once again broken and old, no drapes surrounding. No rain fell outside.

'I am sorry.'

'It's okay,' Alley replied.

'Cale?'

'He was in the bath. She filled the tub and sunk him in the water before coming out to me. They don't know how he didn't drown. He was so young, just a new born. Mrs Duhent found me first. They say he must've been in there for at least half an hour before Mrs Duhent found him and pulled him out. She can't remember how he was, whether he was floating or just holding his breath for all that time. She was in shock, I guess. She says she doesn't remember much. Everyone says that he shouldn't have survived it.'

'But he did. The water could not kill him.'

Alley nodded. 'That's one third of my world; what happened that day. Another third is what happened to Cale after that.'

'Someone hurt him.'

'My mother was taken to Deep Moss Heights. We went to stay with my father's sister up at Ashfall Tops. She was married and they had two little children, twins, two boys, about Cale's age. Her husband wasn't right in the head. It was alright for a few years, though … until Cale was about eight. My auntie's husband started doing things to Cale. He bragged about it on some blog. That's how they caught him. And it all came out. He was a sick man, but he never did anything to his own sons. It was just Cale. He spared his own sons and just went after Cale.'

Pan was turned to the shattered window and the view beyond. 'He was the sacrifice.'

'Sacrifice?'

'Cale. The man knew he was sick, knew that he would hurt them. He sacrificed Cale to spare his sons the hurt. He sacrificed Cale to save something he cared for.'

'Yeah. Something like that. He spent a couple of years in jail. My auntie divorced him, took her boys and moved to the other side of the country. She broke off all contact with my brother and I. I guess she just wanted to forget the whole thing, put it all behind them.'

'That man was evil,' Pan breathed. 'He was a pirate.'

'He was.'

'I am not evil,' he whispered.

'What?'

'I am not evil and I am no pirate.'

Alley looked to him. His chest heaved as he struggled with his breathing.

'I am not like that.'

'I know, Pan.'

'I am sorry. But I cannot stop this.'

'Pan?'

Pan wiped his face, held it and said into his hands, 'I am no pirate. But I must continue.'

Alley stepped back.

'It must be done,' he said, more to himself than to Alley.

'Pan, you're scaring me.'

His hands fell and landed against his chest. 'But I can show you,' he said, turning on her, his expression open and pouring something close to urgency.

'Show me what?' she returned, stepping back.

'Why and what for.'

'I don't understand.'

'I will show you my world now, what needs to be saved.' He reached forward, took her hand before she could hide it from him. 'Come to the Never.'

30.

ANOTHER PARADISE LOST

They lay upon the soiled floor side by side. She could feel the warmth emanating from his body. The chill gusts rushed in through the broken windows and doorless doorways. It circled them like birds of prey, stirring the ash, but never swooped upon them. Beside Pan, Alley felt free from the movements of the world. She never wanted to leave his side.

When the specks of brightness scurried into the room, Alley was unafraid. They kept their distance, watching and darting, striking at those of the creeping shadows who gathered enough courage to move upon the two.

It was easy to doze next to him in that terrible, decaying place. She felt herself becoming ethereal, drifting through the resilient fabrics of space and time and everything else that meant anything.

She raised a hand to a tiny spark inching its way closer. It zipped away from her touch. 'Are you here to kill me, little thing?'

Pan shifted and turned. 'Careful of them. I do not know what they will do to you.'

'You can see them?'

Pan raised his hand over her chest, an inch above her shirt and the skin beneath. The speck moved towards him. Others made their way towards their position.

'What are they?' Alley asked, in a whisper, watching Pan's open hand and the speck so close to her chest.

'To you, I do not know.'

'Please, Pan. I need to know.'

'They come from where I come from. What they are there is not what they are here. Here, these guys need to exist as something else, something that is real in your world.'

'Like what?'

'I do not know, Alley. All I see is what they really are, not what they are to you.'

'But what does it mean? No one else can see them.' Alley rolled her head from side to side. 'Pan, I don't get any of this. None of it makes sense to me.'

'I do not think it is meant to make sense here.'

'But it scares me.'

'I know,' he said.

Pan made a short movement of his hand, tossed the speck into the air and left it hovering above them. Raising a finger, he performed a swirling motion, compelling the spark into an orbit. The surrounding points of light moved in and joined the aerial circuit. Soon the space above them was filled with a revolving glow. It intensified, sped itself and rained down upon them, washing all shade from the room until only unsullied brilliance existed.

The glare forced Alley to close her eyes. The barrier of her eyelids did nothing to shield her sight from the brightness. Unable to tell whether her eyes were open or closed, all she could do was rest in the light, accept the exhaustion she felt and drift.

The moment of transition between light and dark could not be determined. One moment she was held by light, the next she found herself submerged in darkness and a warm breeze. She blinked hard, enticing her eyes to adjust.

Gradually, plants and palms materialised. They were painted a deep green, vibrant, despite the thickness of the night. Pan was above her, bright and smiling, hair exploding outward. He reached down and helped her to her feet.

'Where are we?' she asked.

'This is my home.'

'How'd we get here?'

'The fastest way there is.'

'Light?'

'Light,' he nodded.

'Am I dreaming?'

'Everyone asks that.'

'Well ...'

'No ... But, if it helps, yes.'

The jungle surrounding flowed, yet remained still. Alley moved to a squat plant that poured its large leaves up and out like a fountain. She ran a finger across it, causing its glossy sheen to lighten. She felt something in the plant reaching out to her ... something in all the plants, and in the air and in the sand at her feet. It beckoned her, calling her deeper, calling her to explore all the hidden mysteries this jungle sheltered. There was excitement in there, an endless supply of wonders to see. There was no boredom here, no stricture or dreary predictability. This was life, condensed and squeezed, its drops caught and purified to leave its rare essence enveloping her.

'This place ...' Alley attempted, rotating on the spot, feeling the weight of her physical self seeping away. She stopped and looked to Pan. She wanted to take his hand, break into a run and never stop, be everywhere at once, sweep up every experience into herself and never release it. And why couldn't she? There was nothing to restrain her. There was nothing behind her, no tethers, no qualms. There were only the proceeding moments, each one leading to greater exhilaration.

Pan moved forward, inseparable from this place, just another extension of its wonder. He reached out and touched her arm.

'Cale!' Alley withdrew with a yell.

Pan's expression levelled. The jungle shivered.

'Why am I here, Pan?'

'You just need to see it,' he returned, and moved away into the jungle. Alley was drawn along behind, awed and unable to recall the words she had just uttered.

There was something else nestled amongst this beauty, something tainted. There were memories of laughter and comfort, and the impossibility of loneliness. It lingered on like residue heat. It was of youth, of souls once abused and discarded, now secured in happiness forevermore.

But it was only a memory.

'What happened here?' Alley asked, feeling her senses were too limited to view this place correctly.

Pan stopped. The muffled murmur reached them like a cry. The jungle parted. Thick leaves spreading over the ground recoiled to reveal a crooked form. The naked man was burned and bleeding and bundled upon the ground.

With eyes fearful, the man peered straight ahead. He stilled his trembling, as though they might not see him if he refused to make a movement.

Pan lowered himself and placed a hand on a shoulder blackened and blistered. 'Do you know who I am?'

The man flinched.

'Can you hear me, tribesman?'

'I cannot,' the broken man replied.

'Look at me.'

'With what?' he returned.

'Your eyes.'

'I have no eyes.'

'You do.'

'I have no eyes. No ears. No tongue. I have no body, no memory, no past. There is only nothing. For it has all been lost. The end is here. It is what I am. I am the end.'

'You still exist.'

'No,' the man said, almost laughing. 'I cannot.'

'But I see you.'

'Then where is my light?'

'I hear you.'

'You are kind to say such things. I know I am the end.'

Pan looked up to Alley. 'His mind is lost.' He returned to the man below and said, 'She has returned, tribesman.'

'I know no *she*.'

'The Tiger. Your princess.'

The man blinked, and said, 'Why? Why? You gain little from tormenting the end.'

'I speak the truth. She has returned to you.'

The man sobbed, his eyes filling with tears, and hid his face in the earth. 'Why must you torture this thing that remains? She left. She left us. She is the end with us all.'

'She did leave. Yes. She thought those that remained were all taken into the endless night. She did not know that any of you resisted.'

'We do not.'

'As you say. But she is back, tribesman. Believe me.'

His eyes flickered, locked onto the sand and soil his head rested upon. 'No. No, no, no. She is the end. She did not return, you demon, you pirate.' His words were broken by his whimpers.

'It is true,' Pan said. 'The maidens led her. They returned her … And I am no pirate.'

His body sagged as though it was preparing to liquefy and seep into the earth. 'The maidens of the sea?'

'Are there others like you? Others that are still here to fight?'

'Do you not understand? We are the end. It was pointless of her to return. She will find none of her people here. All of us are lost.'

'And lost things exist to be found.'

'I do not believe you.'

'It is true, tribesman.'

'We shall see.'

'She will find you.'

'We shall see.'

'Believe me.'

'Please, just let me go,' the man said, 'let us all go. It is our time. It is all suffering when you refuse this thing that awaits us,' his eyes turned on the one above him, 'great king.'

Pan dropped his sight, studied the sand and blood below. He stood and returned the large leaves to their position, covering the crippled man from view.

'What's happened to him?' Alley asked, as the jungle drew her away. The stains and inner putrescence was now visible. She saw black mud crawling up trunks and through leaves like veins carrying infection.

'It is a disease. The Dark Anchor. The end.'

Alley shied away from the vegetation as though it was all blistered and ready to burst and spew its septic innards upon her. She wandered, arms tight against herself, searching for the splendour she saw before.

'You see why I will fight against it?' Pan said.

Above, the sky was a perfected surface of nothingness. Alley scanned the spread visible amongst the bowing leaves of towering palms. She counted eight stars … nine, ten … maybe fifteen in total, a mere handful in the entire night sky. One began a spasmodic twinkling. Its light fluctuated as though clawing for escape, then, with a small shudder, it disappeared. The loss could not be overlooked, the blank voids between the survivors becoming much more vast and desolate.

Alley collected her middle in her arms and held tight. She felt as though she would cease to exist in a similar fashion.

Her sight fell and found a subtle blue glow emanating above the distant growths. It was pleasant and calming and reminded her of the luminescent waters in which the three old women took Beanie Lady. The jungle flowed around her as she moved towards it.

'There are still some places untouched,' Pan said, 'some places stronger than others.' He reached forward and grabbed her forearm, halting the jungle's current. 'But I do not think you should see those shores.'

'I need to.'

'Strange things wash upon them. You will not understand it. Your eyes are not meant to see such things.'

'Then, Pan, you need to start explaining.'

He released her arm and turned to the misty light filtering through the dark green vegetation. 'I am not sure I can explain this one.'

Alley urged her body forward, the trees parted and a beach spread out before them. Its sands were rippled, as white as snow and just as soft. Its waters were calm and sparkling, glowing blue and lapping at the white sands with scintillating waves. Palm trees leaned over the beach, inclining in a respectful way.

'Beautiful,' Alley said. Lowering herself, she ran her fingers through the powdery sand and felt its warmth. 'I'd love to see it during the day.'

Pan kicked at the sand with a heavy foot. 'It is always night now. Always.'

As Alley stood she found the beach was spotted with long, glowing bubbles of bluish-white mist. The bubbles drifted around each other. A few were stationary, stretched out along the sand as though in slumber. She turned to Pan.

'They are people,' he said.

'People?'

'This shore leads to a back road, a place that borders death. It connects your home to mine. Some who fall in your home arrive here.'

'Why?'

'To be found, I assume … but that is only a guess.'

'This can't be real,' Alley said, watching one drift towards them.

As the spectral smudge neared it gained substance. Fingers and toes gained definition. Hair could be seen and facial features. Alley gushed. 'I know that one.' The transparent expression before her was serene. 'That's Bryce's little brother, the boy who drowned the other day.'

Without acknowledgment of the ones before him, the ghostly Mitch turned and walked away, his steps leaving no footprints. The details of his being blurred and faded as he put distance between them, until he could not be distinguished from the other misty blobs populating the shore.

Alley's eyes bounced to each glowing form. 'Do you think …' her remaining words caught in her throat.

'Think what?'

'Um, Milly?'

'I doubt it. These ones seem to be after something, holding on until they are satisfied. Your friend was just looking for her release from your world. I do not think she would wish to bind herself to these sands.'

'You sound sure.'

'I think I am right.'

'How do you know? You never met her.'

'I have seen her life.'

'You have?'

'Through her window. I see them all, Alley.'

She wanted to press Pan further. It was the approach of another form that silenced her questions. It was stubby and crooked and its face was crinkled like a scrunched up paper bag.

'No,' Alley breathed.

Without sound, the form of Mr Duhent reached towards Alley with a vaporous hand. When she reached out to take the offering, Mr Duhent pulled back. Confused, Alley dropped her arm. Mr Duhent reached for her once again.

'He wants something,' Pan said.

Alley nodded. 'She does, too.'

*

They crept through the darkness. Upon the black wall before them they saw a small patch of copper light, spreading itself out into the void. It was a portal, through which was an elderly lady pouring the contents of pill containers into the kitchen sink. She turned on the tap, sent the pills into a spiralling departure down the drain.

When the array of small containers was empty, she collected a bottle of wine. The cerise liquid was poured into a glass, lifted to her stretched lips and emptied into her mouth. With a spasm to her stomach, the woman regurgitated the liquid into sink. The wine and splatters of blood were indistinguishable as they stained the reflective metal.

Wearing a look of acceptance and misery on her elderly face, she took a seat at the kitchen table and buried her head in her wrinkled limbs.

They remained at the window for a long time, until the elderly lady lifted her head, eyes red and swollen, switched off the lights and headed out of the room.

As though the motion of the scene dictated the required action, Alley found herself standing at the woman's bed. There was no alarm on the woman's face, no recognition, as Pan roused her and took her hand. The elderly woman said nothing as they led her out into the night.

All three drifted on unseen currents, seeing nothing beside the path set before them.

At the shores of Mystics Bay, Pan released her and took a position next to Alley. The waters illuminated with the familiar blue tinge. The three swimmers lifted their heads, the water static as they broke the surface. The three women, eyes as pale blue as to be white, held out their hands as they floated amongst each other, beckoning to the woman with the gestures of old friends.

As though this was a usual activity, she removed her clothes with unhesitant fingers. Her large old people's underwear was shed and she stood plump and wrinkled in the moonlight and water's glow. She strode forward until her feet were submerged, then the small folds of her hips and stomach, then her chest. Collecting the hands of two of the swimming ladies, she twisted her head behind. In her first display of consciousness, the woman's lips spread thin, before she was drawn out into the depths of the bay and sunk beneath the surface.

31.

THE NATURE OF A WATER-WOLF

He felt hollow, as though the last piece of him had been taken. Even the dark giant existing in his chest was gone, dead, leaving only the thin membrane of his being. And what remained was nauseous with something similar to fear.

The ocean rolled as it always did. The last few surfers were stroking a path to shore as the remnants of daylight waned to dark. They paid him no attention as they peeled their neoprene skins from their bodies and made their way along the sands in a tight cluster, like tribesmen returning from a successful hunt.

Soon he was alone. He stretched back his shoulders and raised his head.

A cloud slid across the sky, revealing a partial moon. There was no howl left inside. He was unable to imagine that he was alone, the final person left in the world. The town was behind, the pressure of it hard at his back.

He could not escape into the beach inside his head. He would need to find other shores. He looked across the waters, wondering how far he could swim.

But even the water was tainted now. Mitch had been murdered by it, the water and himself.

'Cale!' Alley called out.

He stared at the ocean and climbed to his feet.

'Cale?'

He shook his arms, prepared his legs, eyes on the horizon.

'Don't you do it, Cale,' she said, her voice broken. 'You can't do this to me.'

He looked back with eyes of apology and broke into a run, already feeling the icy hold of deep waters. A hand scooped up his middle, lifted him from his feet and threw him onto his back. Cale could not maintain his sneer. With a slack face he watched Pan step away.

Alley sat down next to him. After a moment of quiet, she said, 'You didn't come home last night.'

Cale slumped where he was, drained.

'Or the day before.'

'There's nowhere I want to be around here,' he murmured.

'Did you hear about Mr Duhent?'

He refused to reply.

'Mrs Duhent has left us as well. They gave us everything. Why don't you come home?'

'I could swim across the ocean, I reckon. All oceans.'

'You can have the house all to yourself.'

'There'll be a beach out there somewhere, with no people for miles. That's where I should be.'

'You want to leave this place?'

He had always wanted to leave this place.

'Everywhere you go, there's going to be people.'

'I could just keep swimming.'

'Forever?' Alley watched the coastal breeze dash the lips of the waves. 'Why don't you come home?'

'It's stupid, but I used to imagine that everyone in town disappeared and I was the only one left. I'd live on the beach, this beach. I'd be the king of it. And every night I'd howl at the moon. I'd howl so loud that anyone coming near me would be scared away. I'd be the scariest thing for miles and nothing would come close.'

Alley looked up at the moon. 'Howl.'

Cale shook his head. 'It's stupid. And what's the point? Nothing ever changes. This town will always be here and it will always hate us,' he said, his tone as solid as lead and edges blunted.

'That's not true. There're some idiots out there who treat people like shit because it makes them feel better about themselves. That's all. But who cares about them anyway?' she said, with a quiver to her voice. 'Who cares what they think? It's about us now. Only us. This is our story now.'

Cale's head fell to the side. 'But they're right to hate us. Even mum must have hated us.'

'No,' Alley said. 'No. That's not it. I mean, I don't think it is … not anymore. I actually think she loved us.'

He turned to her with a frown.

'I do. But she wasn't well. She was all mixed up. But when she did what she did, I think it was because she wanted to save us, or protect us from something.'

'From what?'

'I don't know. Like sadness, maybe. She might have thought we were as sad as she was. I know how it sounds, but I really do think she did it because she loved us.'

They sat together, not speaking.

Cale shifted, felt the pull of the ocean, those far off waters unable to be seen by the human eye. 'I don't know anymore. All I know is that I want it all to disappear.'

'Even these waters?'

'Yes.'

'I don't believe you.' She collected a handful of sand and let it trickle into Cale's lap. 'This is your place, Cale. You belong here more than anyone. You are this place.'

He brushed the sand from his legs.

Looking up, she found the shard of the moon. It seemed so far from the sands they sat upon. She threw her head back, drew a breath, filled her lungs and released a mighty, 'HOWOOOOOO!'

Cale started and looked to her. He had never heard such a sound come from his sister before.

With a half-smile she looked to him. Arching her head back once again, she closed her eyes and poured her howl into the sky.

Cale cackled, looking around, checking for any people. 'You're crazy,' he laughed.

'That's what they keep telling me,' she laughed back.

With Alley, Cale tossed his head back and, together, offered the entire town their combined, piercing howls.

Something rushed into Cale, filled him and made him jump to his feet. He opened himself to the night expanse above. Alley climbed up beside him, laughing and leaping around him, leading him into a wild dance as they howled at the sky and the moon, at the town and all the people in it.

Alley threw off her jacket and unslung the camera from her shoulder. She went to toss it to the side but stopped herself. She showed the camera to Cale.

'Go for it,' he said.

Alley paused long enough to take aim and snap a single photograph before continuing on in their dance.

When his throat was sore and his sides ached, Cale collapsed to the sand, looking to the sky, laughing. 'We are crazy.'

'Does it matter?'

He lifted his head to locate his sister and smiled.

'Why don't you come home, Cale?'

Returning to the sky, Cale drew a long breath before replying, 'Maybe a bit later.'

With a grimace and a nod, Alley walked back across the sands.

'Alley,' Cale called out. She stopped and turned. 'You might be right, you know?'

Alley smiled, turned and left her brother to the sand and water.

*

The night winds rushed, skimming the ocean's star-speckled surface, gathering an arctic vigour. They swept upon the shore, iced and sub-zero, and eddied about a small body on its side as it compacted itself to the size of a kidney bean.

Cale trembled in his nest of sand, hugging his legs into his body. He squeezed his eyes shut, and saw his distant beach. The sands were white, the plants a healthy green and the waters shone a crystal blue. He was miles above, looking down upon the warmth, and verdant life and cerulean purity.

His body quaked, rattling open his eyes. He saw darkness and the frozen granules of his bed. Each of his frosted breaths, escaping in a small cloud, pilfered a little more of his fading heat. His muscles were strict with shivering. Every inch of him ached.

Clamping his chattering teeth, he sealed his eyes once again. His beach was rising to meet him as he hung in the upper reaches of this humid place. Like an incoming missile, the sands and vegetation targeted him with aggression. Cale opened his arms, readied himself to embrace this land with his shattering bones and splattering blood.

Through the hurtling blur, he registered the waves upon the shore, the ripples through the sand and the blobs of fruit in the trees. There was a swish and a flicker as he broke through the canopy. The ground struck and Cale was upon his feet.

The prostrate body nearby twitched. The young boy blinked and sat up. He peered at the jungle surrounds, surprised to be awake. Finding Cale, the boy wiped his eyes and said, 'Hi. Did you wake me?'

'Sorry. I didn't mean …'

'No, no, no. It is good that you woke me. I am no longer tired.'

As though rusted, the boy worked his limbs and climbed to his feet. Staining the threadbare vest of the boy was a large patch of glistening dark.

'Are you okay?' Cale asked.

'I am.'

'Your shirt …'

The boy looked down, touched his front with his fingertips and lifted the dabs of blood to his eyes. Unbuttoning his vest and drawing it back revealed a wide opening the length of his chest. 'Curious,' he murmured.

Cale clutched his stomach and turned away. 'Holy shit. What happened to you?'

He replied with a hum and shrugged, and re-buttoned his vest. Ignoring the horror he held, the boy turned to Cale and asked, 'Who are you?'

'Nobody.'

'I have never seen you before.'

'I have never seen you before, either. Who're you?'

'I am Vinny.'

'Vinny?'

'That is me.'

'Actually, I think I do know you.' Cale turned his back on the boy and lowered himself to the ground.

'You do? How do you know me?'

'A while back, in a place like this, there was this Great Wolf. He had you on his back.'

'Yes. I am of their pack. I am a wolf of the water. Although, I do not remember ever riding one of the Great Wolves.'

'You were dead.'

'Oh.' He lowered his sight to his chest. 'Yes. I remember the battle. They bested me and skinned me of my fur.' He looked back to Cale. 'Are you dead, too?'

Cale considered the possibility. 'No. Not yet. The wolf … he told me to save you.'

'You can save me?'

'I don't know. I don't know if I can save anyone.' He bit his teeth, clenching his jaw. 'I couldn't save Mitch.'

'Mitch? Is he one of the lost?'

'He was a … my friend. And he's dead now. He drowned.'

'Drowned? Could he not swim?'

'He could swim. He could swim really well. But he needed help. And I didn't help him.'

'Why did you not help him? Can you not swim?'

'I can swim.'

'But you did not help him?'

'No.'

'I do not understand.'

With the back of his wrist Cale wiped the cold moisture from his nostrils. 'I was scared.'

Vinny scratched his head, troubled by the answer. 'Scared? Perhaps next time you will not be scared and the boy will be saved.'

'But I will be.'

'How do you know?'

'I know.'

'Very well. Be scared, but save him anyway.'

Cale glanced to him and saw the fresh blood seeping through his shirt, running down into his shorts.

Vinny wobbled, steadied himself and turned his attention to the sky. 'It is dark. Far too dark. Where are we?' He shuffled to a group of bowed palms.

'I think this is my place,' Cale replied. 'I'm dreaming.'

'Your dream? That is certainly curious. It looks like the Never. But I do not think it is the Never.'

'The Never,' Cale said, lifting his head. 'Pan's Never?'

Vinny dived at him, gripped Cale's head between his hands and brought their faces together so their noses were almost touching. Dark blood was running from under Vinny's vest and down his arms. The putrid reek of infected wounds and rotting meat filled the thin space between them. Vinny peered into one of Cale's eyes and then the other. 'Am I in there?' he questioned, beneath his breath. 'Is that where I am now?'

With eyes glazing, Vinny released Cale and fell back onto his rump. 'Oh, my!' A large, wearied grin spread across his face.

'What is it?'

'I saw it.'

'What? Saw what?' Cale said, touching the bones of his head.

The boy cackled, blood dribbling from his mouth. 'There is a wolf in you.'

'A wolf?'

'Yes, yes, yes. Are you a water-wolf, too?' He laughed, exposing teeth smeared with crimson goo.

'No. What are you talking about? A wolf inside me?'

Vinny nodded, directing a shaky finger at Cale's chest as though he should be seeing what he was seeing. 'It hides as it sleeps, yet my eyes can sight it. I see you, brother.'

Cale placed a soft hand on his front, feeling for the vibration of a growl, or the pulse of a second heart.

'Can you feel it?' Vinny coughed, spattering his dirt-patched legs with dashes of red.

'I don't know.'

'Look. You are not dead. You do not die easily.'

'You're right. I'm always left alive.'

'Perhaps you are so mighty you cannot be killed at all. There is no reason for you to fear.'

Cale dropped his hand. 'But there is. Heaps of reasons.'

Vinny pushed himself to his feet, coughing violently. 'Wake it up,' he smiled, wiping the trickles of blood from beneath his nose and mouth. 'Wake it up and let us go save the drowning one.' He collected Cale's hand and attempted to pull him to his feet. 'Come, brother. No one will ever die again. We are the water-wolves. We are strong and fearless. We decide who lives and who dies. The choice is ours.'

'That's what the wolf told me. He said that the choice is mine. But it isn't. It never is.' Cale slid his hand free of the slimy, red grip. The boy teetered and collapsed before him. 'Mitch. He's already dead. I can't save him. I couldn't save any of them. My parents died. Mr and Mrs Duhent are gone too. My sister …' he shook his head. 'I haven't got a clue how to help her. And when I was little I was … hurt. All my friends abandoned me. That man made my life worse than what it was. And it caused our only other family to run away from us. The only place I've got now is this town and it doesn't even want me here. I didn't choose for any of that to happen. I had no bloody choice in any of it.'

'You still choose, brother.'

'Didn't you hear me? All that stuff just happened. I didn't have a choice at all.'

'You do.' Vinny's limbs buckled and jolted as he attempted to direct them. His head lowered to the ground. His skin was now grey and the blood had stopped flowing. 'How you stand, brother,' Vinny, his eyes stained and unfocused, wheezed, 'that is your choice.'

Cale watched as Vinny released his last breath and became very still.

Lying down at the boy's side, Cale shut his eyes, squeezing the liquid from them. Opening them revealed the chilled sand before his face. He heard the crashing cheer of the Coalcliff shores and felt the creeping warmth of a hesitant dawn.

*

Everyone was already in assembly when Cale arrived. He made his way across the deserted school grounds towards the school hall. He snuck into the building and was directed to the rear corner by a teacher. The surrounding students, glad for any small distraction, followed his bent shuffle and watched him settle down in the shadows.

The projector dangling from the far-off ceiling cast its bright image across the wall behind the front stage. It was Mitch's school photo, his sly smile enormous and looking so different from the limp expression he wore when he was dragged up from the seabed. The date of his birth, followed by last Friday's date, sat in black, swirling numbers beneath the portrait.

Teachers stood before the podium and spoke of Mitch's academic and swimming achievements, his popularity, the abundance of potential, and how missed the boy will be in the school. The sounds of sniffling and subdued weeping echoed within the cavernous hall and reached Cale as though they, too, had been issued a microphone.

A few parents came. They climbed onto the stage with sullen faces, wringing their hands together and spoke of his politeness, his generosity, how good a friend he was to their children. Mitch's own father never appeared.

When the school principal stood before them all and labelled it a tragedy as everyone before him had done, and began speaking of the importance of not taking dangerous risks, of being sensible, and of looking out for each other, Cale jumped up and ran outside. No one stopped him.

He moved to a small brick wall retaining a neglected garden and sat upon it. Everything was bright out here, the surfaces bleached by the unobstructed sunlight. He braced his arms either side of him and hung his head.

He listened to the school band that closed the assembly. When they exhausted their repertoire of sad songs the students were ushered out to an early lunch. As the first few left the hall a pang within Cale told him to get up and run. He did not know why until he saw his grade flow from the building.

Their eyes found him and locked on. Every glare that seized him recited the story of how Mitch had been abandoned to his death in those savage swells.

It should have been you …

There were small shakes of the head, whispers, and lips twisted in disgust. Cale's mind screamed at him to run, but he could not move.

When they had all moved on, Cale remained. A teacher, Mrs Something-or-other, from the year above, edged over at some point. She sat next to him on the retaining wall and asked if he was alright. He was unable to speak. He only mouthed words like some mentally disturbed mute. The teacher suggested he go to the sick bay and placed her hands around his shoulders in an attempt to direct him there. Cale froze as though that was the only thing he could do anymore. He clung to the bricks beneath with all his strength until the teacher gave up and wandered away.

Alley walked into his line of sight. She stood before him, not uttering a word. She held out her hand and presented a small piece of card. It was a photo. He reached up to take it, hating how his hand trembled. It was of himself, the water filling the background, and his arms raised and ready to strike, as he howled to the night sky with something looking like courage on his face.

He studied the image. It looked like a different boy, a boy with a wolf inside him. This boy was no victim. He was someone who knew suffering, and used it to whet his fangs. This was a water-wolf.

Alley was gone when he dropped from the wall. He would return the photo to her later. He did not need it. He would find something better.

32.

A BROTHER'S GOODBYE

Alley left Cale with the photo and returned through the common grounds, coming to a stop in its centre. The specks of brightness whizzed back and forth at the boundaries. She dared them to attack. If they neared, she would pluck them from the air and squash the light from them.

As though hearing her silent challenge, a speck zipped towards her. Alley swatted and missed. The point of light dodged her other hand, swerved back and collided with her eye. Ache reverberated through her head. She clutched her eye, but refused to drop.

'Hey, Alley,' a voice said. 'They attacking?'

'Huh?' she returned, rubbing the painful glare from her sight.

'Flies?'

Her vision cleared enough to reveal Trent standing before her. She lowered her arm and straightened herself. 'Oh, hi.'

'Where's Pan?' Trent scanned the grounds, his stare level and hard.

Alley shrugged.

'How's your brother holding up? I hear he's copping a bit of flak about Mitch.'

'It's his first day back since the accident,' she said, not knowing what else to say. She turned around and peered through the shifting mass of students. He was gone and she knew he was not staying at school. 'It was no one's fault.'

'Yeah. They're all just upset, you know? They'll calm down.'

'I hope so.'

'Bryce's a mess.'

She looked to him.

'We're having a little send-off for his brother tonight at the beach?'

'That'll be nice for him.'

'You gonna come?'

'Me?'

Trent directed his tilted grin towards her.

'Who's going?'

'Mainly our grade. Probably a few from Mitch's year, too. Some of the girls are building a memorial raft. We're going to set fire to it and sail it out into the ocean; Viking-style or something like that. It'll be good if we can get everyone there. Bryce will appreciate it.'

'Would he?' she said, surprised at the amount of cynicism in her voice.

Trent released a light chuckle. 'It still will be a nice thing to do for Mitch.'

'You're right,' she returned.

'So, you gonna come?'

She skewed her expression into one of indecision.

'Come on,' he whined, playfully. 'If you don't promise me you'll be there, I'll come over and pick you up myself.'

'No, no. I'll go … for a bit.'

'Good. I'll look out for you.'

He gave her a wink, turned and headed back to his friends, leaving Alley with a throbbing brain and a storm of gleaming specks around her.

*

The night was streaked with racing lights. Alley hesitated at the front door, considered returning inside, crawling into bed and hiding herself beneath the covers. But would Trent really do what he said? For reasons she could not quite define, she was fearful of Trent stepping into her home and seeing what was inside.

Closing the front door behind her, Alley lowered her foot from the step to the ground, searching the army of specks for any sign of aggression. Tonight they seemed preoccupied, content to remain distant and merely threaten.

Scanning the surrounds revealed no sign of Cale. It was a vain hope. She knew he would not be returning any time soon. Perhaps he would never return. Perhaps he was planning on living the rest of his life at the beach.

Was he destined to become a homeless person, she wondered. Would he become one of those hairy men, always incensed and grumbling, that mothers hastily usher their children away from? Would he live a life like Beanie Lady?

Alley thought of the woman's end. Maybe that is what Cale wanted, an end like Beanie Lady … and Mrs Duhent. Alley could help him. She knew how to do it. She could lead him to the waters, direct him beneath the surface so he would never return to this world. Maybe there he would be saved from his misery.

Her heart skipped a beat. In response the specks lingered in their flights. What was she thinking? Alley gripped her head and forced a sob from her throat. Her thoughts were a jumbled mess.

'Are you alright?' Pan asked, at her side.

'I don't know,' she returned.

Pan placed a hand on her shoulder. Alley felt the broken pieces of her mind settle and form a coherent whole.

'I have a bad feeling about tonight,' he said.

Alley watched the specks float backwards, forming tight clusters against the deepest of night's shadows.

'Bryce is going to be there.'

'So?' she said.

'He is dangerous right now. And he has been spending too much time with the Anchors.'

'Why are you so scared of them?'

'Ha! I am not scared of them.'

'If you say so.'

Pan released a grating breath.

'I still want to go,' she said. 'Will you come with me?'

'I will.'

Alley smiled her thanks and led them into the streets. Small collections of people were seen making their boisterous way towards the coast. Reaching the sands, the gathering was easy to spot. North, spread out on the rocks beneath Deep Moss Heights, was a large scattering of shadowed figures. A small fire burned, illuminating a large circle of the crowd.

Appearing like some ancient pagan nature-worshipping ceremony, there were those who sang and danced about in the firelight, their swinging bottles glinting with amber light as they swung their arms. The majority were much more passive. Standing in small, open groups, they engaged in quiet conversations, some sipping drinks or scanning phone content in an all-consuming pale glow.

Despite the fitful pockets of animation there was a specific heavy air about the area. It settled upon the ocean, holding enough weight to keep the waves low. They lapped at the base of the rocks in a gentle manner; Alley imagining it as a form of ocean apology or remorse.

'Panny!' Romina bubbled, stopping before them.

Pan's head shot back.

'Alley,' she said, turning to her with her eyebrows arched high, 'I didn't know that you came to things like this.'

'Trent told me about it.'

'Hope you don't feel out of place.'

'Don't worry, Romina, I don't. We're here for Bryce anyway, aren't we?'

Romina beamed, looking to Pan. 'We have to have a *get to know you* chat tonight, Pan. Just me and you. Stick around later on, 'kay?'

'Maybe.'

'That's a yes,' Romina said. She signalled to her friends with bent fingers where a drink would rest and sauntered away.

'A *get to know you* chat …' Alley said, poking Pan in the ribs. 'That sounds sweet, doesn't it, Panny?'

He sniffed the air. 'I do not do sweet.'

'Alley-cat,' Megan said, heading towards them, Taz stomping the rocks at her side. 'Hi, Pan. Didn't know yous were coming. Want a drink?' She presented a stretched green bottle absent a label and a make shift cup made from a jam jar.

Alley shrugged. 'Ah, sure.' She collected a jar full, took a sip, swallowed, gagged, panted and expected to see flames on her breath.

'I know,' Megan said, apologetically. 'My cousin's homebrew. It's all we could get our hands on.'

Pan collected the jar, held it up to his eye and scrutinised the liquid inside. 'What is this stuff?'

'Drink of the gods, mate,' Taz said.

He took a long gulp. His expression crumpled and he stepped back as though dodging an attack. 'Are you sure you are supposed to drink this?'

'Well, you ain't gonna water your garden with it,' Taz smiled, maniacally.

'It tastes like poison.'

'You betcha, boyo. That means it's the good stuff. But it's not about the taste. Only worry about that when it's on the return journey.'

'What?'

'Oh, Pan, you've certainly lived a sheltered life.'

A surging holler tore across the rock shelf. It was punctuated by a massive splash. Everyone turned to the ocean to see someone rolling about in the water like an injured seal. Three boys were at the rocks edge, laughing and swaying about with their drinks raised above their heads.

'Hey,' someone yelled with authority. Rowan, the school captain, stormed towards the edge. 'Get him out.'

'Come on, Matt. Get out,' Trent could be heard calling out in half-hearted support of Rowan.

'Awww, c'mon! Whatever, man!' Matt's friends yelled back.

'No one's swimming tonight!' Rowan roared in return. 'You want someone else to drown …?'

A heavy hush fell over the scene.

'I mean … just get out, will ya?'

The figure treading water swam over and, with a great amount of difficulty, his friends hauled him out. 'I'm bloody freezing,' he whined, loping over to the fire with jeering laughter following.

'What a dickhead,' Taz said, taking a swig straight from the bottle.

Rowan moved over to a group of girls surrounding the memorial raft. Standing on a wooden platform, about the size of a writing desk, was a picture of Mitch. It was the same one projected on the wall at the school assembly. Bordering the picture was a floral wreath and, surrounding this centrepiece, were a collection of cards and Mitch's personal effects sitting upon a bed of kindling. 'Let's get this going,' Rowan said, 'before everyone gets too wasted.'

The girls made their final adjustments and indicated it was ready.

'Alright!' Rowan called out, gathering the crowd closer. 'Does anyone want to say a few words?' None made a movement. 'Bryce? Where's Bryce? Want to say anything, buddy?' There was no reply. 'Alright, send it off,' he said, looking to the girls.

''Scuse me?' one of the girls sung to Rowan. 'I'm not going near that water. These shoes cost two-hundred bucks.'

'Yeah,' her friends agreed in unison.

Trent and a few others moved in and, under Rowan's guidance, ignited the raft and pushed it out to sea with a length of driftwood.

An auburn glow wavered across the portrait of Mitch, causing his smirking expression to twist and warp as though the still image was flexing its facial muscles. As the flame found the kindling, the fire lurched upward with a rolling flare of light. A dirty orange pall surrounded the raft, rocking and dipping on the waters. Everyone watched on in silence as the waves nudged the raft back towards the rocks.

Before the raft was battered against the shelf, Alley collected her camera and fired off a shot.

'Hey!' a voice struck through the quiet like a crack of lightning.

Alley turned, camera in hand, to see Bryce swaggering with an unsteady gait towards her.

He blundered to a stop. His twisted scowl was made more menacing by the puffy black eye, and his lips, bubbled, split, and lined with dried blood. The dancing firelight was a violent frenzy on his face. 'You wanna take photos, do ya?' he sneered, through his teeth. 'You wanna capture this beautiful moment forever?'

Alley stood dumbly, her thoughts stumbling against the sight before her.

With drinks paused halfway to open mouths, all eyes were removed from the raft and fixed on the confrontation.

'Go for it,' Bryce grunted. 'Take all the photos you want. Stick 'em on your wall and every morning you can wake up with a smile as you remember my brother's death.'

'Bryce …' Alley only managed to whisper. She could feel the stares of the others encircling her.

Bryce's head dropped for a beat before it jerked back up. 'What? You run outta film? Well then, I hope you got enough for yourself. Make a bloody collage, you and your damn, murdering brother.'

Alley felt herself enlarge. 'What are you talking about?'

Bryce showed his teeth. The split on his swollen lower lip opened and fresh blood glinted in the firelight. 'He left him to die in that water,' he spat, swinging an arm to display the whole ocean. 'That little shit got Mitch to swim out there and then left him to die. That's the kind of shit your brother pulls. That's what he did last time.'

'Bryce, what—'

'Shut-up. Your brother murdered mine.' His head turned away from the firelight, casting his face in darkness. 'I wonder how you'll deal with it. It's only fair, isn't it? He kills mine so we kill yours.'

'You're talking crazy.'

Bryce charged forward, fists balling, face collapsing into a rage. He stopped just short of running straight into her.

Alley stood her ground, and looked up into the feral stare of the large boy. 'Bryce, you're being stupid. It was an accident. Cale didn't mean anything like this to happen. You know that.'

He stepped back and turned away, faced the surrounding crowd and peered at something beyond them. 'They want to kill him. I wondered why. Now I don't care.'

'What are you talking about?'

'He deserves it. He killed *my* brother.' He spun back to her. 'And you. Someone should kill you, too. You're nothing but a stain.'

'Ease up,' someone said in the darkness.

'Yeah, calm down, Bryce,' said another.

'Piss off,' he growled, targeting the area with a finger, maintaining his glare on Alley. In a whisper, he said, 'Your mum was on the right track. Why don't you go throw yourself off the cliffs, too?' He leaned back and snorted. 'You'll probably do it anyway. You're just a freak like she was.'

Before Alley knew what her body was doing, her arm was swinging and her hand was colliding with Bryce's face. The sound of skin smacking against skin crackled across the area. Half the crowd drew a noticeable breath and did not release it.

Bryce stepped back, as though his body wanted to throw him into a swift retreat. His eyes were large. Blood from his lip had sprayed across his cheek. For a fraction of a second, Alley saw something exposed in the windows of Bryce's eye. It was fear that she saw, a child's fear.

Alley pulled her hand back and held it with the other as though it was going to rampage again. 'Bryce, I'm—'

SMACK!

The force of Bryce's hand sent Alley to the side. She caught the rock before her head collided with it. The camera was not protected as it struck the rock, broke from the neck strap and tumbled into a nearby rock-pool, discarding fragments as it rolled.

Words of condemnation were thrown as a few boys rushed in. Bryce refused to be budged. He stood his ground and shoved back. 'Alright. Alright,' he conceded with a shout. 'Get off me.' The boys stepped back, warily.

The hands that were offered to Alley were discarded. 'No,' she said, 'it's alright.' She climbed to her feet and looked at Bryce. She matched his infuriated glare. 'I'm sorry, Bryce. I'm sorry that I hit you. I shouldn't have done that. And the person who's done that to your face shouldn't have done it to you either.'

Bryce sobered.

'I'm sorry for a lot of things. I'm sorry that you've had a hard life and that you've got a father like yours.'

Bryce shook his head with a tiny tremble, mouthing small words without sound.

'I'm not stupid. None of us are.'

He rushed again, shoulders lifting, arms tensing. Alley did not flinch. He stopped short, leaning his bulk over her.

'But you can't keep acting like you do,' she continued. 'It's such a tired cliché. You see that, don't you? That's what you let the world do to you. That's what you let yourself become; just a tired cliché.'

'Get away from her, Bryce,' Trent's voice was heard in the background. 'I mean it.'

Bryce held himself as though he did not hear. After a few tense beats, he lowered his shoulders and rediscovered the crowd. He glanced down at his feet, lowered himself and collected a large handful of grime and slop from a stagnant pool of water. 'You're just an unwanted nothing, Alley. Unwanted and fit to be smothered,' he said, rising and presenting the muck to her like an ultimatum.

She extended her arm. 'Go on. I'm ready. Do it, Bryce. Do it and watch me suffer. Because it helps, doesn't it? It helps with your own suffering.' She thrust her arm nearer. 'Go on, Bryce,' she said, louder. 'And we can suffer together. Just you and me, the same, except for one big difference; I can take it. I'm strong enough to face it and deal with it. So,' she lifted her arm just below his hand, 'do it.'

Bryce hesitated. He glanced to the surrounding crowd, then down at Alley's arm. With a dismissive laugh he tossed the muck back to the rocks. To Alley, beneath his breath, he said, 'Your brother's dead.'

'He's not afraid of you,' Alley called out, as Bryce turned and moved towards the bulging darkness at the base of the cliffs. 'He's stronger than you, too … the things he's gone through … he's stronger than us all put together.'

Alley turned away also. She thought it odd that her heart was not racing or her breathing was not shallow and difficult.

Pan's sprightly step was heard behind. Alley held out an open hand to stop him. 'I'm fine, Pan. I'm going home,' she said, watching the bright specks retreat from her path as she walked.

As Alley hopped down the rocks and landed on the sand, she heard Megan shout, 'Right on, Alley-cat!'

'Yeah, you go, girl!' Taz bellowed, with the crowd releasing sporadic bursts of cheers and whistles.

Pan held his eyes on her silhouette until it merged with night and disappeared. Everyone calmed and returned to their social circles to review the drama. The memorial raft was now beneath the waves. No one had noticed its descent.

Bryce had taken a seat against the cliff and busied himself with swigging out of a large bottle. He kept his eyes on the rocks before him, occasionally inspecting the others with a sly glance, sneering and shaking his head whenever he did.

Reaching into his shorts pocket, he retrieved a small, plastic bag. Biting his teeth together, he held his bottle between his knees and dropped a pinch of the powder into its opening.

Pan strolled away from the small fire and stood before Bryce. 'Where did you get that?'

'Get lost,' he returned, taking a swig of his concoction.

'Did the Anchors give it to you?'

Bryce lowered his head. Softly, he said, 'Just leave me alone, Pan.'

'You should not touch that dust.'

Bryce looked up to him from beneath his brow.

'It is dangerous to you, especially that amount. The dust will take you deep. Too deep.'

Steadying his glare on Pan, Bryce collected more of the powder and dropped it into the bottle. 'Deep is where I want to be.' He took a long drink.

'Their goal is the end. If they win, they will all disappear. Their goal is to die. Do you understand that? I cannot save them from themselves. They have chosen to seek out death. But you ...'

'What? Can choose life?' He shook his head with a laugh. 'I don't think life ever chose *me*. If I could make it all disappear ...'

'You sound like Cale.'

'Don't use that name around me.'

'Tell me, Bryce. The Anchors know about him. What do they know?'

Bryce's head tipped, his neck lacking the strength to keep it upright.

'Bryce,' Pan said, with force. 'Tell me. Have they told you?'

'All I know is that they want him dead. They know you want him. That's enough for them to kill him. It'll be here soon. They're getting ready for It.'

Pan stood back and examined the night beyond. 'Finally.' He turned back to Bryce, grabbed his shoulders and pushed his face into his. 'How? How is It getting here?'

Drool flowed in a steady run from each side of Bryce's mouth. 'Tell me!'

Bryce stared through him, eyes like that of a possum. Pan released him and took off at a run.

Bryce did not notice Pan's departure. He had had this fairy dust before, but the Anchors had never allowed him to take as big a dose as he had administered himself.

The scene faded as though his senses were falling into slumber while his mind was wide awake.

Maybe Pan was right. Maybe he had taken too much.

The dots of hovering bright were with him as on the previous occasions. They appeared every time the powder was ingested. But never like this, never this many.

They slowly made their way up from the crevices in the rocks, from behind the dark figures that wavered before him. They popped up from the dark expanse he assumed was the ocean. They rained down upon him from the sky. Even the string of lights that trailed after Alley halted their flight and returned.

They all moved towards him, each with their own personality and shine. Some were tentative, hanging back and moving forward at small intervals. Some drifted towards him boldly, trying to intimidate him with sudden bursts of speed. Others led small contingents of light behind them, like a tiny spark of a commander leading a platoon of soldiers.

The shining dots surrounded him, filled every inch of dark space, shoving each other, peeking over each other's shoulders, looking down upon him as though they were to judge his life, weigh his sins and decide his fate.

The thought of going to hospital moved across his thoughts. It was pointless. He could not move, was unable to speak. He was only able to sit there, as the lights jostled one another to gain better position to pronounce their sentence.

One moved forward and landed on Bryce's bare arm. It seemed to fold upon itself, wriggle and burrow beneath his skin. He released a murmur of shock, watching the dull glow beneath his skin crawl up towards his shoulder.

The others drifted down, landed upon him and dug their way into his body. Soon Bryce was staring at his arms and legs, all aglow with a ruddy lustre.

He felt light and intangible. And, as though he truly was insubstantial, he felt himself floating upwards, drifting in the breeze like a hanging sheet caught by the wind.

Unable to see anything besides the shine of his body against the opaque darkness, he could not tell if he drifted into the upper reaches of the atmosphere, or was being drawn across the seas to distant lands.

It could have been hours when shapes began to form, or seconds. Time existed no longer. He saw what looked like tall, thin trees with massive leaves. Bordering white sands were waters so pure they shone blue, and the shape of a young person … a boy … his brother.

Mitch was clean and unhurt, smiling as though content. He walked across the white sands towards him, his spotless feet leaving no footprints. He raised his arm and extended his hand towards Bryce's face. His fingers brushed the dark rim of his eye and the bloody lump that was his lower lip.

This is too cruel, Bryce thought, as his brother mouthed words of apology. Bryce released his scream. It began deep down inside him. It rose to the surface and ripped from his throat. The vocal rage was enough to give his body movement, allowing him to thrash the image before him. He continued thrashing until the light beneath his skin faded. He was thrown into darkness and felt himself fall into a waiting emptiness he welcomed without resistance.

*

Pan tore across the sand. The Anchors knew of Cale. And It was coming …

He did not have to run for long. He knew the boy was close. Through the darkness, Pan could see him standing knee deep in the water, the waves rubbing themselves against his legs.

'Cale,' Pan called, coming to a stop before the waves could lick his feet.

Cale looked out to the darkness of the ocean. 'I was there.'

Pan inspected the surrounds. 'Have you seen any of the Anchors about?'

'I was over there, in the shadows. I heard it all.'

'Bryce?' Pan asked, returning to him. 'Do not worry. I will make sure he will not get to you.'

'I'm not worrying. It's Alley, my sister, it's what she said.'

Cale watched his legs as they sloshed through the water towards the shore. He stood and faced the distant fire on the rocks. Pan stood beside him and was just able to discern the glow of the young man's body that no other appeared to have noticed.

'You remember, all that time ago, when you told me about those water-wolves?'

Pan raised his brow.

'That's what I want to be. I don't want to run and I don't want to hide. I don't want to be afraid. I don't want to let what happened to Mitch happen to anyone else close to me. I can do it. I can prove my sister right. That's how I can help her. I can become a water-wolf.'

'You can, Cale. But, I do not know anymore.'

'I do, Pan. You can help me, can't you? That's why you're here, isn't it?'

'Cale …' Pan exhaled, and was unable to draw more breath.

'Please, Pan. I already feel different. I can almost see it.' He reached forward to stroke the night with his fingertips.

'You will have to kill. Are you ready to do that? Are you ready to kill?'

'To protect the things I want to protect? I'll do whatever it takes.'

'If you're certain of this …'

Cale stepped to his side.

Pan, his closed eyes and furrowed brow hidden in the night, placed a hand on Cale's shoulder and directed him away from the water.

33.

THE DARK OF
A MOTHER'S EMBRACE

The throb in Alley's head was incessant, broken only by sudden attacks of a pain, sharp and serrated, through her mind. It was as though one of the specks had tunnelled its way into her brain to run riot. She hoped it was no more than the anxiety of being ill-prepared for these exams, or the intense cramming wearing on her mental capacity.

The textbook open beneath her nose was a blur of black and white streaks. She repeatedly checked the title, reminding herself what exam she was attending today … Biology … great, she thought, the one subject where recall was a necessity.

She lifted her eyes to the variegated latticework of the library shelves surrounding. The students of her year sharing the study area were faint projections of real people. If Alley stopped focusing on their quiet chatter, the world fell silent. If she overlooked them, they would all disappear, leaving only a flat plane of smudged colours, and the specks of light that shivered in small bundles far from where she sat.

Did they fear her now?

Laying her pen upon the desk, Alley raised a hand and pointed to a jittery cluster of specks at the base of a bookshelf. The cluster froze, caught in the beam of her acknowledgment. She drew her finger in a straight line, level with the floor. The bunch of specks followed the direction, stopped where her finger indicated and waited for her next command.

Alley squeezed her eyes shut. Her head was cleaved by agony. Collecting her belongings, she threw them into her bag and staggered for the library's exit.

'Alley!' Trent headed towards her. Romina and Sarah were at his side.

'Hi,' she croaked.

'How have your exams been going?'

'Ah …'

'Got any on today?'

'Um …'

Romina tapped away on her phone. 'Seen Pan?'

'I, ah … haven't.' Pan … that was what she needed. He had a way of smoothing the creases and healing the fractures that travelled through her mind.

'If you see him, remind him the party's tomorrow night. Starts right after the last exam.' She lowered her phone. 'You should come as well. That was pretty cool what you did the other night.'

'Yeah,' Trent said. 'You were right. It's a shitty thing his brother died, but Bryce seriously needed to be put in his place. I just hope he wakes up to himself a bit now.'

'I wanna be nice to him, now that his brother's dead,' Sarah added, sighing. 'But he's always such an asshole to me.'

Alley nodded.

'Least he gets special consideration for his exams, the lucky bastard.'

Alley stared at the girl.

'Hear what happened?' Romina said, sharing a laugh with Sarah. 'After you left, Alley, Bryce totally flipped out. Don't know what he was taking but he completely lost his shit. It was hilarious. That kid's lost it.'

A collection of adventurous specks were drifting around the three before Alley, inspecting them and casting patches of bright to glow upon their skin. Alley flicked her head, sending the specks whizzing away in retreat.

'So you'll come along tomorrow night?' Trent questioned. 'Me and you gotta have a farewell drink or two.'

Alley looked to him.

'End of exams and all that.'

'Um, sure. We'll see.'

Trent gave her a wink, which Romina looked to with a blank stare.

*

The whole exam, like those previous, was a swift, gut-twisting blur. Her saving grace was the amount of multiple-choice questions.

The specks maintained their presence about her. They could not be dismissed entirely, only ordered to stay out of her way. Looking behind as she walked home revealed a tail of tinsel connected to her back that trailed down the road into indistinctness.

Reaching the Duhent's property, Alley stepped towards the closed garage. It took a further three steps to remember Mr Duhent would not be there, nor Mrs Duhent in her house. Loneliness, a sensation she thought she had surpassed, released the trapdoor within and let her insides drop.

The thought of standing between the walls of her and Cale's little home caused the emptiness within to surge. She moved to the backdoor of the Duhent's house, reached through the broken flyscreen and unlocked the latch. In a neat pile on the kitchen table, stacked one atop the other, largest to smallest, were all the keys to the house.

Feeling drained and alone like she never felt before, Alley moved through the Duhent's home. She lifted her arms, her hands outstretched to travel along the wallpaper and pieces of furniture, now absent all their trinkets and decorations. In the bedroom, she collapsed on the bed and curled herself up in the linen sheets. Their scents lingered here; musty and aged and thick with memories.

She tossed herself onto her back and stretched out, staring up at the ceiling. The specks were attentive, maintaining a respectful vigil against the walls of the room, like a family would surround the deathbed of a beloved relative.

Alley lifted her arm and found it burdened with an incredible weight. Drawing deep breaths, she gestured to the specks, reflecting the movements she had watched Pan perform. The points of shining light recoiled from her gesture. Alley held her arm steady and performed the command with greater insistence. The specks rolled through the air and nudged those alongside them, sending themselves into a swirl around the room. They spun faster and faster, becoming a tornado of light. A gale grew, rattling the furniture. The bed juddered, turning on the spot. The walls groaned and the ceiling buckled, and the rush of lights grew faster and brighter.

Alley dropped her arm, afraid, but the swirl of lights did not stop. It felt as though the whole room would combust into howling conflagration.

Her voice would not release the screams in her throat. She wanted to throw herself from the bed, escape this storm of light, but her body would not respond.

The hurricane intensified and pushed down upon her. The wind whipped up her hair, shrieked in her ears. The brilliance heated her skin, singeing the fuzz on her arms. It swept her up, pulled her in all directions at once. Her mind was stretched, pulled across a distance unimaginable. And the wind halted its assault. Everything became calm.

Alley blinked, washing the glare from her eyes. Her sight returned to reveal the darkness of a dense night. Tall palm trees reached overhead. Spread out before her were the powdery white sands of a familiar beach. The waters stroking the shore were liquid crystal, shedding a pale-blue sheen.

What am I doing here? Alley asked herself. But she knew. For there a figure came walking. Dressed in a simple white slip, the woman moved towards her with a flowing grace.

Alley, her thoughts struggling to stay afloat in a cloudy gel, trembled in response to the woman's nearness. When the woman stopped a short distance before her, expression flat, Alley lowered herself to her knees, and wept.

The woman looked preoccupied, her eyes studying the distances at Alley's back. When the title was uttered, the woman twitched, as though a small electric current had travelled through her body. Her eyes drifted over Alley, not lingering on her daughter's face, as they focused on the sand to her side.

'Mum? It's me.'

The woman's head tilted. Her sight did not shift. 'My child,' she breathed, her voice seeming to leach from the air.

Alley wanted to run to her, like a wounded toddler runs to their mother, bury her face in her stomach and weep until all the sorrow of her life had seeped out.

Climbing to her feet, she remained where she was. She was a child no longer and, no matter the vision before her, she had no mother to hold when this dream world released her. 'Mum, won't you look at me?'

Her mother's sight was glassy. Her expression was a reflection of nothingness. 'My child,' she said, with melody. 'My dear, sweet child.'

'Why? Why did you do it?'

'Do what, my darling?' Her head rose and fell to the other side, her eyes drawn along with it, passing over Alley to land on the sand beside her.

'Everything,' Alley whispered, with a breaking voice.

'Whatever do you mean, my sweet? I only wanted you to be happy.'

Alley watched her hands as they strangled each other. 'You did love us, didn't you?'

'I want you to be happy.'

'Yes. But you hurt us, mum. You hurt us both.'

'Oh, dear.' Her mother released gentle laughter, the sound of scattering pebbles that echoed across the shores. 'Oh, dear, I would never hurt you. I only wanted you to be happy. Be happy, my darling.'

'But you did. Aren't you listening? Don't you remember? You … You hurt us. Years ago, when we were kids.'

'Oh, no, my dear,' she laughed again.

'You did. And you left us. Right when we needed you. And things got worse. So much worse. And we were all alone. Why did you do it? Our lives were ruined because of you. You wanted us to be happy but you hurt us so much. I need a reason why. I need … something, anything.'

Her mother twitched. Her brow lowered. 'The past is sad. There is only unhappiness in life. I want you to be happy. You need to be happy. Come, my sweet. Come here.' She raised her arms to her daughter, her sight still focused on the sands. 'Come and be happy. Stay here with me.'

Alley lifted a hand to her mouth, placed a thumb nail between her teeth. 'Mum …'

A dense gloom fell over the scene, seeming to emanate from the awaiting embrace before her. Alley shivered. The temperate air was drained of its warmth. Her mother's face fell into shadow.

Her mother stepped forward, arms reaching towards her. 'Come into my arms, child. Just for a moment. Down here in the dark, there is no life, no sadness. I will show you happiness. Let me hold you.'

The thick goo in which Alley's mind was suspended oozed down to the rest of her body. It sapped her strength, enticed her to fall into the embrace and drift away from all the problems of her life, sleep like she had never slept before. 'Please. I don't understand.'

'There, there, my dear. It will be alright. Come into my arms. Come down, deep into the dark. I only want you to be happy.'

Alley's legs wobbled. Her eyes fluttered and closed. 'I want to believe you.'

There was a pause before her mother released, 'Life is full of sadness. No life, no sadness,' in a croon like a lullaby.

Alley's body collapsed forward. There was the sound of heavy feet and Alley was thrust backwards. She toppled and found herself sprawled on the sand. Pan was before her, facing her mother, as the woman recovered from a strike to her front.

'Pan,' Alley coughed, climbing to her feet.

'Stay back,' he said.

Her mother, doused in shadow, staggered forward, arms spread wide, ready to collect those before her.

'Keep away,' Pan shouted at the woman. He leapt and drove his foot into her stomach. The woman withstood Pan's driving kick for a beat before succumbing and stumbling.

'Pan!' Alley squealed. 'That's my mum!'

'Not really. Maybe only a part of her is,' he said, turning to reveal a face taut with desperation. 'The darkest part. You should not have come here without me.'

A rumbling groan came from the woman. She threw her head back, opening her mouth wide in a silent cry. Her fingers curled, went rigid and were ready to claw. She brought her nails to her forehead, dug deep and drew down her face with a savage slowness, shredding skin. Her open mouth did not release a whisper.

Alley screamed for her, cried her name and begged her to stop. Her wail dissipated as shock replaced the horror.

In the wake of her mother's nails no blood poured. The torn gashes were jet black. They each seeped a viscous dark that ran down her face and neck, dripped from the end of her nose to land dark spots of complete absence in the sand.

'Run,' Pan said, turning to Alley.

The sight of her mother and the fear in Pan's expression filled her with an immobilising dread.

'Run, damn it!' Pan cried, grabbing her hand and yanking her into flight.

Stumbling and lurching, Alley glanced behind to see her mother convulse violently then explode into a mass of darkness. Like the breaking of a reservoir, the dark flowed outward, growing immense. It was a mighty tidal wave, rolling forwards and upwards, climbing into the heights of the sky.

Alley's foot collided with something solid. She fell. Pan hauled her to her feet, shouting at her to keep moving.

The surrounding vegetation lost its glossy sheen, turned brown and wilted. Tall palm trees swayed, tipped and crashed into the undergrowth in billowing puffs of ash. The sand and leaf litter at their feet rotted, became a grey sludge that filled the air with the foul stench of putrescence.

They rushed through the decaying jungle, Pan smacking at the massive, dying leaves that stood in their way. They slapped against Alley's body with weak attempts to knock her down, crumbling as she charged them. The slope underfoot threatened her stride. Rocks and logs were impossible to see until she was tumbling over them, Pan pulling her up with fearful shouts.

When he told her not to look up, she looked up. The vast wave of darkness arched over them, reaching across the sky as though wanting to collapse its weight on all the land in one great fall.

'What is that thing?' she yelled.

'The greatest Anchor of them all,' he said, between his gulping breaths.

Large chunks of dark stuff fell from its height. They crashed into the jungle around them, sending out resonating detonations that shook the ground.

Alley watched a huge mass of inky black land nearby, exploding a tight thicket of palms into a cloud of splinters and dust. The solid block then erupted in a liquid burst, splashing a syrupy darkness over the jungle. Everything it stained became a big, gaping hole of nothing.

'Do not let it touch you!' Pan cried, tugging at Alley harder as a spray of dark landed in their wake.

The dark wave had travelled far ahead of them. Its jagged lip struck downward, bringing the thing upon the world.

Don't let it touch you …! 'It's going to fall on us, Pan!' she called forward.

He continued running.

'Pan!'

'Just keep running … I need to think.'

'Take us back!'

Pan yanked her forward.

'Pan! Wake me up!'

He stopped, spun and cried into her face, 'I cannot!'

'Why? You did it last time.'

'Look at it!' He flung his arm towards the black sky. 'You think It will not stop us returning!? You think It is that feeble? It has found me. It has come and … and he is not ready,' he breathed.

He glared at her with a face overflowing with anger, as though she was the cause for the thing coming upon them … Was she?

'Did I do this?' she gushed. 'My mother …?'

Pan turned his gaze to the spoiled roof of the world. There were no stars to be seen. All were dead. The emotion drained from his face, his desperation dissolved. 'It does not matter. One way or another it would have reached me.'

'Pan,' Alley breathed, barely audible above the whooshing drone filling the air. He focused on the falling edge of the wave in the distant skies. 'Pan,' she said, noticing her hand still in his. She tugged at him. 'Come on. Let's run.'

He shook free of her hold, scanning the dark dome above. 'Must I really die?' he asked the world.

'Pan, no,' Alley said. She collected his hand again, compelling him to meet her stare. 'Not today. Not like this.'

'I fought well,' he nodded. 'I did try. I just ran out of time … me, of all people.' He released a solitary note of laughter before turning to her. 'But sometimes there are no happy endings,' he murmured, through a weak smile. 'That is what you told me.'

Alley's eyes prickled as they moistened. The fear was now a small hum behind an ache ballooning in her chest. 'It depends on how you look at it.'

Pan's weak smile turned into a large grin. It pulled apart as he broke into laughter. He fell onto his back, arms and legs spread wide. Wiping the humour from his face, he angled a gaze up to Alley. 'I am sorry you will die here with me.'

Alley, feeling the smile stretching her mouth, said, 'Is this even real?'

'No, Alley. Not at all. Come,' he said, reaching a hand to her. 'It was always just a dream.'

She lowered herself next to Pan. The sludge clung to her body with a cold grip.

Together, on their backs in the putrefying jungle, they watched darkness collapse upon the world.

In the side of Alley's vision, a dull gleam streaked. She turned her head to see a tall, thin mass, wearing an ochre sheen, leap into view. It considered them for a beat before darting away into the shadows. She sat up.

'What is it?' Pan asked, sitting up beside her.

The surrounding plants shivered, the ground shook and a horde of misty figures appeared, streaming through the withering vegetation. They were hard to define, their shine and swiftness smearing their features. Each was a different shade, burnished in earthly colours; the deep copper of firelight, the glaze of polished oak, the rich olive of a drenched rainforest. They coursed around the collapsed pair, rushing like a rainbow gale towards the base of the dark wave.

Alley released a gush of a breath sounding close to a question.

Pan crowed, 'It is her,' indicating a form larger and brighter than the rest, patterned in a shine that combined all the colours of the figures that flanked her. She halted, leaving her shaded contingent to continue.

'Greetings, Never King!' The woman's voice reverberated through the jungle, vibrating the trees, producing a soft light to fall from them like burning pollen. The flood of decay paused. 'Do you see me now, Pan of the Never?'

'I know that woman,' Alley said, scrambling to her feet.

'I see you, Tiger,' Pan said, rising.

'Correct. It is I, the Tiger of the Lilies, the Huntress Chief, the bearer of the spirit of this timeless land.'

'Out for a midnight hunt?'

'As we were born to do!' She turned to the wall of dark beyond. 'It has come, Never King, to complete the story of our world. Yet is It so dim-witted to believe It will sweep us away with such ease? Ha! We are the souls of the earth incarnate. It may take everything that we are, but only from a grip that is drenched in its own blood.' She released a war-cry and pounced into the jungle.

'Look,' Pan said, directing Alley's bewilderment to the side.

One of the figures was stationary amongst the others. It appeared to be a young man, dusted in an ochre sheen, the colour of clay earth baked under a summer sun. There was no clothing on the man except for a skirt of material that shared the colour of his lustre. He wore no weapons, his hands free and open. The way he stood before them, eyeing them with a steady sobriety, suggested weapons would only slow his attack.

'You should not have returned,' Pan said.

Alley blinked at the young man. It looked like the stoic Eran she knew, and it did not. He appeared as a version of Eran that had been purified, all blemishes removed, his insides filtered of any contaminate.

'Eran, is that you?' Alley murmured.

His glowing brown eyes considered her for a quiet moment. 'The boundaries of this place have fallen. I'll get you back home,' he said in a voice that filled the area and pushed back the muffled roar of the dark wave.

'There is no victory for the Tiger in this battle,' Pan said. 'She will not defeat It.'

'It is not her intention to conquer,' Eran said, studying the distant wave. 'Her intention is to meet the end as she has lived; as a warrior. She has realised that that is the only way to do justice to her life and the life of her tribe. Cowering in the shadows and beating her fists against the unavoidable demeans the great life she has lived. I am glad she came to that realisation. I am proud of her.' Eran glanced to Pan from the corner of his eye.

Pan chuckled. 'As you wish to see it, tribesman.'

'We are all proud of her, and of ourselves. See us, Pan. We have regained our light, the spirit of the land. This is what we are. This is how it should be. This is our end at the end of the story. And we write our final sentence with pride.'

'I am the Never. I can save it, bring it back.'

Eran turned on him. 'Should you?'

Pan looked to Alley. An almighty quake travelled through the wave above them. Fractures of dull light streaked through its seething black wall. It recoiled.

'She has struck,' Eran said. 'Come,' he said to Alley, 'you may wake now.'

'Yes, let us get out of here,' Pan added.

Eran's hand lifted, separating the two.

Pan stared at the barrier. 'You will stop me?'

'It is not my place to direct you. However, if you remain, It will end … right here. If you run, It will chase you down … anywhere you go. Even forever must come to an end.'

'But you will give me time. My plan …'

'And if you win this battle, the war will not be over. The war will never be over.'

'Good,' Pan said, planting his fists on his hips. 'That is how I like it. I am a warrior, too. I am nothing without the fight.'

'And how much will you sacrifice in your *fight*? The boy has suffered enough. Will you prolong his pain to extend the length of your own existence?'

Pan kneaded the muscles on the back of his neck.

Eran spread his arms, displayed the rush of warriors. 'Look at these beings. Look at what we do. When this land woke and uttered its first words, we were born. We are its voice.' He squared his shoulders. 'What are you, Pan?'

Pan, with quiet words, said, 'I am the Never.'

'Then?'

'You are my voice.'

'So, hear us. Take wisdom from our choice.'

The dark wave, trembling, cracked and bled light.

'Look at what we do and know we are at peace.'

The wave halted its retreat, appeared to heal the widest of the ruptures.

Pan shook his head. 'But everything I am …'

'… Will still be. You did live. You were here.'

Drawing a large breath, Pan lowered his sight to the failing greenery.

'We grant you this,' Eran said, 'one final gift from the last of our power; we can spare her life, return her to her brother. She is not of this place. She does not deserve to die here.'

After a few beats of stillness there was a small movement to Pan's head. It looked like a nod.

'Pan?' Alley said, stepping around Eran's arm. 'You're coming, too.'

Pan sniffed the air. 'You know what? I might remain.' He strolled a distance away and smiled at what he saw. 'Yes. This place is mine. I am going to stay.'

'No. Will you die?'

Pan lowered himself into a crouch and pushed a finger into the sludge beneath him.

'Eran,' she said, 'will he die?'

'All things must end, Alley.'

'No. Pan, I won't let you. Come back. Come with me. I'm not going to leave without you.'

Pan looked to her. 'You should leave. You cannot disappear in that thing. Cale needs you.'

'And what about me? I can't face what's back there without you. I don't want to.'

'I cannot return.'

'Why?'

'Because.' He drew a wavy pattern in the muck, the scribbling of a name.

'Pan!'

'The price is too high!'

'I'll pay it. I'll pay anything. I want you to come back with me.'

Pan looked to her from beneath his brow. 'Really? You will pay anything?' He stood, wiped his fingers clean and shook his head. 'No, Alley, you do not—'

'I know I don't understand. I haven't understood a damn thing since the first day I met you. But I don't care anymore. I just know what I want.'

'That I should live?'

'Yes.'

Lifting his foot, Pan wiped his markings from the sludge. He stood motionless, reading the ground as though his writing still remained. 'Alright,' he said, looking up to Eran. 'As she wishes. It is not my time yet, tribesman.'

With a hard glare on the one before him, Eran spread his arms.

Alley's mind reeled. The ground rose up around them. The plants and trees folded in upon them. She felt her body gain an incredible weight. Her eyes were unable to be held open. Lying upon the ground, Alley felt her mind disperse into the air, drawing her body along behind.

34.

A MIND OF LIGHT AND DARK

Where am I? Alley squinted through the gloom, stretched out her hands and felt the sheets entangling her on the large bed, the Duhent's bed. She was back … if she had left at all.

'Pan,' she whispered. Where was he? Why wasn't he next to her?

Her head splintered, as though a sharpened wedge had been driven down through the top of her skull. She pushed herself up, feeling exhaustion tempt her back to the mattress.

The light specks sped around the room, raging, as she believed a bright spark could rage.

Shielding her sight, she sought the time. She stared at it a long while before she could decipher its message and the significance behind it. Her final exam was in an hour. She needed to get to school.

Crawling to the edge of the bed, Alley froze. She was not alone. There, in the dense shadows of the far corner of the room was a dark form. Twisted and bent, it reached out to her with hands that clawed the air. Its face was a distorted, ravaged mess that screamed silently and bled black.

Terror gripped Alley's chest as she watched her mother take a shambling step forward. Alley squeezed her eyes shut. 'No.'

Lights burst under her eyelids, puncturing her brain with barbed pikes. She opened her eyes and found the room absent of the perverse memory.

The specks in the room zipped towards her, stopped short and darted back to the shadows at the edges of the room. They harassed the creeping dark, forcing the seething things to settle. The shadows obliged, resuming their stillness. Alley utilised the moment to slip from the bed and make her way to the door. The specks rushed against her. Alley ducked her head, swatted the swarm of light.

Is that it? she thought. Do they think I'm one of those shadows?

She felt her mother reach for her once again. Alley ran and her mind flickered.

The day was fogged by grey. The sun was a pale disc above. The streets were lifeless and cold. Everything felt wrong. A hand reached for her over her shoulder, a dark hand, dripping ink. When she turned there was nothing there.

Then she was against a brick wall, head in her hands. Looking up, a car tore down the road, fleeing from her.

A shadowy figure shifted in the gloom of a side street. It vomited shadows down her white dress.

The exam was before her. Each page she opened exploded with small dots of light or slithered with thin ribbons of night. She turned in her seat, searching the hall. The desks were arranged neatly, evenly spaced and supporting a copy of the exam on its top. No student was seated, no living soul in the entire hall.

Alley rubbed her eyes, wiped the sweat from her forehead and looked again. The other students hunched over their desks, scribbling away on their papers. The teachers wandered the perimeters like diligent spectres, faces ghastly and absent of human expression. One raised her arms, hands clawing.

Returning to the exam before her, Alley saw nothing. She shut the paper and left the hall at a sprint.

Like raindrops down a windowpane, the town streamed in grey around her. And the woman was everywhere, draped in white, gushing darkness. The specks of light jittered and flew in frantic dives, but they did not stand a chance.

Reaching the Duhent's house, Alley locked herself in, threw her back against the door, and fell to the floor, breathing hard. She managed to crawl a short distance across the room before collapsing.

*

The rhythmic pounding found her in the depths. It wrapped around her, tightened and drew her up. Alley surfaced, squinting at the wavering glare that held her.

The light specks had merged into one encompassing blaze. It climbed the walls, travelled along the ceiling and snapped at her with blistering teeth.

Alley drew a breath. It scraped down her throat and stopped before reaching her lungs, causing her to hack it back up. Her eyes stung. Her skin cooked and the pungent stink of burning hair rested on the back of her tongue.

Keeping low, she scrambled for the door. Enduring the heated doorhandle, Alley released herself into the cool night. On hands and knees she sucked clean air, washing ash and embers from her airway.

Timbers in the house snapped, weight and flames fell, driving scorched air upon her. Alley crawled, coughing, her eyes seeping. Pulling up before a set of legs, she raised her head and discerned the face of Bryce through the blur.

He lifted a foot, placed it on her shoulder and kicked, tossing her onto her back. After another spasm of coughing, Alley climbed to her knees. Bryce lurched forward. Alley raised her arms, protecting her face from another strike. None came. Bryce had stopped. She searched the surrounds.

In the quivering amber glow that flooded the Duhent's property were a scattered crowd of dark individuals. With Bryce, as though entranced, they glared at the infernos that savaged the house and the rear shelter.

'Bryce …' Alley huffed. On the back of his right hand was a black mark, a tattoo of an anchor.

He looked down upon her, face absent of emotion. 'Your brother's not here.'

Alley gulped. It was a painful move. Her throat was damaged.

'Where is he? We want him.'

'Don't … don't you hurt him.'

'It's too late.' Bryce let his sight drop. 'He's set to die. Even Pan … he'll kill him if we don't, Alley.' He shrugged. 'It'll be better if we kill him.'

'No. Pan wouldn't. I don't believe you.'

Bryce turned his weary attention to the roaring blaze. With a yawn, he said, 'Who cares what you believe …? Who cares what any of us believe anymore? The end is here. It is all ended.'

35.

THE WAKING OF
THE WATER-WOLVES

T he child was on his stomach. He reached out, dug his hand into the earth and dragged his body through the mud in a slug-like fashion.

Cale watched Sticks inch himself nearer and nearer the running stream, hand after hand, his face encrusted and his limbs encased in grime. When the small child reached the water and sunk his head beneath the surface, Cale stood, placed Touch to the side, and walked over. He collected the child's feet and hauled the little body back up the bank and released him under Tree-home.

When Cale returned to his seat on the elevated fig roots, Sticks once again began his slug crawl for the water. 'Stop it, Sticks,' he pleaded.

The greyness that tainted Coalcliff had found its way into the clearing. It was once bright and magical, coloured in the richest shades of autumn. Now it was awash with a charcoal film. It was cold, damp and unwelcoming. Tree-home had dropped all its leaves. The floors and rooms that Sticks had constructed were rotting and buckling.

'It is Dark Anchor,' Pan had explained, before dashing off. It had found a way to get them. And his sister was in danger.

Cale could feel it, everything that Pan said. He collected Touch and placed it on his lap. With the bottom of his shirt he scrubbed at the hilt, leaving a clean patch of wood above the collection of carved runes.

The sound of distant rustling was followed by Pan staggering into the clearing. He stopped and found Sticks's head submerged in the stream, sucking at the water. Grabbing the collar of the boy, Pan lifted Sticks up and dragged him back up the gentle slope, where he released him into the leaf litter. With an open gaze, he looked to Cale.

'What happened?' Cale asked.

'I was right,' Pan answered, his voice hollow. 'It found a way here. It used your sister … like It knows …' He trailed off.

Cale gave the hilt one last polish with his shirt. He reached to the side and collected a sharp stone chip. 'Is she alright?'

Pan stepped around the clearing, placing his hand on solid things then withdrawing it with a jerk. 'I doubt it. She is back, but … I doubt it, Cale.'

The edged piece of stone hesitated above the scrubbed patch of wood. Cale could see the images in his head; the cracked crown, the broken pieces of camera, and the collection of tall waves. He understood he could only etch one. Looking up to Pan, he asked, 'So, whose story is this?'

Pan stopped his manic movements around the area. His eyes shifted back and forth, his thoughts appearing to be performing somersaults. 'I do not know anymore.' He moved before Cale and dropped to his knees, reaching his eye level. 'I do not know, Cale. Whose do you think it is?'

Cale opened his mouth and was stopped by Pan's hand.

'Tell me what you want to do.'

Pulling away Pan's hand, Cale said, 'I'm ready. I want to do this.'

'Now?'

'Now.'

Pan stood.

'Sticks,' Cale indicated the boy, moments from dunking his

head into the stream once again.

Pan considered the boy with a knuckled brow. 'He is too ill to come with us. And if we leave him here he will drink until he drowns.'

'What should we do?'

He examined the area, and nodded to the side. 'Tie him to the tree.'

From one of the suspension bridges over head, Pan tugged at the makeshift rope rail and the entire thing fell to the ground, along with one of the larger walls of the construction.

'Do not be concerned for it,' Pan said, noticing the injured look Cale wore. 'There is no more use for this place.'

Untying the rope from the timber planks, Pan gathered up Sticks, sat him against the tree and lashed his body to the trunk. Sticks, head flopping forward, was too weak, or too unaware, to resist.

With the boy secured, they both looked to the other, and each gave a nod.

*

Night had fallen. Cale could not have said when. He stood on the boundary of the world; that thin line separating what is real and what is not. He had found it without Pan's guidance. It could be felt, always resting there, waiting for one who knew how to step around reality and place foot upon it. All he needed to do was close his eyes and see a void upon which he could paint his pictures.

Distances became irrelevant. Objects were only there if he chose to see them. The directions were much harder to grasp. Pan needed to lead him. And now they had arrived, standing side by side, buried in darkness, before the cave that hid the terrible beast.

'He's not in there,' Cale said.

Pan placed a hand on Cale's shoulder, directed him to the open night, and receded into the shadows.

There, illuminated by dim moonlight, lumbering in his direction, was the vile creature. It was huge, hairy and directed its limbs with savageness. Dangling from the end of its arms were large bulbs, possibly severed heads from its countless victims.

Cale viewed the beast's bounty, refused the disguise that coated it, and saw they were not severed heads, just plastic bags, bulging with produce from the grocery store.

The beast raised its snout, locked red eyes on Cale and came to a stop. With Cale, the beast assumed the stillness of the surrounding night.

Like the gradual solidification of water to ice, Cale's body began to seize. No unfamiliar hand was upon him. It were the eyes of the beast that immobilised him. The beast had power enough to stop him with no more than a stare.

'Who's that?' the beast grunted.

Cale was powerless.

The beast stepped forward and angled its beastly face closer. 'Oh, shit. What the hell are you doing here?'

Cale saw the dark wave approach, preparing to drown him. He thought of Mitch, battling within that churning chaos. He trembled, felt his anger bubble up, loosen his body, and he released the howl of a water-wolf.

'Hey, shoosh, keep your voice down. You're not supposed to be here. I could get in a lot of trouble if I'm caught talking to you.'

Cale snapped into movement. He rushed, Touch slicing through the air. He slashed twice, attacking each bundle of bags the beast held. The items fell to the pavement. Packets landed with a thud. A few jars shattered or rolled into the street. A carton of milk split and spread a milky puddle between them.

The beast flinched, surprised by Cale's rapid attack.

'Stop this,' the beast growled.

Cale leapt and swung his foot into the beast's groin. For a moment Cale believed he had not struck with enough force. The beast stood, swayed, clutched itself with both paws and collapsed to his knees with a constricted gurgle.

As the beast continued his fall forward, Cale attacked again. He drove his foot into the beast's chest, sending it onto its side. It rolled onto its back. No vicious roar was released and no attempt was made to get to its feet. It lay there, head angled upwards, watching Cale as though the massive creature was afraid of him.

It was a ruse. Cale knew the beast to be evil and dangerous. He levelled the point of Touch to the beast's throat. 'I want it back.'

'What? What?'

'What you took.'

'Yes. Yes. I'll get it to you. I promise I will. But you have to leave and never come here again. They'll bloody chuck me back in there if they find out.' Its red eyes shifted, searching the night as though there were scarier monsters out there than a water-wolf with a blade to its throat. 'So, what is it? What do you want back? I'll post it to you. Just tell me what it is.'

'But you can't,' Cale said. 'You can't give it back.'

'Look, Cale,' the beast said, 'I don't know—'

'No,' he breathed, pushing the tip of the blade into the leathery, hairy hide. In the pale light, a dark line travelled down its neck, glistening, to drip onto the ground

'What?' the beast cried, through a whisper. 'What the hell do you want, kid? Do you want an apology? Is that it? You want to see me beg for your forgiveness? Hell, it was years ago. I've paid the price, haven't I? What more do you want?'

Cale applied more pressure. The beast's face creased. Its rumbling fell quiet. 'Maybe I just want to kill you.'

The beast snorted. It was amused by his statement.

'Look at me,' Cale said.

It stared up at Cale and its breathing became heavier. 'Just like that, you'd kill me? You'd really kill me? Come on, it was nothing, Cale. It was just a bit of fun. I never hurt you. It was just play.'

Cale secured his grip on Touch.

'You think I'm just going to a let a kid try and kill me?'

The beast rolled to his side. Cale raised a leg and stomped down on the beast's throat. It fell back and Cale drove his heel into the beast's clawed paw, spread out on the rock.

The beast wanted to roar its pain into the night. Only a stifled grunting did it allow to escape.

'I could kill you.' He raised Touch, gripped the hilt in two hands, its point targeting the chest below. 'I could just stab your heart and walk away.'

The beast's black lips quivered.

'I'm told I should do it. It would be justice. It would be the price for what you took from me. I should do it. But I won't.'

'You won't?'

'Not yet.'

'… Why?'

'You can wait for it. I thought you were scary. I thought you had my life in your hands. But you don't. You never did. You have nothing. And you're weak. It's me now … I'm the one who's holding your life.'

Cale lowered Touch and extended his open hand, directing it to the prone beast. The beast watched Cale's hand for a long while. The night turned around them and the beast resigned, placing his paw in Cale's hand. Cale could not do much in the way of helping the large thing to its stubby legs. The beast was forced to do most of the work.

'Don't think you'll ever be free,' Cale said, releasing the beast to his feet. 'People like you never are. Now it's your turn to be afraid.' He wiped his hand on the grass to his side and stood back to inspect the beast. It seemed frail. 'I'm going to be the king of your world now,' he said, and turned his back on the beast, 'before I decide to end it.' With Pan falling in beside him, Cale led them away.

The substance of the world faded as Cale directed them both back to Coalcliff. Before he lost himself in the spaces between worlds, he offered Touch towards Pan.

'Are you planning to kill him, Cale?' Pan asked, looking down at the weapon.

'No. I don't need to. Whether he lives or dies doesn't matter. It was never about him, was it? It was about me. And it's better this way. It's better for me.'

Pan accepted the wooden sword, considered it for a moment and then presented it back to Cale. 'The king bears the blade …'

Cale nodded, reached forth and took Touch into his hands.

36.

ALL IS ENDED

Fires burned. Sharpened gusts split the skin, embedding cold. Cries of panic ricocheted through the streets. Small collections of howling individuals carried violence and destruction through Coalcliff. The whole town fumed.

Where am I going?

Alley staggered through it, shying from the cars engulfed by flames, spewing rolling funnels of toxic black smoke. Sirens hit her ears and skewered her brain, adding to the incredible ache thumping in her head.

… He'll kill him if we don't, Bryce's words repeated in her mind.

It could not be true. Pan would never do such a thing. She needed to find Cale. She needed to find Pan. Pan would protect Cale. And her. Just his presence was enough to settle the whipping of her thoughts and ease this migraine that would not relent. If Pan was with her, everything would be alright.

… I'm not here to save you, Alley, she heard Pan's voice resonate in the air.

She turned and lunged for him, crying his name. There was no one behind her. Pain struck, leaving her blinded by light.

As her sight cleared, she found herself lying in the street. For a beat there was quiet. The street was calm. The asphalt against her cheek was warm and the distant fires comforting.

Then the bray of havoc fell. The dark of the town heaved and a woman draped in white, hidden at the distant edges, tore at the night, making it bleed.

Alley stood and attempted to run. Her legs lost all strength. She stumbled and toppled into a garden, a low lying spread of junipers cushioning the fall.

'I didn't think you had it in you, Alley-cat.'

On hands and knees, feeling the needle jabs of the bristling plants, Alley looked up to see Megan and Taz.

'How much have you drank, girl?' Taz laughed.

They each collected one of Alley's arms and helped her to her feet.

'Want anymore?' Taz offered a bottle of wine with her free hand.

'Don't be stupid,' Megan said, slapping it away. 'She's out of it. She needs some water.'

'I'm fine.' Alley mumbled, her lips refusing to cooperate with her brain.

Somewhere at the far reaches of the town, a gun released a succession of shots. The reports spread and settled comfortably within the violent clamour.

'Geeze,' Taz huffed. 'Was that gunfire?'

'Everyone's going bananas,' Megan said, shaking her head as they watched two youths raise a garbage bin above their heads and launch it through the window of a lightless house.

'End of school,' Taz shrugged.

'Nah. It's not just that. Look … half these maniacs don't even go to our school.'

'Yeah. I dunno. Let's just get back to Romina's. Things are getting nuts out here.'

'Come on, Alley,' Megan said, leading her away. 'You need to recover.'

Alley submitted to the two. There was solace in the sturdiness of their hands. If her head had not been threatening to implode, she could have slept as she staggered between them.

The writhing mass they approached was decorated by a rainbow glow. Garlands of multi-coloured light bulbs had been strung between the trees and the three story house. They directed Alley with hands on her back through the tide of bodies on the front yard. The front stair reverberated with the rapid thump of the music. In the house the air was thick with sticky warmth. Like a school of salmon in a skinny river, clammy bodies slid against each other, spilling drinks ensuring the shifting crowd was well lubricated. The smells became more varied the deeper they wriggled. The stink of sweat and beer-breath mingled with the overly sweet scents of perfumes and spilled liqueurs that decorated the walls and carpet in incandescent shades. Alley felt her stomach retreat.

Reaching the kitchen, Alley discovered a bubble of clear space. A blur of faces moved around her, wild smiles filled with teeth, and large eyes that peered through everything. Megan presented a glass of water which Alley took and drank, bracing herself against the counter.

'Alley!' a voice sang. 'You made it.'

Trent's face bobbed through the sea and settled before her. It glistened with a fine film of sweat. She stared at him, holding the glass to her lips.

'She's had a bit too much,' Megan said, above the discordant cheer of voices and coughing beat of the music.

Trent's face dipped up and down. 'Don't worry, I've been there. Want to go out the back for some fresh air?'

He took her hand and led her through the muggy hive. Noticing Megan and Taz on their tail he turned, and said, 'It's alright. You guys enjoy the party. I'll make sure nothing happens to her.'

Megan and Taz turned their high eyebrows on their friend.

The self-assured smile he directed at Alley reminded her of Pan. He coaxed her onwards. She placed her eyes on his level wall of shoulders and followed.

Escaping the sweaty humidity of inside, they passed into the night. Cool freshness washed over them and pushed against the open doorway behind.

The backyard spread deep into the night. Feature trees and hedged gardens, vine-covered archways and elegant timber seating transformed it into a loose maze of objects and colour. A few small groups and couples were scattered amongst it.

Romina, doing the rounds with Cynthia and Sarah in tow, and a colourful cocktail in hand, stepped towards them. 'Hi, guys. Having fun?' she said, in her suggestive way.

'Just looking for some quiet,' Trent said, over his shoulder.

'Whatever you say,' she giggled. 'Well done, Alley,' she called out after them and collapsed into Cynthia, laughing.

Trent led Alley to some wooden seating situated at the rear fence. Large gardenias in full bloom encircled them, filling the area with an aromatic air. He collapsed on a bench, pulling Alley after him.

'I just need to rest for a bit,' she said. 'I have to go find Cale.'

'Yeah, just for a bit.'

He placed his arm around her shoulders and drew her close. The warmth of his body caused her exhaustion to condense. She tilted her head back and rested it on his arm. Like being with Pan, the pain in her head was now a muted throb.

'Been having fun?' he asked, taking a drink of his beer.

She hummed indecision.

From their position, the jittering electronic beats were hushed. The wrestling and dancing bodies looked small and harmless in the lights as they thrashed about. The house and its revelling infestation looked like a vision from another time.

Back here, the mess of the party could not reach them. The pandemonium in the surrounding streets could not find them. They were king and queen, high in the tower of their impenetrable castle, watching the senseless rampage of their subjects with a vague interest.

She wished she could stay here all night, hidden within Trent's arm, an arm that Pan was not prepared to offer. The thought of her brother made her tense.

'I should get going,' she said, pushing herself from Trent's body.

'You sure? Just a bit longer. It's nice just sitting here with you.'

He held her with an unflinching gaze. She broke away. 'Cale.'

'He'll be alright for another half-hour.'

She shook her head. 'Pan … he might be up to something.'

'Don't worry about that guy. Stay.'

Her attention turned to the dark green leaves of the surrounding plants. *I'm not here to save you …* 'He might not care about any of us.'

'Who?'

'Pan.'

'What's everyone's obsession with Pan. Stop thinking about him. He's a nobody.' With a light touch on her cheek, Trent turned her head to meet his eyes. 'I'm here.' He lent in and pressed his lips against hers.

Alley stiffened and was transported back to her early teenage years. She was at school, before the knowledge of her mother's madness and her brother's assault landed like an atomic bomb. Normal, well-liked Trent, with his grinning face and rosy cheeks, was with her. He reached out and grabbed her hand and her life unfolded from that touch to this present moment.

She wrapped her arms around his neck and pulled him closer. She fell into the motion of it all, the rising warmth. A floating awareness felt his hands travel up her back. They rested on her hips, holding her for a moment before they ran up under her shirt and brushed across her stomach. There was a pause, a fumbling at her jeans.

She leaned back, broke contact and felt the chill of the air.

He looked at her, questioning.

'I … now's not the time. I have to go do something.' She stood and backed away from him.

'Are you coming back?'

Alley glanced over her shoulder at the party. It had gained an unpleasant amount of detail. Before turning away, she offered Trent a small smile.

Reaching the house, Alley was shoved back as a body doubled over and ejected a green shaded liquid from its stomach onto the back patio. Those standing nearby cast their amused groans at the culprit.

'Alley, Alley!' came an urgent call.

She turned to Taz.

'The cops!' she blurted, her bewilderment stretched wider by inebriation.

'*Outta-da-way! Keg comin' through!*'

Nudged to the side, Alley peered at her, not understanding.

'They're here, looking for you.'

'*Beer me! Beer me!*'

'Me?'

'Something about a fire at your place.'

Alley's mind became static fuzz and threatened to switch off. She caught herself on a wall, knocking a small body into a stumble.

'My drink, you stupid …'

'You were the last person there?' Taz blinked. 'And that old lady. She's missing or something.'

'Shots! Shots!' A tray full of shot glasses drifted above the crowd.

From the front of the house the rumble of noise had softened. Jeers and taunts filled the empty air, moving like a wave towards the rear of the house.

'Pigs! Pigs!'

'Take it off, boys!'

The tray floating above the heads tipped and clattered onto the floor. The shot glasses shattered.

'Awww!'

'I think they want to take you to the station, Alley.'

Fear gripped Alley's chest. 'I can't. Cale.'

'Yo! The cops!'

'Shit! Run!'

'Do you want me stall them? I can stall them if you want?'

A few people dashed past them, glancing over their shoulders. Alley nodded.

'I'm on it.'

Alley staggered back through the crowd and out into the backyard.

A swaying face, swollen red and eyes rolling back, popped up before her. 'Where … bathroom?'

Alley swatted the air between them. The person tilted one way, then the other, and toppled backwards. She moved into the backyard at a quick trot. Trent would help her.

Navigating a tight collection of shrubby trees, adorned in tiny white lights, she found a huddle of people. On the bench, Trent was sitting centre. Romina was on one of his sides, and Cynthia the other. A few others stood before them, forming a circle. All, except Trent, were hunching over a small light.

Moving closer, Alley saw the phone, held in the hand of Sarah.

'Got the whole thing,' Sarah said.

'Put it away, you perv,' Trent said, with a bored sigh.

'Wait, wait, wait,' she laughed. 'This is the best bit.' Everyone leaned closer. 'Look at the moves … go Trent, you sly dog,' she said, leading the others in their laughter.

Trent joined in with a light chuckle of his own.

'Here, I'll play it again.'

Romina sat back and eyed Trent. 'Whatever. Your moves were shit. You couldn't get her to give it up, not even that weirdo.'

'Hey, the night's still young,' he said.

'You better,' she said, and turned to Sarah. 'And you so have to film it and upload it. It would be so, so funny.'

'Hell yeah,' Sarah returned, looking up to Trent. 'Giving hope to freaks all over the nation …'

He laughed in reply.

Alley tripped and caught herself on the shrubbery beside her.

'Oh,' Cynthia breathed, directing everyone's attention to Alley.

'Whoops,' Romina bleated.

'Alley, wait,' Trent said, standing as she turned to flee.

'Let her go,' Romina beamed. 'What the hell was she doing here anyway?' she called out into the yard.

So stupid … her mind repeated as she charged down the side of the house, bouncing off people as she went. Her head was down and she counted her steps, growling the sequence through her teeth.

A strong arm reached out and blocked her path. 'Hold up there, miss.'

Alley's eyes travelled up the uniform to find the square face of the officer. He shouted over his shoulder, 'Is this her?'

Another officer, examining an ID of a swaying and scowling individual, returned it and made his way over. 'Yep. You got her.'

'Alrighty,' the first officer said, 'let's go.' He gripped Alley's arm and led her towards the road and the awaiting patrol car.

Everyone kept a respectable distance, lobbing their corny taunts from the safety of the crowd.

'No,' Alley yelled, shaking the hand from her body.

'Easy there. We just want to talk to you.'

'I … Cale,' she stumbled, her sentences liquefying as they made their way to her lips.

'How much have you had to drink tonight, miss?'

Alley shook her head. 'I …'

'There was a fire at your residence tonight.'

Alley nodded.

'According to neighbours, you were seen exiting the property as the house was burning.'

She stared at him.

'The woman who lived there,' he flipped through his notebook, 'Mrs Duhent, hasn't been seen for days.' He tucked the notebook back into his pocket slowly. 'Where is Mrs Duhent, Miss Cord?'

Alley gaped.

'What's wrong with her? Drugs?' said the other officer.

'Probably. We better cuff her.' He reached to the back of his belt and retrieved the metal handcuffs.

'*Piiigs!*' the stretched shout poured, just as an empty bottle of beer collided with one of the officer's heads and shattered.

Alley protected herself from the shower of fragments.

'Christ! Mate, you okay?'

'Damn these little shits! They're out of control!'

Uncovering her face, she saw streaks of red running down the man's irate expression. Both officers turned to the crowd, retrieving their pepper spray.

Alley turned to the night and ran as the officers hosed down the partiers. She ran as fast as she could, the cries of her former classmates ringing out into the night.

37.

A BRUTAL TRUTH

The alert lights of the emergency vehicles spun, washing the scene in a sequence of blue and red. The house had been levelled, wiped from the land and all memories vaporised. Police officers and fire-fighters shuffled through the scorched remains. They kicked at blackened objects and lifted warped things close to their faces with pincer fingers.

Alley prowled the edge of the property. On the breeze were hints of soaking charcoal, melting plastic, charred fabrics and all the other wrong smells associated with the incineration of a lifetime of possessions. It was enough to make her raise her shirt and cover her nose and mouth.

Reaching the forest, she was forced to drop her mask and raise her arms, protecting herself as she searched. This was the domain of shadows. Her mother's wraith drifted alongside her, haunting this place. The woman did not need to spill her darkness here. This area was already alive with it. It slithered with black streamers, all moving in a certain direction. Alley, her skin crawling, followed the current.

For comfort, she murmured Cale's name over and over, and to remind her leaching mind what she was doing amongst this tide of death.'

The clearing opened before her. The creeping dark did not enter. They circled the area, prodding the air, searching for a weakness, hungering to strike at something within.

Before her was a once mighty fig tree, opening itself up to the skies. It was close to death now, all its leaves shed and its branches cracked and rotten. In sagging limbs, the tree heroically held a disintegrating construction aloft. It was a tree-house, more a house than a cubby.

Below it, at the base of the trunk, a child sat. His small head was tilted forward. Binding him to the tree was a bundle of rope.

Alley rushed over and fell before the child. She lifted his head and peered into a face gaunt and mud encrusted. The child's eyes fluttered. A weak groan purred in his chest.

'It's alright. I'm here. I'll get you free,' she said, tugging at the lashings. 'Hold on.'

The rope was tight around his body. The knots were complex and unyielding. She collected a sharp stone and pounded the rope until it snapped. Yanking off the restraints, she held the child by the shoulders to keep him from falling.

'Who did this to you?'

The boy's eyes drooped. His head fell from side to side. With a feeble arm he attempted to move her from before him.

'No, no. It's alright. I'm not going to hurt you. I can help you. Tell me who did this. Was it Pan? Did Pan do this to you?'

The child blinked his eyes into focus. He found her and smacked his dry lips together. 'Pan ...'

'Why? Why did he do this?'

'I wanted water,' the boy panted. 'I was thirsty. They tied me to Tree-home.'

'It's alright. I'm here. I'll get you some water. But first, do you know Cale? He's my brother. He might be with Pan. I need to know where he is. Is Pan going to hurt him?'

The child yawned large, finishing it with a loud honk. 'The boy with Pan?'

'Yes. Where? Where did they go?'

'To crown the boy in blood.'

'What? You mean Pan's going to kill him?'

'No. Pan makes him king. That's what Pan will do … Then he sends boy to death. King first. Then death,' he said, as though she should know the correct order of events.

'Why would he do such a thing?' she said, only half to the child.

'The end is coming. The end is coming,' he teased, melodiously.

'The end? Pan said something about the greatest Anchor. Is that it? The end?'

'Yep. The big Dark Anchor. It will come and it will eat Pan.'

'Eat? Like death? This Anchor wants to kill Pan?'

The boy released a yawning laugh. 'But Pan is too tricky,' he sang. 'Anchor will eat other boy instead. It will think he is real king and go away. But he is not the real king. Pan is. And Pan will steal back home.'

'The Never?'

'Uh-huh. Pan will win and save home. He will save home and bring it all back, and bring all us back, and we will all have fun and go on adventures … except that boy. He won't come back. He will be dead, forever.'

'So the Anchor who wants to kill Pan will kill my brother instead, thinking its Pan? And Pan will let this happen?'

The boy cackled and coughed and threw his head around in circles, eyes closed and gaunt expression twisted in delight.

Alley stood and stumbled back.

There was only one other place she could think her brother would be.

As though they knew of her intentions, a handful of bright specks dropped from the skies. They harried her run, weaving between her pumping legs, and striking at her face, blinding her. The ache in her head became a pressure that threatened to collapse her.

Battling a few low hanging branches, Alley tore from the forest, throwing her fists at specks that drew too near.

Her heart lurched as she remembered the assemblage of authorities filling the property.

'*Hey, that's the girl!*'

'*Quick, go that way.*'

The officers that remained spread out. Alley dodged an arm, sidestepped another. She saw an opening and charged. A strong set of arms wrapped her up and pushed her to the ground. She felt the bite of thin metal around her wrists.

Breathing heavily, she was pulled to her feet. 'I …' she stammered. Concentrating as best she could, she released the one word that mattered. 'Cale!'

The bright specks swarmed.

'Cale?' one officer said to another.

Alley could no longer see. The lights filled her eyesight.

'That's the brother … Where is Cale?' a droning voice asked.

'Cale!' Alley screamed. In a sudden rush, the brightness fell upon her mind. There, it detonated, destroying itself as it attempted to destroy her.

Her body seized and she felt herself go limp. She was on the ground once again, staring across the grass as the land quaked. Polished shoes stepped before her, shuddering. The world was shaking itself apart.

'*What's wrong with her?*' the echoes of a voice pattered upon her awareness. She could see and hear, but was unable to move. Another slice of agonising pain ripped through her mind. It lasted only a moment as everything faded to nothingness.

'*She's having a seizure,*' came another echo. It resonated in her head, dispersing the final remnants of consciousness Alley possessed.

38.

TO KILL A WOLF

Her world was now comprised of parcelled sections of time. Each one was separate and distinct from the others. There was no connection, only an incomprehensible collection of images and sensations, each one associated with a specific level of fear; straps around her body; the solid surface beneath her; the bleached white walls ensuring her containment; unrecognisable faces peering down with grave expressions; small pricks on the inside of her arm.

Why straps? she questioned, without sound. Why the walls, the hard surfaces, and the moving, flat on her back, the walls sliding and the ceiling rushing away? And the machines? Those massive machines in which her body is fed …? The humming and whirling and droning and clicking? And her stillness? 'Stay very still, please,' the voices say over and over. *Why?* she wanted to ask. Stay where? But she cannot. She had no voice of her own anymore. All she had were these inexplicable, disjointed moments, and the perpetual waves of fear as they peaked, spilled and spread throughout her body.

*

The morning was a murky grey. Pan followed Cale as he limped into the clearing. The boy was exhausted. He, himself, felt drained of something essential. They stood, their limbs dangling, gazing at Tree-home without a word between them.

Cale dropped to the ground, cradling Touch in his lap. His fingers stroked the runes on the hilt as though he was reading brail. With eyes shedding a dull gleam, Cale viewed the hidden horizon and the great thing that approached.

Pan stared at a large tangle of rope for a beat before he understood what he was seeing. He staggered to the tree and lifted it towards Cale.

'How?' Cale mouthed the word.

They both turned to the water. Face down, snagged a distance downstream, was Sticks.

'No, Sticks. No,' Pan heard himself mutter, as they wandered over.

Reaching the child, Pan turned him onto his back and looked down at a face bloated and blue, eyes sunken and black. He had been dead for many hours.

Dragging him from the stream, Pan laid the sodden body on the bank. Cale joined his side and they both looked down on the lifeless child.

A misty cold sidled into the clearing and accompanied the two in their vigil.

'His parents died when he was little,' Pan murmured, bending down and adjusting the boy's arms into a more comfortable position. 'It was a fire, or something like that. He was given to a couple. They were not very good people. They lived in this rundown little house. Every two weeks, when they received their support payment for the kid, they locked him in the laundry room and went away with the money. Sometimes they would not come back for days and days.'

Cale let Touch hang from his hand, the wooden tip digging into the mud.

'They would leave him some food, and just let him drink from the laundry faucet that had this big, metal sink beneath it. This one time, when they locked him in the laundry, as was usual, he climbed into the sink and tried to turn on the tap for a drink. But the tap handle twisted off, leaving only a little metal screw that he could not turn with his fingers. The water was trapped.'

Pan turned and strode away. He swept his foot through the dead leaf litter. The leaves stirred as it passed through them and then lay still. He was unable to kick them back into the branches as before. Time no longer bowed to his whims.

'I saw him through that window,' he continued, seeing that Cale had not moved from the child's side. 'I saw him break the tap. I saw him cry. I came back every day to watch him.' He faced Cale. 'It is hard, you know?'

Cale tilted his head, listening while keeping Sticks in his sight.

'It is hard to know which ones to save and which ones to leave to their fate.' He looked up. The wintry sun hauled itself above the trees, the light thickening the turbid grey hanging like mist. 'After the third day the boy started to get really sick. He kept vomiting up yellow and red goo. And he could not stand properly and walk. His fingers were all bloody and torn from trying to turn that little screw that would never turn for him. He was going to die in that room. Just before he breathed his last breath I took him. I took him to the Never where there is no such thing as thirst, or hunger, or exhaustion.'

Turning from the child, Cale looked to Pan. 'You saved him.'

'I have saved many ... the Never and I.'

'Can you save him now?'

Pan shook his head. 'When they die here, they are dead. They may appear in the Never, but not as how they were.'

'He doesn't deserve to die,' Cale said, lifting Touch before him to inspect the hilt.

'Many do not. But it is hard, Cale, deciding which ones to give life and which ones to kill.'

Cale nodded and turned to the east. Quietly, he asked, 'Do I deserve to die?'

Pan lowered himself to a crouch, watching Cale steadily. 'No, Cale. Not at all. But I am going to kill you.'

Cale drew in a long breath through his nose. He scanned the trees before him as though measuring the massive thing rushing towards them from distant lands. 'I know why. I know what's coming for you.' He turned, lifted Touch and released it to the ground. 'I can feel it. And it's okay.'

'Damn it, Cale …'

'You're still my friend, Pan. My only friend.'

'No, I am not!' Pan roared, leaping and kicking Cale in the chest, launching him onto his back. 'Do not say that. Do not tell me it is okay. Tell me it is wrong. Tell me you want to live. Tell me my time is over. Cale, you have to convince me not to do it. Just one word. Please.'

Cale watched him from the ground.

Pan stormed away and studied the forest. 'Your sister is in trouble.'

'I know,' Cale wheezed, pushing himself into a sitting position.

'She needs you.'

Cale pulled his knees up into his chest and stared at Sticks beside him.

'Did you hear me?'

'I did.' Cale shifted closer to Sticks. 'When will It get here?'

'Cale …'

'When?'

'When the sun falls on this day it will never rise again.'

'Ever?'

'Not for this town.'

Cale nodded.

'Most are already gone, disappeared,' Pan said. He drew his hands close to his face, feeling the heaviness of his limbs, the restriction of the world upon him. It was close. 'This town has been dying for a long time. And now it is over. The Dark Anchor is its final breath. And there are only two ways to stop it.'

'Me or you.'

'The choice was so clear before.'

'I can save her,' Cale mumbled.

'What?'

Cale climbed to his feet. 'What if I choose?'

'But it is my choice.'

'I can save them. I can save him,' Cale said, displaying the prostrate form on the bank.

'Sticks?'

Cale nodded.

Pan inspected him for any signs of insanity. 'He cannot be brought back if he dies here. I already said that.'

'No. *You* can't bring him back. You can't bring him back into your Never. Can't you feel it? Your home is gone. It's all eaten up.'

Pan gripped each of his arms, fearful they may begin trembling. 'You are the only piece of the Never that's left. But me …'

'What are you saying?'

'Let it be up to me now.' Cale retrieved Touch from the mud. 'Let it be my choice. I am the only one that can save them.'

'Are you? You think you have ascended so far?'

'What if I was always ready for this? Maybe I was born for it.'

'That weapon must be poisoning your sense.' Pan charged.

Cale raised the wooden blade and targeted his heart, halting him.

Pan grimaced at the threat. 'You direct Touch at my chest?' He straightened as much as his body would allow. 'I am the Never King. You merely warm my throne, kid. For an eternity I have watered my land with the blood of thieves and pirates. Do you think you can stop me with a weapon? A weapon I am as familiar with as my own skin?'

The wooden splinter was secure in the boy's hand. The blade was steady as it hung in the air. Pan watched it, feeling the muscles of his body tightening.

'I don't want to stop you,' Cale said, letting his wrist go limp, lowering the tip of the blade. 'But you know you're not meant to survive this thing. And you don't know what I'm capable of, what I'm capable of surviving.'

With a gentle hand, Pan lowered Touch and stepped back. 'I am aware,' he breathed.

Cale slid Touch through his belt, resting the blade against his leg. 'I want to face it, Pan.'

The sky overhead was darkening. The air filled with a soft drone. Pan dropped his sight and searched the ground. 'You will take the decision from me?'

'No. I won't take this off you. I'm not like that. You must give it to me, freely.'

'You want the decision?'

'I want to choose for myself.'

'And you will choose to defy It?' Pan said, shaking his head. 'It is impossible, Cale.'

'I know it is.'

Each moment that passed sapped more of Pan's strength. An urge to lie down and sleep almost took his legs from beneath him. 'It could all disappear. All of it … me.'

'It could.'

'You think you can save me?'

'Water-wolves protect. They save. But It has to take you. For me to find you, Pan, you must give yourself up to it.'

'Cale, do you know what you are asking me?'

'You have to trust me.'

Pan read all the lines on his palms as though they documented the tales and adventures of his life. 'This thing is beyond us all. Do you understand? It is a thing that is,' he blinked, and closed his hands, 'inevitable.'

'Exactly.'

Pan looked over to see Cale, his eyes gleaming and his hair wild above a toothy smile.

39.

THE NEVER KING

This was who she was. She was a thing of white walls, a bed of white sheets, a pillow of white, and the confusing things beside her, tethered to her, dripping and blipping, and always watching.

Occasionally there were those faces, all blurred and topped with grey. *Stay still … This will only hurt for a moment …*

There were other words, spoken in whispers between those hovering faces. *Tumour … brain … inoperable …* They drifted around her, slithering like black ribbons caught in a breeze.

Just make her as comfortable as possible … That was the worst one. It made her feel terrible and she did not know why.

There were crucial details hidden behind all the white; colours and faces and objects. Sensing them, she wanted to climb from the bed, scratch at the wall, peel away the paint to find out what they really were. She knew everything would be alright if she could only push through these walls and find the things hidden there.

Her body refused her want. The straps were absent, yet her limbs lay like dead things around her.

Why was it so hard to move? Why was it so hard to remember and think?

Was this death? Was she dying, or already dead? Like her brother …

A flicker of awareness zipped through her mind. 'Cale,' she breathed.

Was he already dead? But why would he die?

Pan!

She felt a chill calm seep through her mind. Her thoughts congealed, became solid things that meshed with those alongside them. Memories returned, dragging with them a thumping pain.

Alley pushed herself up in the bed and inspected the thin gown she wore. It reeked of hospital. It was a familiar smell; one remembered from her visits here when she was a child. Her arm was connected to an intravenous drip. Her finger was clipped with a peg that led to a monitor. Not a visitor, but now a patient.

Questions on what had happened were shuffled behind thoughts of her brother. Would Pan go through with his plan? Was Cale already dead?

Her head ached and she wondered how long this consciousness would last before another attack.

She could say yes. She could say Cale was dead. That would release her. She could then lie back and submit to what she knew was coming.

'Enough,' Alley growled, gripping her head, attempting to squeeze such thoughts from her brain.

Exhaustion swamped and she dropped her arms. She gazed at her hospital cell. This had been where her mother spent her final days. Trapped within these bleached white walls, the air soaked with disinfectant and sanitiser. Alley could not bear the stink of it now. She would sink her face in a pool of mud just to escape it.

My darling child …

The whisper bled in from the walls, as though her mother had infected this place.

Come with me. Stay down here forever.

Alley wrapped her knees close to her chest and buried her face.

I only want you to be happy …

'Leave me alone!' she screamed to the ceiling. Her voice reverberated off the walls then disappeared. Silence thickened and made the air heavy.

She dropped her head again. 'Don't leave me alone.'

The fluorescents above sputtered.

'Help me.'

The lights buzzed, straining, and then blinked off. The monitors fell dead. Darkness flooded the room.

A power outage? The nurses would be rushing to all the rooms, checking on the patients. She turned to the door, expecting to hear the jingle of keys and the turning of the lock. There was only quiet and the vague silhouette of a woman before the door.

Sliding from the bed, Alley watched the image evaporate into the dark. The door clicked opened and Alley removed the drip and clips tying her to the monitors. Creeping out into the hall, she stood still, breathing without sound, the linoleum chilling the soles of her feet. The place appeared abandoned. No voices could be heard and no dance of torchlight could be seen at the far extents.

She shuffled to the nearest door and tested the handle. It was locked. She tested another and another and another. All were locked.

In the lightless hall, a sweep of greater darkness rolled through. Alley followed the wafting void to a door unlike the others. Testing the handle granted her access to whatever was on the other side.

Moving forward with her hands wobbling in front, her toes collided with something solid. Pain arced up through her leg. She flexed her toes, tested their functionality on the attacking object. It was a stair. She climbed, her hands feeling along the walls for any opening. The stair turned upon itself as it ascended. It was a stairwell. On every landing there was a door that Alley tried to open. Again, they were locked, forcing her to climb higher.

It seemed endless, a continuous stair which she would climb for all eternity; her personal, lightless purgatory. Her pain was the only indicator her heart still beat.

When the muscles of her legs ignited and her breathing became rapid, a ripple in the emptiness caused her to reach out a hand. A wall blocked her path. The stair had ended. Sliding her hand over the flat surface before her, she found the opening bar. She threw her hip against it and the door swung outwards. A rush of fresh air swam around her. She drew a deep breath and examined the night sky. The sound of distant waves could be heard. The smell of sea salt was on the wind.

The concrete was craggy, grating the bottom of her feet as she stepped towards the spread of stars. Her gown whipped against her body as ocean gusts tugged it playfully. She moved forward until a waist high concrete wall halted her. Far below was the ocean, sparkling beneath the starlight. Upon the horizon was a wall of hollow darkness.

Alley looked to the cliff edge below. She thought of her mother, wondering if she felt as calm as she did now.

The wind pressed against her back, or possibly a hand. Alley gripped the wall, feeling the grittiness of the concrete, and pulled herself up onto its edge. With arms extended from her sides, she stood, eyes on the stars above as they were slowly being devoured by the dark.

'You think you can fly?'

She twisted her head. 'Pan.'

He stepped forward.

'Are you really here?'

'I am.'

Alley smiled.

'But I am not here to save you.'

'I know,' she replied, watching him hop onto the ledge at her side. 'But you're here.'

Leaning forward, Pan inspected the distance to the ground.

'Cale?'

Pan looked up and viewed the dark stretching itself along the world, separating sea from sky, and consuming them both. 'I really do not know. It is on him now. I guess, I have to trust him.' He looked to her.

She nodded. 'You can trust him.'

Pan held out his open hand. 'So, is this a happy ending?' he asked.

Alley took his hand, smiled and they both tipped into the fall.

*

The child was weightless in Cale's arms, his skin cold. The streets were absent of all sounds, all except for the penetrating drone in the air. No one was left. He was the last living thing in Coalcliff. Where they had all gone, he could not have guessed.

He remembered when he dreamed of being the last. He had imagined himself as a wild child, all alone, the people of the town vanished.

That was not what he wanted now. He wanted the town to be filled with people, never bound to the path beneath their feet, every step forward a chance to change direction

Reaching the coastline, Cale placed the child to the side, sat down and removed his shoes. With his feet bare, he collected the child back into his arms and walked towards the waters, feeling the sand between his toes, savouring each grainy step he took.

Pan had doubted. But Cale knew this thing well. It was not meant to be hid from or attacked. It was something that needed to be accepted and withstood.

Cale lowered the body onto the damp sand. 'Hold on, Sticks,' he said.

Rising, Cale stepped from the land and into the ocean. It held him up to his waist. He turned his head from left to right and stretched it back to view the sky. The dark wave filled it all, climbing higher, consuming the stars as it rose. The ocean waves that collapsed around him were silent. The great thing's hum, now a rumble, removed the capacity for other sound.

The dark mass reached far overhead, preparing to lay itself upon the whole town. Cale drew Touch from his belt and held it at his side, greeting this thing of endings. It had consumed much from his life, and Pan's. But a residue of memory remained in It. The memory always remained. It was memory of Sticks, and that boy Vinny, of his sister, and of Pan, and all the others. He would swim the eternal distance of this mighty wave, enduring all its efforts to purify itself of his existence. He would gather all he required into his arms, finding them all. Then, he would swim on, swim through the infinite expanse, along its timeless currents. He would not stop until he broke through, surfacing on the other side of time and death. There, he would ascend into a land of creation, a true Never King, and his throne would be shared with the damaged and the lost and the despairing.

The ancient thing spoke. It recognised the death and loss that bound this little being standing so far below. It jolted, nodding to him in a grave, respectful manner.

He was ready, feeling a hand on his stomach that was not really there.

This is what his life had been about; surviving the impossible.

Cale lifted Touch above his head and howled into the night as the great, dark wave fell to meet him.

ABOUT THE AUTHOR

In 2006 Arron self-published his novel *Dark Blessings*, the first book in a series of five, under the pen name of Arron Houghton. His short story, *The Water Fox* was published in *[untitled]* issue seven and in the *2017 Write Well Award Anthology*.

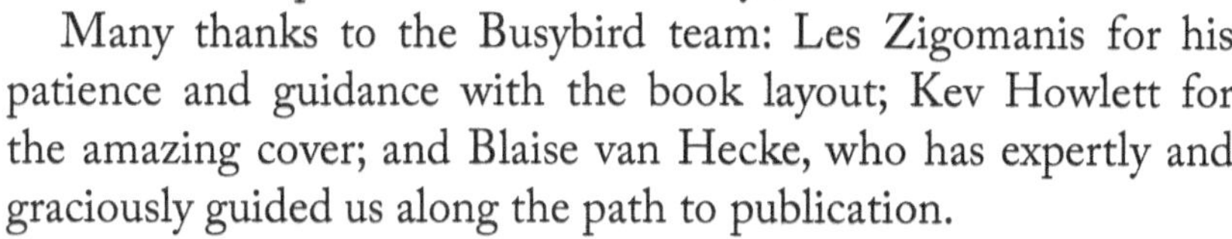

Sadly Arron passed from us in 2015 aged 31.

He was passionate with his writing and was excited with *The Never Ones,* which we have published in his memory.

Many thanks to the Busybird team: Les Zigomanis for his patience and guidance with the book layout; Kev Howlett for the amazing cover; and Blaise van Hecke, who has expertly and graciously guided us along the path to publication.

Thank you to Laurie Steed. Words cannot express our graditude for the Foreword.

To anyone reading this who may be struggling, you are not alone. Help may be only a phone call or email away.

A donation from sales will go to Beyond Blue and to an Author Program at Busybird.